"The twists and turns of the plot, the ..... development of the
colorful characters and the fascinating subplots drew me right
into the story as if I were part of it. A terrific read, I loved it."
—Lando Klassen, Chairman of the Board,
Christian Booksellers Association of Canada

"James Coggins has written an intriguing and highly readable
mystery with plot turns and enough suspects to keep the reader
guessing until the end. I look forward to more John Smyth
books."
—Linda Hall, author of *Steal Away* and *Chat Room*

"James Coggins weaves a compelling mystery through solid and
believable law enforcement characters and an intriguing plot.
He's captured the true essence of a homicide investigation."
—Mark Mynheir, homicide detective
and author of *Rolling Thunder*.

"James Coggins has created an enjoyable novel combining a
main character I identify with, a story that holds my interest,
and some intriguing insight into the work of the church."
—N. J. Lindquist, author of *Shaded Light*

"Jim Coggins has done it again: penning a sizzling 'murder mystery,' this time in the heart of the Canadian Bible belt, Abbotsford B.C. It reads like a British 'Whodunit?,' which keeps the
reader off-balance to the end. On a deeper level, Mountaintop
Drive is a telling commentary on the clash between culture and
faith."
—Vern Heidebrecht, Pastor of Prayer and Discipleship,
Northview Community Church, Abbotsford, B.C.

"James Coggins is a splendid storywriter and Mountaintop Drive *is a gripping read. So gripping that I took it to the beach with me and forgot to use sunscreen. That wasn't my only injury. I sprained my wrist turning pages. Read this book, but use caution!"*
 —Phil Callaway, speaker and author of
  Wonders Never Cease

"A slick, crisp read. It has just about everything. Mystery, suspense, action, twists in plot and a lot of extras you won't find in too many mysteries these days—morality, spirituality, and theology. Mountaintop Drive *is a page turner but it's far more than a weekend's entertainment. It will take you places you never expected to go. A good ride."*
 —Murray Pura, pastor of Heartland Community Church
  and author of *The Poets of Windhover Marsh*

Mountaintop Drive

A John Smyth Mystery (#3)

JAMES R. COGGINS

MOODY PUBLISHERS
CHICAGO

Scripture quoted in chapter 5 of this book is 1 Corinthians 12:30; 13:4–8, 13. Scripture in chapter 16 is John 3:16. Scriptures in chapter 19 are Proverbs 30:7–9; Philippians 4:12–13.

Library of Congress Cataloging-in-Publication Data

Coggins, James Robert, 1949-
    Mountaintop Drive : a John Smyth mystery / James R. Coggins.
        p. cm.— (A John Smyth mystery ; #3)
    ISBN-13: 978-0-8024-1769-5
    1. Periodical editors—Fiction. 2. British Columbia—Fiction.
3. Mountain resorts—Fiction. I. Title.

PR9199.4.C64M68 2005
813'.6—dc22

                                                                    2004028014

ISBN: 0-8024-1769-8
EAN/ISBN-13: 978-0-8024-1769-5

1 3 5 7 9 10 8 6 4 2

Printed in the United States of America

*For Sharon
and other inquirers*

Also by James R. Coggins

Who's Grace?
Desolation Highway

Prologue

She strolled in the terraced garden, admiring her flowers, pausing now and then to pluck off a withered blossom or imbibe the fragrance from a bush of late red roses or a sprig of lavender. Out of habit, she took stock of little chores that needed to be done—a bit of mulching here, some pruning there, some weeds among the pebbles, a patio plant in need of repotting. But she wasn't in the garden to work. Not right now.

She glanced over at the fence and wondered if he would talk to her today. Instinctively she straightened her tailored shorts and tee-shirt, fluffed out her expensive short haircut, straightened her posture. Then she shook her head and gave a little laugh at her own vanity.

Sylvan knew she was beautiful. Being beautiful was a fact of her life, an asset she'd long ago learned to use and maintain. But now, in her midthirties, she found that the maintenance took more work, and increasingly she wondered why she bothered. She knew now that she wouldn't be young and beautiful forever. For the first time in her life, in fact, she was beginning to see her own mortality as something besides a remote possibility.

The neighborhood was silent, as usual, except for a dog barking a few doors down. No sign of a fellow human being. She frowned, took one more turn around the garden, climbed the steps to the sundeck on the second floor, and glided gracefully into the elegant house adjoining the garden.

The hours passed, darkness settled in, and Sylvan walked around the house as earlier she had walked around the garden—straightening pictures, rearranging cushions, putting books and magazines back on shelves. She tried to read but was unable to concentrate, warmed up some soup but couldn't eat it, wondered why she felt so restless.

She was accustomed to being alone in the house while her husband was away. Usually she welcomed the quiet, the freedom to follow her own schedule. But today she felt distracted and disquieted, haunted by questions she was not yet able to answer.

She thought of something he had said once—that it was not good to be alone, that she was meant for something more than what she currently had.

But did she want something more? She thought she did.

Was she willing to do what was necessary? Perhaps.

And what would happen if she did?

It was only later still that the answer came, and it came in a way she had not expected. She didn't see it coming, in fact, until an arm slid across her throat and a hand gripped her shoulder. Terror seized her as well, in a choking stranglehold. She struggled desperately, flailing with gym-toned legs and arms and elbows, but her assailant was too powerful for her. Then the blows began, and her screams quickly subsided to a gurgle.

She hit the floor, a jumble of thoughts surging through her failing brain.

She died reaching up.

Chapter 1

MONDAY, JULY 5 – WEDNESDAY, JULY 7

I don't want to go on another working vacation!"
Ruby Smyth had long since outgrown stomping her foot,
but her face flushed and her green eyes flashed.

"We *always* go wherever the annual convention is, and you
end up working all day while the kids and I sit in a hotel room
watching reruns on television!"

Her husband sighed. "But the church will pay most of the
cost of the trip, and you know . . . otherwise . . ." He brightened. "Maybe we could leave the kids with my parents and
drive out, just the two of us—spend some extra time and just
be tourists. It could be fun," he coaxed.

"But I want to go to the Maritimes! I want to see Louis-
bourg and Green Gables and Oak Island and Peggy's Cove
and Newfoundland!"

She was softening, but she hadn't changed her mind. "I'm
glad you have the job you do. I think it's what you're supposed

to be doing. But this year, I just don't want to go on holiday with the Grace Evangelical Church."

That conversation had taken place in February, but it was still very much on John Smyth's mind in July when he guided the battered old gray station wagon out of the lane behind their modest story-and-a-half stucco house in inner-city Winnipeg. It stayed in his thoughts as he and Ruby turned onto the Trans-Canada Highway and headed not east toward Canada's Maritime Provinces, but west, across the vast prairies, toward British Columbia.

Ruby, on the other hand, seemed to have forgotten about their earlier disagreement. She sat next to him with an un-folded map on her lap and an iced cappuccino in her hand, ready to make the best of the vacation she hadn't wanted. Her flaming red hair glinted in the early morning sun.

John looked at her and sighed. He loved his wife. He would have liked to have taken her to the Maritimes or, for that matter, on a cruise around the world. But in the end there had been no real choice. His meager church salary dictated that they either took their vacation where the annual con-vention was or didn't take one at all. And Ruby knew that as well as he did. It was an inevitable consequence of the deci-sion they had made years earlier to serve the church. They had both learned to accept things that could not be changed and to look for the positives even in generally negative situations.

"Do you think your parents will be able to handle the kids all right?" Ruby asked as the towers of Winnipeg receded slowly in the rearview mirror and the old car settled into a steady pace, like an ant starting to crawl across a football field. "We're going to be gone three weeks," she added. "We've never left the kids that long."

"That's precisely why we're doing this. You need a holiday

from your job too. My parents are perfectly capable of taking care of the kids. They raised me, didn't they?"

"Turn the car around right now!"

"Very funny. Matthew and Elizabeth are going to spend a week at camp, so you wouldn't be with them for one week anyway."

"I know, but Anne is so little."

"She's six."

"Yes, and Michael is thirteen." There was a long silence before she continued quietly, "Do you really think your parents can handle Michael? He's already taller than your father, and your mother is . . . well, when it comes time for the meek to inherit the earth, I think she's got a lock on it."

"Michael," John sighed, staring at the empty road ahead and thinking of his sullen, angry firstborn. He had no idea why Michael had been so hard to live with recently—or what he and Ruby should do about it.

He sighed again. "Well, they'll probably handle him as well as we've been doing."

The afternoon sun shining in through the cheap Venetian blinds drew dark bars across his face. He was looking down, as if it took all of his concentration to keep the band of his wristwatch rotating slowly on the fingertips of both hands.

"Not this weekend," he said stubbornly. "I don't think it's a good idea."

"Come on, Mike," the other was saying earnestly, leaning forward on the edge of the other bed. "It's the perfect weekend for it."

"But they're right there in the house. They're gonna notice somebody sneaking out in the middle of the night."

"Naw. The kids'll be asleep, and the old folks—you know

they're totally clueless—always believe the best about everybody. They'll never suspect a thing."

"I don't know." His eyes were still fixed on the rotating watch. "I still think we should wait."

"I'm tired of waiting, man. Tired of being pushed around. You know?"

"Yeah, I know."

"So I'm gonna do it, no matter what. I just need to know if you're in or not."

There was just a moment's pause before the answer came. "I guess I'm in."

That first day, John and Ruby passed out of their home province of Manitoba and most of the way across the neighboring province of Saskatchewan, a distance of about four hundred and fifty miles. Other people traveled faster and farther in a day. But other people weren't driving battered old station wagons, and they did not enjoy the same sense of peace that was gradually settling over the Smyths.

There was something relaxing about being alone with no phones or children or any responsibilities other than driving. It provided opportunity for conversation, for being quiet together, and for reflection.

On the second day, they continued on along the Trans-Canada Highway, through the dusty grazing lands of southern Alberta, and into the heart of the Rocky Mountains, the first and most beautiful range of mountains in Canada's westernmost province, British Columbia.

"John," Ruby asked as they neared the mountains, "do we keep secrets from each other?"

He glanced at her in surprise. "Why do you ask that?"

"I don't know. I was just thinking about Deborah."

"Your friend Deborah from church? Whose husband left her?"

She nodded. "She thought he was traveling on business, but he was really seeing another woman."

"You think I'm doing that? When I say I'm at a church convention in Calgary I'm really with a call girl in Grand Forks?"

She rolled her eyes. "You know perfectly well I don't suspect you of anything. I just think it's easy for couples to drift apart, to start leaving things out of conversations."

"And that's another reason we need a vacation, right?"

"Right. But you didn't answer my question. Do we really tell each other everything?"

"I think we tell each other everything that's important."

"But how do we know what's important?"

He didn't know how to answer that, so he just shrugged, and she had the grace to let the matter drop.

A black late-model Oldsmobile lurked in the shade of trees lining a quiet side street. The muscular, surly-faced man at the wheel stared straight ahead, as if totally disinterested in what was taking place beside him. Next to him, a paunchy older man with a ragged goatee leaned against the passenger-side door, talking through the open window to a slender, blond teenager in a gray jacket.

"Come on, kid," the older man said. "You know I deal in cash only. No credit. You don't bring me money, I don't give you nothin'. Got it?"

The boy outside the car swallowed hard and nodded but said nothing. As he turned and slouched away, there was anger in his eyes.

The third morning took John and Ruby Smyth through more mountains, green and forested, in contrast to the gray rock and snow of the Rockies. Then they traversed a flatter, drier, hotter section between mountain ranges before following the Coquihalla Highway up and over a final mountain range and down into the lower Fraser River valley. As they neared their goal, their conversation turned from what they were leaving behind to what they were heading toward.

"Did we really need to allow three weeks for this trip?" Ruby asked.

"I think so. The convention will take up the rest of this week, and then I want to write articles on the Grace Evangelical churches in Abbotsford."

"There are only two of them."

"I know." John grinned. "But they are quite different churches, and I want to attend a Sunday service at each of them." John Smyth was editor of *Grace* magazine, a periodical produced by Grace Evangelical Church, a century-old Christian denomination based in Winnipeg.

"John, promise me you're not going to spend the whole three weeks working."

"Of course not. I've already told you that. There'll be plenty of time for vacation, too, side trips and things. We can go to Vancouver, see Stanley Park and the ocean. And some days we'll just sleep in and relax."

"Relax? At Doctor John's place?"

"You don't like Doctor John very much, do you?"

"It's not that I don't like him. It's just that I find him . . . well, cold. It's like he's always thinking, and you never really know *what* he's thinking. And why does everybody call him *Doctor* John anyway?"

"Well, no one calls him that to his face, of course. It's just a sign of respect. He's one of the few real intellectuals in the Grace Evangelical Church. He's only in his late thirties, but he's already written three significant books, not to mention all the money he and his family have contributed to the church."

"Oh, I know they're very generous, and we should all be grateful."

"Remember when his parents lent us their cottage on West Hawk Lake for our honeymoon? We couldn't have afforded a place like that, maybe not even a honeymoon at all— and yet we got it all for nothing."

Ruby smiled in remembrance. "When they offered us their cottage, we pictured a rustic log cabin out in the bush. We weren't expecting a two-story house with wall-to-wall carpet, six bedrooms, three bathrooms, a fireplace, and satellite TV."

"I suppose that may be the Robinsons' idea of rustic." John became serious. "One of the pitfalls of being rich, I guess. But anyway, why don't you like Doctor John?"

"That was his *parents* who lent us their cabin."

"Yes, but he's the one who invited us to stay at his house for the convention."

"That's okay for you. The two of you will sit and discuss theology and church politics for hours on end, but there will be no one for me to talk to. He has a large house, and he hasn't invited anyone else to stay there but us. He could probably put up a half-dozen delegates without any crowding."

"I don't think Doctor John would feel comfortable with a lot of strangers in his house. In fact, it's really an honor that he invited us. He's pretty careful about guarding his privacy. And he's been even more private since Deirdre died."

As the Trans-Canada Highway winds down out of the mountains following the Fraser River, the enclosing mountains abruptly angle off in both directions, and the road enters the broad triangular floodplain of the lower Fraser River valley, a land as flat but not nearly as extensive nor as dry as the Canadian prairies. The vast majority of British Columbia is covered with mountains and dense fir forests, but this is one of four broad, fertile river valleys where agriculture flourishes. The mighty Fraser runs sedately through this fertile land for a hundred miles before pouring its mud-brown waters into the Pacific Ocean near Canada's major west-coast port and third largest city, Vancouver.

More than half of British Columbia's four million people live in this tiny corner of the province locals call "the Lower Mainland," their burgeoning suburbs pushing up the sides of the mountains in order to preserve the fertile valley floor for agriculture. Halfway along the valley, perched atop a series of low, rounded, sand-and-gravel hills and surrounded by raspberry and dairy farms, sits the city of Abbotsford. The homes and businesses of Abbotsford's 130,000 people have now covered almost all the low hills available and have started to drift eastward up the western end of an even higher prominence known as Sumas Mountain.

It was to this higher, newer Abbotsford that John and Ruby Smyth were headed.

"There's Whatcom Road," Ruby said, pointing to the sign.

John guided the aging station wagon off the highway. With Ruby reading off directions, he followed the twists and turns of various streets up the side of Sumas Mountain. As they rose higher and higher, the homes became larger and newer and more expensive, perched like castles on the rocky cliff side. The fire hydrants, instead of the usual red-and-white painted metal, were faced with polished brass.

"Turn right here," Ruby said, "on Mountaintop Drive. That's Doctor John's house—number 36031."

John pulled the old car into the wide driveway of a two-story pink stucco house with a sculptured cedar-shake roof and white pillars holding up a front portico. Off-white mini-blinds covered all the visible windows. The front yard was artistically landscaped with large brown granite rocks, cedar chips, and spiny bushes.

John and Ruby sat for a moment looking at the building.

"Welcome to our home for the next couple of weeks," John said.

"That's not a home. That's a . . . a . . ."

"It's just a house, Ruby, the home of Dr. John Robinson. If it had a white picket fence out front, it would look just like our place."

"Yeah, right." Ruby gave him a lopsided smirk as they climbed from the car and started up the walk.

When John pressed the doorbell, a chorus of deep bells reverberated within. He looked puzzled.

"Westminster chimes," Ruby said.

"Oh."

The door swung open to reveal a tall, well-built man in his late thirties with neatly trimmed dark hair and a dark mustache. He wore expensive casual clothes—a cotton knit shirt and pressed khakis—but he was the type who would look distinguished in ragged blue jeans.

"Ruby," John Smyth said, "I think you have met Dr. John Robinson."

"Call me John," the tall man said.

Ruby smiled, looking across at her short, bearded, bespectacled husband and then up at her elegant host.

"Two Johns," she said. "That might be a bit confusing."

As they were unpacking their suitcases in a spacious guest-room, Ruby whispered, "This place feels like a first-class hotel. Did you see that living room—white carpet, powder-blue velvet upholstery, those glass and polished-brass end tables?

And the bedrooms . . ." Sitting on the bed, she slid her stockinged feet back and forth on the plush carpet. "They're as nice as the living room."

"So, enjoy it. We don't often get to stay in a place like this. Let's get unpacked and go down for supper."

"Doctor John cooks?"

"I think he has a housekeeper."

"Housekeeper?" Ruby thought about that for a moment. "I'm not sure I could live in a house like this and not even have to clean it. I think I would feel—I don't know—guilty or something. Do you think Doctor John ever feels guilty?"

They ate their supper of assorted salads and grilled steak outside on a wide sundeck. The house, cut into the steep hillside, turned out to have three stories instead of the two it showed to the street. Each floor commanded a panoramic view of the Fraser Valley, with bright green squares of farmland stretching out to the south, the U.S.-Canadian border two or three miles away an invisible line on the valley floor. To the west, beyond the rounded hills, houses, and trees of Abbotsford, the valley ran on to the Pacific Ocean forty miles away. A row of fir-covered mountains angled southwest. And behind them, to the south-southeast, dominating the view in almost every part of the valley, rose a majestic cone-shaped white peak.

"What a beautiful mountain!" Ruby enthused. "What's its name?"

"That is Mount Baker." John Robinson smiled. "It is actually in Washington state, but some of the best views of it are in British Columbia. It's volcanic of course, over ten thousand feet high, and receives more snow than any other mountain on earth—a hundred feet a year. That's because of the prevailing southwesterly winds coming in off the Pacific. There is a joke about our rainy season lasting from January 1 to December 31 every year, but the heavy rain actually only lasts from October to April. Summers are generally dry. It is a remarkably efficient system. What falls as rain in the valleys falls as snow on the mountains, and the melting snowpack from the mountains provides water for the valleys all summer. That makes agriculture possible in the valleys and sustains the rain forest on the mountainsides."

"Oh," Ruby said. This was a little more information than she'd been asking for. "Anyway, it's a fantastic view."

"Yes, you can see the whole valley from here. That view is what makes the houses up here so expensive."

"That and the fact that they all look like mansions," John Smyth put in.

Robinson smiled. "There are some disadvantages to living up here."

"Like what? Icy roads in the winter . . . ?"

A chilly silence suddenly descended on the conversation, and John and Ruby Smyth exchanged embarrassed glances.

Ruby hurried to break the silence. "Is it a friendly neighborhood? Do you know the neighbors?"

"Not really. The people on that side are Chinese or Korean, I think. They keep their blinds drawn, and I hardly ever see them."

"What about the other side—that lady over there, for instance?"

The two men looked down at the neighboring yard, where a well-proportioned, thirty-something blonde woman in shorts and a tee-shirt was weeding her flower garden.

John Robinson seemed to take a moment to collect himself. "I don't have many women friends. I've met her husband. He's a lawyer. We've talked a couple of times and exchanged

21

business cards." Robinson brightened. "Did you know that Abbotsford is known as Canada's Bible Belt?"

"Of course," John Smyth replied "I want to write some articles about that while we're here."

"There has been a very fine doctoral thesis written on the subject. I'll get you a copy. Weekly church attendance here is still almost 60 percent of the population. That is not very high, certainly not when compared to the Bible Belt in the United States. But with the Canadian average for church attendance now at less than 20 percent, 60 percent is unusual indeed. Churches flourish here—there are about eighty-five of them—and Christianity still influences a lot of people. A majority of the city council, in fact, are evangelical Christians. They put restrictions on bars, and a referendum a few years ago turned down a proposal to establish a casino. That kind of thing makes Abbotsford an attractive place to live for many Christians, but it is also an anomaly, out of step with trends in the rest of the country. There are few places left in Canada where Christianity is as accepted as it is in Abbotsford, though even here you'll find a lot of indifference and even hostility toward the faith."

Robinson seemed to have settled into a comfortable groove, as if he were lecturing one of his classes at Abbotsford College, and it appeared he might go on for some time. Catching a pointed glance from Ruby, John said, "I'm sorry to interrupt this, John, but we're feeling pretty tired, and we have a busy day tomorrow."

Chapter 2

THURSDAY, JULY 8

There it is," John Smyth told Ruby. "Athens has the Parthenon. Paris has Notre Dame. Toronto has the CN Tower. And Abbotsford has this."

Mountaintop Grace Evangelical Church was two curves and a quarter of a mile down the road from John Robinson's house, set back over the brow of a hill in a slight depression. It was not a traditional church building—a rectangular box with a steeple—but was designed to fit into its affluent neighborhood, all glass and brick with a green steel roof sculpted to look like a range of mountains. A paved driveway curved through a landscaped front lawn and under a covered portico so that passengers could be let off at the door in bad weather without fear of getting wet. The drive then continued around behind the church to a multistoried parking garage designed to take advantage of the natural depression in the terrain.

Inside, the wide, curving foyer was already filled with jostling people, their excited chatter drowning out serene gospel music played over speakers. A number of light oak doors on the inner curve of the foyer gave access to a spacious amphitheater that sloped toward a hundred foot-wide central stage. The royal blue carpet supported row after row of pews, made of more light oak and cushioned with more royal blue. The space could seat twenty-five hundred people, about five hundred more than had actually shown up for this annual North American convention of the Grace Evangelical churches.

"This place reminds me of Doctor John's house," Ruby whispered to John.

A tall, good-looking man in a well-cut dark-blue suit strode to the podium. "Good morning! I am Marv Andreason, senior pastor of Mountaintop Church."

The audience erupted into applause. Mountaintop was a success story. One of the wealthiest and most dynamic churches in the denomination, it had grown from the handful of people who started the congregation twenty years earlier to a weekly attendance of over four thousand.

John Smyth, sitting in the very front row with Ruby, took a photo of Andreason and noted the man had the politician's knack of reacting to the click of a shutter, so that he always appeared in photos face on and smiling.

Smyth took a few more shots of the dignitaries seated on the stage behind Andreason and then began taking notes. Writing a full report of the annual convention was one of his regular job responsibilities. He had been doing it for a dozen years and had developed a level of competence at it that the church now took for granted. He didn't really mind. The annual convention was also where he met ministry colleagues, old friends, and interesting people.

At midmorning, when the convention adjourned for a half-hour coffee break, Smyth took advantage of the break to catch Andreason's arm as he stepped off the stage. "Marv, we agreed we would find some time to get together and talk about your church."

"Hello, John." Andreason gave Smyth a fully attentive smile that seemed as enthusiastic as a bear hug would have been from a lesser man. "It's good to see you. As my secretary told you in her e-mail, Monday is my day off, Tuesday is the day I spend in prayer, and Wednesday is reserved for sermon preparation. Why don't we meet in the Starlight Café for breakfast on Thursday? You know where it is? Good. Now, I know you want to talk to some other people in the church as well, so I had my secretary set up some appointments for you. You can get the list from her."

Before Smyth could say anything further, Andreason had laid a hand on his shoulder as if in blessing and slipped off into the crowd.

The brown-haired, broad-faced man gripped his expensive briefcase with a manicured hand and shifted his weight, impatient for the door to be opened.

"Good afternoon, Mr. Halvis," said the guard.

"Afternoon!" the other grumbled. "It was morning when I got here."

"That was five minutes ago. Sorry you had to wait for the shift change." Ralph Hearne grinned. "I suppose you're here to bring justice and freedom to another of our unfairly convicted residents?"

Halvis grunted. "I'm here to see a client, yes, but that has very little to do with freedom and justice. If it was a matter of justice, most of my clients would never leave this place."

Hearne nodded. For once he was in complete agreement with the lawyer.

"As for freedom," the lawyer went on, "the only freedom

I'm interested in right now is my own. I am trying to discharge my obligations here at Matsqui so I can get away. I was at Ferndale earlier this morning, and a couple of my clients asked if I could come back to see them on Saturday to work on their appeals. I told them I was going to Kelowna to negotiate a multimillion-dollar real estate deal, and that was far more important than their appeals."

Hearne nodded again as he swung the door open and stepped aside.

Sunset comes late in the Canadian summer, and darkness falls even later. It was well past ten when the boy in the gray jacket first hit the streets, moving with practiced silence from shadow to shadow, his blond hair catching a gleam from a street lamp. He intentionally avoided the woman who stood forlornly on the street corner by a bank. He knew what she was there for, and he despised her for it. For that matter, he despised all women and their weak, silly ways.

But he forgot about the prostitute almost as soon as he rounded the corner. He had things to do that night. And it was still a long walk to where he wanted to go.

About the same time, nearing the end of a long shift, Ralph Hearne was also walking—down long, artificially bright institutional corridors, looking for trouble as surely as the boy, and just as likely to find it.

Chapter 3

"**M**y name is David Michael Black, and I am a convicted criminal."

John Smyth, in the front pew, snapped a shot of the man standing on the stage of Mountaintop Grace Evangelical Church. Small and wiry, the man had black hair and a thick, droopy black mustache. He wore an ill-fitting suit, white shirt, and crooked tie.

During the day, the convention had focused on business reports. But this evening meeting, like the others, was devoted to sermons, music, and "testimonies"—people talking about the difference Christianity made in their lives. These personal stories were often the most interesting and moving parts of the convention.

Black spoke with an earnestness and passion that Smyth found convincing. He told of his early life in Montreal with an alcoholic mother and an abusive father, but he made no excuses for his later behavior. He described an ever-widening spiral of petty crime, drugs, and violence, ending with a conviction at age twenty-nine for manslaughter. That, in turn, had brought him to Matsqui Institution, a medium-security federal prison in Abbotsford.

"I couldn't believe it when this short, pudgy guy said he wanted to come visit me every week. I figured he wanted something. He said he just wanted to be my friend. I said he was a liar. He just smiled and said he would come visit me anyway—and he did. Said his name was Bob."

At that point, the convention delegates interrupted Black's story with applause and laughter as they realized that the "short, pudgy guy" was Bob Young, pastor of Shadow Valley, the other Grace Evangelical Church in Abbotsford.

"Pastor Bob come to see me every week for two years," Black continued. "And I didn't make it easy for him. Sometimes I cussed at him. Sometimes I yelled. I told him he was a short, ugly loser who was wasting his time. See, I figured he was gonna reject me like everybody else, and I just wanted to get it over with. But he kept coming. So finally one day, when he was getting ready to leave, I told him not to ever come back, and if he did come back, I'd have him killed. And you know what he did then?"

The man paused, swallowed hard and looked out into the silent amphitheater.

"Pastor Bob said, 'See you next week.' And that—well, that broke me. It was like—like he was even willing to die, just so he could help me. I mean, nobody ever gave up anything for me. But this guy was ready to give up his *life*."

That had been two years ago. Black had since been transferred to Ferndale, a minimum-security institution across the Fraser River in Mission, B.C., to serve out his last months before release from prison. He was now allowed weekend passes, and on one of those passes he had been baptized as a Christian at Shadow Valley Grace Evangelical Church.

"My name is Kurt Hallbach." Black's companion was somewhat taller, blond, and handsome. His story differed from Black's only in the details. He had grown up in British Columbia, his parents had divorced, he had finished high school but he had then drifted into fraud, break-and-enters, and finally armed robbery. Another member of Shadow Valley Church, a small white-haired man, had been the one who had visited him. "Then he stopped coming, and I figured he gave up on me," Hallbach said. "But then, after a couple of weeks, Pastor Bob came and told me Allen was dead. His wife was dead, and all the time he was visiting me, he was dying of cancer. I couldn't believe it—he chose to spend his last days with a convict. Pastor Bob told me that Allen was like Jesus, who spent his last hours with two criminals . . ."

At this point, Hallbach broke down. Smyth got a picture of him sobbing with Bob Young's arm draped around him. He also noticed with chagrin that the "short, pudgy" pastor was at least five inches taller than he himself was.

Smyth whispered to Ruby, "I think I should do a profile on these two."

"You're not going to spend our whole holiday chasing down criminals for interviews, are you?"

The two of them were talking quietly at the end of the day. The voices were low, but the tension was high.

"Tonight's the night, Mike."

"I still don't know. It's risky."

"They'll be asleep. They'll never suspect a thing. Besides, I thought you agreed he has it coming."

"He does."

"It's a good way to get even with him, right? And I could use a little cash."

"Me, too."

"So, you gonna do it or what?"

The other took a deep breath. "Yeah. Okay."

Ruby didn't know what woke her, and her eyes were still half-closed when she sat up in bed. Disoriented, she blinked and looked around.

All was silent and dark. Her husband stirred in his sleep, grunted, and turned over. He looked, somehow, farther away than usual. Squinting, she peered over his shoulder to see the time, but the clock was gone.

Only then did she realize their lighted alarm was back home in Winnipeg. She and John were in John Robinson's house, in a king-sized bed in a mansion in the middle of the Bible Belt.

Shaking off the sense that something wasn't right, she settled back into the pillow and stretched out under the smooth, expensive cotton sheets. Sleep was already closing back in.

Chapter 4

"Did you hear anything last night?"

John Smyth stretched in the bed. "When?"

"I don't know. In the middle of the night. Something half woke me up."

"Are you sure it was something here, and not something back in Winnipeg?"

She considered. "Let's call the kids tonight."

"Sure."

A packed suitcase was waiting at the bottom of the stairs when they came down for breakfast. John Robinson stood beside it. His face seemed strained.

"I need to go away," he said. "My plane leaves in about ninety minutes. Breakfast things are on the table. Henriette, the housekeeper, comes in Monday, Wednesday, and Friday mornings. She cleans, prepares some meals, and does laundry, so if you want anything washed or want her to cook something for you, just ask her." He handed John Smyth a small black box and a card. "This is the remote burglar alarm. The code is 7347. Push the number and then 'set' when you leave the house and the same number and 'off' before you come back in. If you forget and the alarm goes off, push the code and 'off' and then phone the number on this card."

"A burglar alarm?" Ruby asked. "Is that necessary in Abbotsford?"

"It's a sensible precaution," Robinson replied. "Virtually every house on this street has this type of burglar alarm. Is there anything else you will need?"

John Smyth, bewildered by the sudden change in Robinson's plans, tried to think quickly. "We need to get some cash out. Is there a bank nearby?"

Robinson replied in the same tone he had been using before. "Not on the mountain. You'll have to go down into old Abbotsford."

Ruby asked, "While John is in his meetings, I thought I'd get out and get some exercise. Are there any walking trails around here?"

"Not on the mountain. The terrain is too steep, and there is still the possibility of running into a bear or cougar up here. Why don't you go down to Mill Lake? It's in a big park in the middle of Abbotsford with a paved walkway all around. A lot of people walk there. I often walk there with . . ."

Robinson didn't finish the sentence. He just turned and walked out the door.

"Thank you," Ruby said to his retreating back. "I'll try that."

Watching him drive away, John said, "He didn't even apologize for leaving us. I wonder what made him leave so suddenly. I hope you don't mind."

"Mind? We'll be here all alone in this beautiful house. It'll be just like our honeymoon."

"So it will." John paused for a moment, still staring out at the street. "Was Doctor John at the convention session last night?"

"I don't know. I don't remember seeing him there. But I was talking to Arlene White during some of the breaks and might not have noticed. Did you see him?"

"I don't remember seeing him at all."

By late afternoon, John Smyth was dragging. For three days, convention delegates had listened to reports, debated issues, and worshiped together. Now the convention was almost over, with one item left for discussion—a two-page document on "The Nature of God" presented by the denomination's Theological Commission. The carefully worded document defined God as a personal Creator (not some impersonal force). It also affirmed a belief in traditional Christian morality, declaring that God condemns actions such as adultery, theft, dishonesty, and murder.

After some discussion over minor points, the document had been approved by an overwhelming majority of delegates. This was scarcely surprising since the resolution merely restated what most of the church had believed for two thousand years. But Smyth knew that, in passing the resolution, the denomination had reaffirmed a position that was radically different from that of the surrounding society, except perhaps in isolated places like Abbotsford.

Smyth had in his files a survey showing that fewer than 20 percent of Canadians still believed in a God who "punished sin." Smyth wondered what that meant other people believed. That God didn't exist at all? That evil was acceptable to the vague force that ruled the universe? That there was no such thing as right and wrong—or that individuals were free to define right and wrong as they themselves saw fit?

What were the practical implications of such beliefs?

Smyth wondered how many people, given the right motivation and circumstances, would lie, steal, or commit murder and see nothing wrong with it.

It was early evening when the tall, brown-haired man turned his silver BMW Roadster into the driveway, got out of the car, and plucked his suitcase and briefcase from the passenger seat. He walked up the sidewalk, unlocked the front door, called, "Hello, I'm home," and shut the door. Leaving his bags by the door, he disappeared into the living room.

After a few moments, he stumbled back out to the front hall and punched three numbers into his cell phone.

They arrived about twenty minutes after the first cars, their white unmarked vehicle rolling to a stop in front of Tom Halvis's place. Detective Randy McNoll was a six-foot, sandy-haired, twenty-year veteran of the Abbotsford Police Department. The man with him was thinner, darker, and younger, and his off-the-rack suit fit him better. They did not speak as they climbed from the car, ducked under the yellow police tape that was already strung around the property, and walked up the sidewalk to a knot of men by the front door of 36033 Mountaintop Drive. It was a two-story stone-and-stucco house with two magnificent chimneys rising from a cedar-shingled roof.

"What've we got?" asked McNoll, a man given to speaking in clipped half-sentences and occasional proverbs—particularly when dealing with underlings and colleagues.

A uniformed police officer glanced over at a brown-haired man leaning against the wall of the house on the small slab of concrete that served as a front porch. The officer led the two detectives out onto the driveway away from the porch.

"We have a dead woman in the living room," he said quietly.

"Her name is Sylvan Halvis. I don't know how to spell that yet."

"Guess—drugs or domestic?"

"My first guess would be neither. No evidence of drugs, and the husband"—he jerked his head in the direction of the man on the porch—"is the one who found the body. Evidently he was away for the weekend and just got home."

"Drugs and domestic disputes are the usual reasons to get murdered in Abbotsford," McNoll muttered half to himself.

"Well, maybe this case will be different. You were first on the scene?"

"Yes. With Marcia—uh, Officer Scranton." He nodded to a woman officer with a blonde ponytail who stood at the front door of the house. "The husband, Thomas Halvis, was standing on the porch like that when we got here. He didn't say anything, just pointed toward the living room. It's a big room —runs the width of the house, front to back. The body is at the back, by a door that leads out to a deck. We checked to make sure she was dead."

"Was she?"

"Oh, yeah. For some time. Body's stiff. Blood all over the place."

"Shot?"

"Looks more like stabbed, though I didn't see a weapon. There's blood spattered everywhere. Some tables and chairs are pushed back, as if there was a struggle."

"You check the rest of the house?"

"By the book. Woods and Briggs were here by then. They secured the house front and back, and we did a quick walk-through. Nobody in the house. Then we got out and waited for the scene-of-crime people and the coroner. And you guys, of course."

"Coroner's here?"

"Yes. Dr. Evans just went in."

"Good."

McNoll turned away and looked out at the street. His partner looked at him and waited. He had learned to let McNoll speak first.

"Stabbing sounds more like domestic than drugs," McNoll said at last. "More typical of passion or of panic than premeditation. Guys involved in the turf war usually use guns. But can't rule drugs out either. Knife could be a kirpan."

Darwinder Sandhu stared at his partner. He spoke stiffly. "Probably not. Most of the Indo-Canadians involved in drugs are second generation. They've abandoned their Sikh beliefs —don't believe in much of anything—which is why they're involved with drugs in the first place. And that means they don't wear the Sikh ceremonial daggers."

"Traded kirpans for guns? That's an upgrade in technology, not a character change."

There was a strained silence. Both men knew that at least two of the main gangs fighting a turf war over drugs in the lower Fraser valley were predominantly Indo-Canadian.

McNoll spoke again. "Could also be a break-and-enter gone wrong. Thief didn't expect to find anyone home." Then he added, "Could still be a kirpan."

McNoll turned toward the uniformed officer. "Cooper, go door-to-door, say a block in either direction, and ask if anybody saw or heard anything unusual in the past twenty-four hours or saw any activity at all at this house. Take notes. Don't tell anyone anything. Just say we are investigating a possible crime. We'll do more thorough door-to-door interviews later. But right now it's Saturday evening, a lot of people will be home, and maybe you'll get a hot lead. Start with the people on the other side of the tape there." He nodded toward a dozen or so people standing awkwardly in twos and threes on the sidewalk.

McNoll then walked over to the brown-haired man

standing on the front porch. "Mr. Halvis? I'm Detective Randy McNoll, and this is Detective Darwinder Sandhu. We are very sorry about your wife. Can we get you anything?"

The man looked up, his broad face showing shock, grief, and pain.

"Would you like us to call someone?"

The man shook his head. "No, thank you."

"Mr. Halvis, the police will be in the house for quite a few hours yet. Is there somewhere you could stay tonight—with a friend maybe?"

The man shook his head again and cleared his throat. "I'll get a hotel room."

"We can make a reservation for you. The hotel down at the foot of the mountain okay?"

The man nodded, and McNoll turned to Sandhu, who was already pulling out his cell phone. McNoll turned back to the man on the porch.

"Mr. Halvis, I wonder if you would be able to talk to us for a few moments? Why don't we sit over there in my car?"

Halvis was a big man in his late thirties, his immaculate gray pin-striped suit expertly tailored to fit his large frame. McNoll held the back door of the car open for Halvis, then climbed into the backseat after him and pulled the door in until it was almost closed. Sandhu joined them a few moments later, sitting in the front passenger seat.

"The reservation's all set," he said.

"Mr. Halvis, some of the questions I'm going to ask you are routine and technical, and some of them will be hard. Please answer them as well as you can. Your answers will help us find out what happened to your wife."

Halvis nodded.

"Your name is Thomas Halvis?"

"Yes."

"How do you spell that?"

"H-A-L-V-I-S."

"This is your house? You live here?"

"Yes."

"How long have you lived here?"

"Six years. This was one of the first houses on the street."

"The woman in the living room is your wife?"

"Yes. Sylvan. S-Y-L-V-A-N."

"How old is she?"

"Thirty-four. Her birthday is February twentieth."

"How long have you been married?"

"Ten years. We got married in Winnipeg, just after I finished law school."

"Does anyone else live in the house?"

"No. We have no children."

"Tell me what you did and what you saw when you came home this evening."

Halvis took a deep breath. "I was up in Kelowna on a business trip. I left on Thursday and got back tonight around seven. I walked into the house and called out to Sylvan that I was home."

"Was the door locked?"

"Yes. We always keep it locked."

"Burglar alarm?"

Halvis considered. "I never thought to check it. It's not dark, and Sylvan was expecting me home." His eyes widened. "But it might have been dark . . . I don't know when . . ."

"It's all right, Mr. Halvis. Did your wife usually turn the alarm on at night?"

"Not always. Sylvan doesn't like—didn't like—the alarm. A lot of the time she didn't set it even when I was away, especially if she was expecting someone. I was always getting onto her about that."

McNoll was watching the large man appraisingly. He said in a softer voice, "Okay. You were telling us what you did when you got home."

Halvis took a breath as if steeling himself. "I unlocked the door and went in. I set my suitcase and briefcase down in the hall and walked into the living room. Sylvan was—she was lying on the floor at the other end of the room. I could see . . . the blood—"

"I know this is difficult, Mr. Halvis, but it is important. Did you check to see if she was alive?"

"I think I touched her hand. It was cold." He shivered. "I didn't want to disturb the scene."

McNoll stole a glance at Sandhu.

"I'm a lawyer," Halvis said.

"Of course. What did you do then?"

"I went back into the hall and called 911. Then I went out onto the porch and waited."

"Did you go back in and look at your wife again?"

Halvis shook his head. "I—I couldn't."

"Did you hear any sounds in the house? Could anyone else have been here when you got home?"

Halvis shook his head. "I didn't hear anything."

"Did everything seem normal in the house, other than what had happened to your wife?"

"I think so."

"The temperature in the house was normal?"

"The air conditioning was on, I think. It's been a hot day."

"You didn't adjust it when you got home?"

"No, of course not. It's on a thermostat."

"Nothing out of place?"

"I didn't look around. Didn't go into the rest of the house. But I didn't notice anything."

"We will have you go through the whole house in a day or

so, if you feel up to it When was the last time you talked to your wife?"

"Last night, around seven. I phoned during a dinner break."

"How did she sound? Did she sound worried or frightened, or excited?"

"She sounded . . . normal. We only talked a couple of minutes. I had to get back to my meeting."

"Was anyone here with her then?"

"No, I don't think so. I asked her what she was up to, and she said she was planning to spend the evening at home."

"Mr. Halvis, excuse me for asking at a time like this, but we have to ask hard questions in order to properly conduct our investigation. How were you getting along with Mrs. Halvis?"

"What do you mean?"

"Did you have a good marriage? Have you quarreled recently?"

"We were getting along fine. We had a good marriage. We didn't always agree on everything, but we had a good life. We hadn't had any major arguments for months."

"Did you have any *minor* arguments recently?"

"Not that I can remember. As I said, we didn't always agree, but we hadn't really argued about anything for a long time. We—we're just not that kind of people."

"I'm not accusing you of causing your wife's death, Mr. Halvis, just trying to determine her state of mind. If you two had quarreled, she might have called a friend to come over and talk, for instance."

"We didn't quarrel . . . about anything."

"Another difficult question. Could your wife have been having an affair or some kind of relationship with another man?"

"No—at least, I don't think . . ."

"Did you suspect something was going on?"

"No. It's just . . . I can't accuse . . ."

"Even if it's just a suspicion, it might be helpful. I promise we won't give it any more weight than it deserves."

"No. My wife loved me. She wouldn't . . ." Halvis broke off, his throat catching. "Look. Once I came in and heard her talking on the phone to someone she called John. When she heard me, she hung up immediately and said it was a wrong number."

"Did you ask her about it?"

"What would be the point? If she was having an affair, she could just deny it. And there must be a hundred innocent explanations . . ."

"Okay, we can leave that for now. Mr. Halvis, did your wife have any enemies?"

"No."

"Do you?"

"Not really. As I said, I'm a lawyer, so I might have some disgruntled clients, but no one in particular comes to mind."

"Can you think of anyone who might have reason to kill your wife?"

"No. Of course not. She was a wonderful, beautiful woman."

"What kind of law do you practice?"

"Mostly business and contract law. But I do some criminal law, especially legal-aid cases."

"Were you in Kelowna in connection with your law practice?"

"Yes, I was helping a local group negotiate a deal to buy a mall up there. There was a swap for some land here, so it was a pretty complicated deal."

"And such deals are normally negotiated on weekends?"

"Not usually. We thought we had reached a deal earlier, but some complications arose. There were some deadlines involved, and the weekend was the only time we were all available on short notice."

"Were the negotiations successful?"

"Yes, we completed an agreement this morning, had a late lunch together, and then I drove home. Traffic was terrible. Why are you asking all this?"

"Just checking out every detail. Where were you staying?"

"The Ogo Inn. It's a big new development on the east side of the lake, near the bridge. Listen, am I a suspect?"

"Not really, Mr. Halvis, but you know we have to check all possibilities. We can't take a suspect to court and have the defense lawyer ask if we checked the husband's alibi—so we're checking the husband's alibi. Now, would you please write down the names and addresses of the people who were with you in the meeting?"

When Halvis had done so, McNoll said, "Thank you, Mr. Halvis. I am sorry to put you through this. You have been very helpful. Is there anything we can do for you? Would you like us to contact your wife's family or anyone else?"

"No, thanks. I can do that. I should do it."

"Let me know once you've contacted them." McNoll handed Halvis his business card. "We don't want family members finding out about this through the press, so we won't release your wife's name until we hear from you."

"I appreciate that. I should be able to contact them tonight. There's only her mother and two brothers, and they're all in Winnipeg. Is that all?"

"Just one more thing. In a few minutes, we will ask you to step over to the house. The scene-of-crime team will take your fingerprints and shoeprints and samples from your clothes. As I'm sure you know, this is purely for comparison purposes. Your prints will be all over the house, and we need to eliminate those so we can see who else was there. After that, you can go down to your hotel."

McNoll and Sandhu left Halvis in the backseat of the car with the door open a crack and walked toward the house.

"Do you still think it might be domestic?" Sandhu asked.

"Like I told you—drugs or domestic."

"You mean you suspect the husband?"

"I mean we check his alibi and see. Doesn't pay to get ahead of the facts. And domestic doesn't always mean husband. She could've been having a 'domestic' relationship with someone else."

On the porch they met a man in brown slacks and a checked shirt coming out of the house, pulling plastic coverings off his shoes. His hair and short mustache were iron gray, his face tanned.

"Gerald," McNoll nodded briefly in greeting. "You okay?"

"Good, Randy," the coroner answered. "A lot better than that woman in there."

"You done with the body?"

"Yes. Do you want to see it before they take it out?"

McNoll nodded again. "Any preliminaries?"

"The cause of death appears to be multiple stab wounds, at least six or seven. I presume she bled out."

"A lot of blood then. The killer would have blood on him?"

"Don't see how he could have avoided it."

"So, not an efficient killing. An amateur?"

"Possibly."

"Is the weapon still there?"

"No. At least, I didn't see it. It was probably a knife or a letter opener, something like that—not very sharp judging by the tearing and bruising around the wounds."

"A crime of opportunity then—not planned?"

"That's for you to decide, not me."

"Any thoughts on time of death?"

"Hard to pinpoint precisely. The air conditioning was on

automatic. But I'd guess about eighteen hours, give or take a couple of hours either way."

"So we're talking sometime between midnight and four o'clock this morning."

From a distance, she might have been asleep, a beautiful woman sprawled on the plush carpet in a nightgown of creamy silk. But the blood gave her away. It covered her chest and abdomen and spread on both sides of her. She had fallen partially under a small coffee table, one table leg by her shoulder. Her once-beautiful face, now contorted in pain amid matted clouds of blonde hair, lay half under the table. Abstract patterns of blood spattered the floor, the walls, nearby pieces of furniture, and some books and other items that lay scattered across the floor.

"She been moved at all?" McNoll asked. He and Sandhu, encased in plastic suits and shoes, moved carefully around the room.

Tony Mangucci, the plastic-covered scene-of-crime man conducting the tour, said, "No. She was obviously dead, so Cooper didn't do more than check for a pulse. The coroner didn't need to move her for his examination. She may have moved herself a bit, though, after she fell." He pointed toward a bloody heel print a few inches below her right foot.

"What else have you got?"

"There are bloody footprints leading out the back door and blood smears on the door. We haven't analyzed them yet or checked for fingerprints. The door has been pried open with a crowbar or something like that. I don't know where the footprints lead. Storch is following them now."

"Have you checked the husband's suitcase and briefcase?"

"Not yet. Do you suspect him?"

"I suspect everyone. At the very least, the bags were on

the scene, and I want to get them out of here. He might have a bloody knife in a side pocket, but I doubt it. Check for cross-contamination of the site. Maybe something in the bag will corroborate his alibi. Then check the husband himself— prints, shoeprints, and such."

"Okay. I'll do it in a few minutes, as soon as we get the body out of here."

"Thanks."

The late evening sun was setting on the western horizon when John and Ruby Smyth's old station wagon rolled down Mountaintop Drive to John Robinson's house. They slowed as they slipped through a knot of emergency vehicles and bystanders at the house next door and turned into the driveway of Robinson's house.

"What do you suppose is going on there?" Ruby asked.

"I don't know. A robbery, maybe? Doctor John said they'd had trouble with break-ins around here. Maybe I should go see."

"Maybe you shouldn't."

He hesitated, still looking next door. "You're right. We can check the news tomorrow." He pulled the little black box out of his pocket and turned off the burglar alarm. "At least the break-in wasn't here."

Wearily, they unlocked the front door. John kicked off his shoes by the door and sank into the blue velvet couch in the living room. Ruby slid her shoes off as well and sank down beside him, massaging her feet on the plush carpet.

"Want to watch television?" John asked.

"What on television?"

"Anything, as long as it's mindless. It's been a long weekend."

McNoll and Sandhu took off their plastic suits on the front porch.

McNoll had not said anything since they looked at the body. Sandhu squared his shoulders and asked, "What do you think? Somebody does a B and E, pries open the back door in the middle of the night, she hears him and comes down to investigate, so he grabs a knife and kills her?"

"Maybe. Let's see what Storch found."

They walked around to the side of the house.

"Don't come any farther," Bobby Storch called. He was Mangucci's scene-of-crime colleague. "Put your shoe covers back on." He was a thin man of medium height and a swarthy complexion, sweating in his plastic suit.

The two detectives complied and returned.

"The footprints cross the deck and come down the steps," Storch explained. "There are a lot of blood smears on the grass here. I think maybe the killer tried to wipe the blood off his shoes. There's also a lot of blood on the cedar hedge—he may have tried to use the hedge as a towel to wipe off the blood. The trail continues down there across the lawn to the street—just traces by that point."

McNoll surveyed the eight-foot cedar hedge that separated the Halvis property from the house next door. The hedge ran right down to the sidewalk, where a dozen or so people were milling around, kept back by a line of yellow police tape. "Anything on the sidewalk would be contaminated or obliterated by now," he sighed.

"Yeah," Storch answered. "Not much point sealing it off now. Perp probably just got into a car anyway."

"Try anyway. Maybe we'll get lucky and there'll be a trail down the sidewalk."

Walking back around to the front, McNoll said, "Woods, clear the people off the sidewalk. Move 'em back a couple of houses or so, so Storch can see if there are any blood traces there."

"What now?" Sandhu asked.

"Don't know. Don't want to start the in-depth door-to-door interviews until we know a little more, and it'll be hours before we get anything definitive from the scene-of-crime guys. Might as well go back to the station and see what we can dig up on the background of the victim, then go home. Be a busy day tomorrow."

"Aren't you going to talk to them?"

McNoll followed Sandhu's eyes to a place across the road where a rotund thirty-something man and a casually dressed twenty-something woman waited under a streetlight. "The press?" He swore. "You do it," he said. "Make the department look good—show 'em the affirmative action program is working."

Sandhu allowed himself a slight roll of the eyes but responded matter-of-factly. "What do you want me to tell them?"

"Just that we're investigating a suspicious death—and that the public information officer will release the victim's name and other particulars tomorrow morning."

"I think I will try that walk around Mill Lake on Monday," Ruby said as she and John lay in bed reading that night.

"Okay," he said. "You could do that while I'm working on my reports. I'd like to get started on them while the convention is still fresh in my mind. I don't have any interviews scheduled till Tuesday."

"I guess you might as well write them up. If you tried to take the day off, you'd still spend all the time thinking about work."

"Do you want me to go with you on the walk? Do you think it is safe there to walk alone?"

"Doctor John said people walk there alone all the time, so I'm sure it'll be okay." She paused. "He has a funny way of talking, you know."

"Who?"

"Doctor John. We're sitting on the deck, looking at the view, having a conversation, and all of a sudden he launches into a lecture about weather patterns on the Pacific coast."

"Occupational hazard for a professor, I suppose," said John Smyth, who was trying to focus on his reading.

"Yes, but we're not his students. And I think it's something more than just habit. Have you noticed that whenever the conversation ever shifts toward anything personal, he clams up or changes the subject?"

"Well, he's always been that way," John said. "I guess he's just a private person." He changed the subject. "What do you think all that was about next door?"

"The police, you mean?"

"Yes," he said. "Probably a break-in or something."

"You're probably right. It seems like such a nice, peaceful neighborhood, but I suppose Doctor John's burglar alarm is there for a reason." She paused and looked hard at John. "Whatever it was, it doesn't have anything to do with us."

"Mmm," John said and turned his attention back to his book.

"John."

"What?"

"You have too many other things to do, and this is our vacation. Promise me you won't get involved."

"Involved in what?"

"Involved in whatever is going on next door."

"I'm not going to get involved. Why would I?"

Chapter 5

The sun was well above the rim of Sumas Mountain by the time the Smyths emerged from John Robinson's house the next morning. Police vehicles were next door, and yellow police tape surrounded the property. As the Smyths backed out of the driveway, they saw two men carrying plastic bags out of the house and putting them into the back of a white van while two uniformed police officers watched. A white car rolled up and stopped behind the van. Two men in suits got out.

"The police are still there?" John asked as they pulled away. "That seems a long time for just a robbery."

The Smyths parked their old station wagon on one of the middle levels of the parking garage behind Mountaintop Church—in a row that also contained two Volvos, a Jaguar, a BMW, six SUVs, four minivans, and a Corvette. The eleven o'clock service was packed, with a few delegates from the convention joining the regular worshipers. John Smyth looked over the crowd, almost by habit recording and analyzing what he saw. They represented a range of ages, from babies to seniors, but the majority of adults seemed to be in their twenties, thirties, and forties. Dress ranged from blue jeans to three-piece suits. Some of the younger married women were dressed as if for work in a large company office, sporting perfect makeup and well-tailored dresses and suits. Many of those in attendance, of all ages, were singing enthusiastically, with arms raised and heads swaying, eyes closed.

The music was loud, contemporary, and flawless, led by a "worship pastor" named Jared Lincoln. Dressed in pressed black jeans and an open-necked yellow shirt, Lincoln fronted a professional-quality band of eleven singers and musicians. Smyth knew the band had released three CDs of worship songs written by Lincoln and other members of the church. He sometimes played them on the inexpensive player the Smyths had picked up for Christmas one year at Wal-Mart.

Video screens twenty feet wide on each side of the stage showed close-ups of Lincoln and other worship team members, followed by the words of the worship songs projected against scenic backgrounds of mountains, trees, and fields. One line on the screen caught Smyth's attention: "All of are days, were going to sing your praise." A thousand-dollar sound system, he reflected as he mentally corrected the errors, was no guarantee against five-cent typos. And proofreading things he was not supposed to be proofreading, he noted, was an occupational hazard for people like him.

After thirty minutes of singing, a pastor made announcements and ushers took a collection. Then the lights slowly dimmed and the two screens began showing scenes from a television court show where married couples shouted insults at each other and insisted they wanted a divorce. After a minute or two the scenes faded, and a single spotlight revealed Marv Andreason, dressed in an immaculate gray-brown suit, standing in the center of the stage.

"They started out merely being impatient with each other," he read, "but over time their impatience has grown into intolerable cruelty. They are envious of each other's success and of the happier lives of other people. They are boastful, proud, rude, completely selfish, and angry all the time. They keep a record of every little thing the other has done wrong. They distort the truth, lying to each other, themselves, and everyone else. They delight in doing evil things to each other, and they no longer trust each other or anyone else. They have no hope left and have given up. Now only three things remain: anger, despair, and hate."

The spotlight faded, and another spotlight illuminated another part of the stage a few feet away. In the spotlight stood an elegant blonde woman in an immaculately tailored blue suit. In her hand was a Bible. "And now I will show you the most excellent way," she read. "Love is patient, love is kind. It does not envy, it does not boast, it is not proud. It is not rude, it is not self-seeking, it is not easily angered, it keeps no record of wrongs. Love does not delight in evil but rejoices with the truth. It always protects, always trusts, always hopes, always perseveres. Love never fails . . . Now these three remain: faith, hope, and love. But the greatest of these is love."

Marv Andreason now joined the woman in the spotlight and put his arm around her. "What Nancy just read was from First Corinthians, in the New Testament part of the Bible. When it comes to love, I want to tell you today that God really does have a more excellent way. Nancy and I will celebrate twenty-five years of marriage next summer, and we can tell you from experience that God's way is definitely best. Thank you, Nancy."

As Nancy walked off out of the spotlight, Andreason continued, "I want to talk to you this morning about two kinds of love—romantic love, in which we are looking for Mister or Miss Right to come along with flowers and candy and to make us feel good, and God's kind of love, in which we sacrifice ourselves for the good of the other person. The first kind of love is essentially selfish and leads only to unhappiness, anger, and separation. Only God's kind of love can make us truly happy. If your marriage or your experience of love seems more like the experience of those couples we saw up on the screen, then I am here to tell you there is hope. You don't have to live that way, because God can change the way you love. God can change your life."

Mangucci and Storch, carrying evidence bags to a police van, stopped and watched McNoll and Sandhu drive up.

"Morning," McNoll said. "Long night?"

"Yeah," Mangucci said. "And we're not done yet. I think I want to be a detective—so I can sleep nights."

"It's not as easy as it looks. All you have to do is collect the evidence. We have to make sense of it. Want to show us what you found so far?"

Mangucci and Storch led the two detectives around the side of the house.

Storch explained, "Two sets of bloody footprints lead out of the house onto the back deck and down the steps. Whoever made the footprints went off the cement walkway and onto the grass. They seem to have pushed into the hedge here and left a lot of blood on the leaves. We couldn't get distinct footprint impressions off the grass after this point, but there are traces of blood all the way down the lawn to the sidewalk. We found some minor traces on the sidewalk and on the storm drain grate—we assume one of the killers stepped on it getting into a car that was parked there. There are no further traces of blood in the neighborhood."

McNoll nodded. "And inside the house?"

Mangucci led the detectives in through the back door. "You can see the mark here where the door was pried open. But while the door jamb is bent, the lock isn't broken, which means the door probably wasn't locked in the first place. The perps probably didn't realize that. The body was found here, of course. From the blood spatter, we think she was originally standing a few feet farther from the back door, about here. Again, from the spatter, we assume she was grabbed from behind and stabbed by someone who is right-handed. There is uniform spatter in all directions from here, so there was no one standing in front of her. She may have tried to struggle toward the door, because she moved forward two or three steps while the stabbing continued. She seems to have collapsed and been dropped about where we found her. Perps then ran out the door. She continued to bleed for some time."

"*How* seems pretty clear, but the real question is *who*. Any evidence in that regard?"

"We lifted lots of prints, but none of them bloody. It's going to take a long time to analyze them all and see which ones don't belong."

"So nothing remarkable that would break the case open?"

"I wouldn't say that."

McNoll and Sandhu became very quiet, giving Mangucci their full attention.

"This is the coffee table that was by the victim's head. Remember that she had pushed herself with her heel so she was lying partway under it."

"Yeah," McNoll said. "What's the point? The killer was still here, and she was trying to crawl under the table to protect herself?"

"That's what I wondered. Anyway, I dusted the table for prints, in case the killer might have touched it. I dusted the top, and then I turned it over."

Mangucci, using gloved hands, picked up the table and set it upside down on a bloodless patch of carpet. McNoll and Sandhu leaned in for a closer look.

"Wow," Sandhu said. "What's it mean?"

"I don't know. You're the detectives. I just collect the evidence, remember?"

"One thing it means is she was probably still alive when she hit the floor," McNoll said. "Must have taken her a little while to bleed out."

"But did she write this, or the killer?" Sandhu asked.

"If she pushed herself under the table, she probably did," McNoll said impatiently.

"Unless the killer wrote it and then put the table there by her head."

"You mean like Charles Manson's people scrawling 'helter skelter' on the walls?"

"Maybe."

"If it's a message, then why hide it under the table? Why not write it on the walls?"

Sandhu replied uncertainly, "I don't know. I'm just trying to think of all the possibilities. Maybe it was a message for her to read while she was dying. If it is like the Manson killings, then the perpetrators are probably crazy anyway, so it doesn't have to make sense."

"Forget what's possible," McNoll said. "Let's stick to the evidence." He looked at Mangucci, who took a deep breath.

"Well, it's blood, and it seems to have been written with a finger. From the drips, I would guess that the table was standing upright on its legs when that was written or was turned upright shortly afterward."

"Any fingerprints in the blood?"

"In the *1* here, I got one partial print, I don't know whose finger yet. The finger seems to have paused at the bottom of the *1* and then trailed away."

"As if she was writing and then lost consciousness at that point," McNoll said, glancing at Sandhu.

The four of them stared at the inscription. Scrawled in an unsteady hand on the bottom of the table was "John 31."

"What's it mean?" Sandhu asked. "Who's John?"

"Don't know," McNoll answered. "If the victim wrote it, then maybe she was trying to name her killer--that it was John somebody."

"Wait. Didn't her husband say he overheard his wife talking to someone named John?"

McNoll grunted. "So her lover killed her?"

"Maybe," Sandhu said. "On the other hand, maybe her husband found out about the affair and killed her and she was appealing to this John for help. Or maybe to some other John. Isn't there a Christian Saint John?"

McNoll shrugged as if to imply that he wouldn't know about such things. He was not a religious man. "Then what's the *31* mean?"

Mangucci suggested, "There is a book in the Bible called John, and Bible verses are written like that, with the book and the chapter number. But the book of John doesn't have thirty-one chapters."

McNoll scowled. As far as he was concerned, there was too much religion in this city, Christian, Sikh, and otherwise, and he wished people like Mangucci who were religious would keep it to themselves.

Mangucci continued, "Maybe it's not *31* at all. If she passed out at that point, maybe what looks like a *1* was intended to be a *B* or a *D* or some other letter. We don't know what else she intended to write. For that matter, I'm not even sure the *3* is intended to be a *3*. She might have been trying to write a capital *B* and got the strokes mixed up as she was dying, putting the straight line after the bulges instead of before them."

"So who is John B?"

None of the others had an answer.

The two were arguing again. "Stop worrying, Mike. Nobody saw us. We were back in our beds before anybody knew we were gone."

"I know, but that was too close. It wasn't worth it. What if they find out we were there?"

"Nobody'll find out. We took care of it. No one will ever know."

Abbotsford's Indo-Canadian community dates back more than a century, when workers from India came to work on the railroads and in the lumber operations. In the last half century, their immigration rate has dramatically increased, and they have taken over many of the area's raspberry farms, as the earlier wave of European immigrants moved off the farms and into city professions. The Indo-Canadians who own the farms live in newly built "monster houses" with stuccoed walls and cedar-shake roofs on the front edge of their properties, where several generations of a family live together. Lower-caste immigrants often work as field hands on the farms and, like many other working-class and lower-middle-class residents of Abbotsford, live in thirty- or forty-year-old urban "ranchers."

It is usually the marginalized who immigrate. Most of these Indo-Canadians have come from the Punjab, where they belonged to the minority Sikh religion, squeezed out by the majority Hindu religion in India, their hope of a separate Sikh state in the Punjab growing dim. They brought their culture with them, although that culture is changing with each successive generation.

The grandfathers, bearded, turbaned, and wearing a kirpan, the ceremonial Sikh dagger, at their waists, tend to cluster in parks, in malls, and on city buses, playing cards and chatting in Punjabi. Their wives, dressed in saris, walk three steps behind them as a sign of respect, their husbands conversing with them over their shoulders. The second generation, however, now middle-aged adults, have largely abandoned their kirpans but still attend the Sikh temples on Saturdays, their minds largely preoccupied with earning a living in a new land. Many of the youngest generation of teens and young adults are thoroughly Westernized, speaking English without an accent and focusing on fashionable clothes, fast cars, and electronics purchased at A&B Sound and Future Shop.

Darwinder Sandhu was halfway between the second and third generations. At thirty-seven, he was one of several Indo-Canadians on the hundred-seventy-person Abbotsford police force and the first one to be promoted to detective. But his nine-month partnership with Randy McNoll had proved less than satisfying. Detectives work in teams, but Sandhu was always acutely aware that he was the junior partner in his team. McNoll never let him forget it. No matter how thorough and professional Sandhu's work was, McNoll still managed to imply it was not quite good enough. And rather than sharing information and ideas as an equal, McNoll tended to lecture and give orders as if Sandhu were reporting to him.

Sandhu was willing to take it—for now. He liked the work, and he didn't expect to be paired with McNoll forever. In the meantime he had managed to work with the man without throttling him—or stabbing him with a kirpan—mostly by keeping his mouth shut and treating the whole thing as a learning experience. McNoll could be rash and careless, but he had a lot of experience, and his solve rate was pretty good.

It was almost five o'clock in the afternoon when he

approached McNoll's desk in Abbotsford police headquarters. His partner was reading a report but wearily dropped it when he saw Sandhu. "What did you find out from Kelowna?"

"I asked the Kelowna detachment of the RCMP to check out the Ogo Inn," he answered mildly.

"And what did the Mounties find out?"

"Apparently Halvis checked in late Thursday afternoon and left Saturday afternoon. His bed was slept in Friday night. I talked to two of the three people Halvis was meeting with—a lawyer named Medford and a businessman named Gill. Their meeting Friday night lasted till ten; then they had a couple of drinks in the bar and went to bed about ten thirty. They resumed meeting again over breakfast at eight Saturday morning. Halvis left a wake-up call for seven thirty."

"Anybody see him or try to contact him between ten thirty and seven thirty?"

"Nobody tried, but why would they? The people I talked to also said they didn't think he seemed tired Saturday morning, at least no more tired than everybody else in the meeting, and it would have taken him all night to drive here from Kelowna and back. It's at least three hours one way—a good hour to Merritt, an hour to Hope, and another hour here."

"Yeah, three hours even with a fast car and no traffic."

"I can't see doing it in much less. Tricky to speed on those mountain highways without running off the road or getting a ticket."

"So check for tickets. And see if he used his credit card."

"I checked. No tickets. I can't get the credit card information till tomorrow. There was only one phone call charged to his room in Kelowna. It was made to his home phone on Friday night at seven sixteen, just like he said. Lasted three minutes."

"You checked Halvis's cell phone?"

"Are you sure he even has one?"

"He's a lawyer."

"I'll check it tomorrow—his home phone too."

"Okay. What about the third man Halvis was meeting with?"

"He's an Abbotsford businessman named Charles Baker. He traveled separately from Halvis and is evidently not back yet. Do you think it's worth tracking him down?"

"You know who the most important witness in an investigation is?"

Sandhu spread his hands.

"The one you don't talk to."

Sandhu nodded. "Have you seen any forensics reports yet?"

"Just got the first ones. They're still working on fingerprints—lifted hundreds of 'em from the scene. Nothing significant in the rest of the house, no signs of struggle. She was killed where we found her. There was a struggle there, though."

"Did you read Cooper's reports?"

"Yeah. No one saw or heard anything."

"So, then—shall we call it a day?"

"Sure. Go get some supper. Then come back. I've got four uniforms assigned to us tonight. We'll start the door-to-door interviews at seven."

Sandhu stiffened. It was another decision made without consulting him. McNoll didn't seem to have noticed.

On Sunday afternoon, exhausted after three days of convention, John and Ruby Smyth had taken a nap, putting off their other plans.

"Hello." It was Michael who answered.

"Hi, Mike."

"Just a minute. I'll get Grandpa."

"Mike, wait . . ."

There were several moments of silence before another voice came on the line.

"Dad?" John Smyth asked.

"Hi, John. How are things in B.C.?"

"Good. The convention went okay, and we're having a relaxing day. How is the project going?"

"Project? You mean Michael?"

"No, Dad. The other one."

"Ruby's not there?"

"She's in the kitchen making a late supper."

"Oh. All right then. It's going fine. I've got the old doors off and the kitchen cabinets stripped down. I'll start refinishing them tomorrow. Should be finished on time."

"Good. I can't wait to see Ruby's face when she sees it. How are the kids?"

"We got Matthew and Elizabeth to camp this afternoon. The other two went along, but Michael wasn't too happy about it. He seemed tired and out of sorts all day."

"I gathered that when he didn't want to talk to me."

"What's that?"

"What's what?"

"That sound."

"The Westminster chimes."

"What?"

"The Westminster chimes. It's what passes for a doorbell out here in the Bible Belt."

"Well, aren't you going to answer the door?"

"No. It's okay. Ruby's getting it."

"John," Ruby called. "There's a policeman at the door."

"Well, let him in," Smyth answered. "Sorry, Dad. Gotta go."

"Wait. Did Ruby say policeman?"

Smyth hung up before he had to answer.

Constable Cooper was twenty-five, tall, athletic, and very handsome, with his dark hair cut in a military brush cut. "Good evening, ma'am," he said. "We are investigating the incident that occurred at the house next door on Friday night. I wonder if you could tell me if you saw or heard anything unusual there."

"Well, we saw the police cars," Ruby said. "Could you tell us what happened?"

Cooper ignored her question. "The police cars were here on Saturday, ma'am. We're asking about Friday. Did you see any activity at all then?"

"We were at a convention all day Friday," John Smyth said, emerging from the living room. "The Grace Evangelical Church convention at Mountaintop Church down the street."

"How long were you gone?"

"We got back close to ten o'clock in the evening."

"What about after that, during the night? Did you see or hear anything?"

"No. Sorry," John Smyth said. "What happened next door?"

"Well, something did wake me up," Ruby said, almost simultaneously.

Cooper's eyes riveted on Ruby. "What time was that?"

"I don't know. In the middle of the night sometime."

"What woke you up?"

"A sound, I think, but it had stopped by the time I was awake. I don't remember it—just had an impression that there had been a sound."

"Did you hear it too, sir?"

Smyth shrugged. "Sorry. No."

"When was the last time you saw your neighbors?"

"Did something happen to them?"

"I would rather not answer that until you tell me what you saw."

"We only saw one of the neighbors once," John replied. "On Wednesday evening. There was a blonde woman weeding her garden in the backyard."

"They're not really our neighbors," Ruby explained. "We don't normally live here."

"Where do you normally live?"

"Winnipeg."

"We came for the convention," John explained. "We're staying here with our friend, Dr. John Robinson."

"Could I talk to him, please?"

"I'm sorry. He's not here," John said.

"Where is he?"

"He left yesterday morning. He caught a morning flight."

"To where?"

"I'm not really sure. He didn't say."

"When will he be back?"

"He didn't say that either."

"Doctor John is a, well, somewhat unapproachable man . . ." Ruby started.

"I see. Could you tell me your names, please?"

"Smyth. John and Ruby Smyth. No, that's a Y."

"What?"

"Smyth is spelled with a Y."

"Y?"

"I don't know why; it's just the way my ancestors spelled it. Maybe a typo on a birth certificate or something. In the past, there were no dictionaries, and you could use whatever spelling you wanted for a word as long as it approximated what the word sounded like . . ."

The policeman looked confused. "Could I see some iden- tification, sir?"

"John," Ruby said after he had gone. "He never told us what happened next door."

"And we forgot to check the news today. I wonder what did happen."

"I guess we'll find out soon enough," Ruby answered.

Chapter 6

MONDAY, JULY 12

Abbotsford's city council describes Mill Lake Park—located in the heart of Abbotsford, in an area of subdivisions and schools next to Abbotsford's main shopping district—as "the jewel of the city." The lake is an old mill pond from the period a century or more ago when the early settlers' first preoccupation was logging and clearing the valley floor for agriculture. Now the area is a park, a pleasant refuge for fish and birds, dogs and rabbits, children and adults.

There were still pink streaks in the morning sky when Ruby Smyth parked the old station wagon in one of several parking lots around the rim of the park. She sat on a nearby bench to retie her sneakers and sat just a moment longer to get her bearings and enjoy the fresh morning air. Then she stood, stretched, and began walking the paved trail around the lake.

McNoll and Sandhu sat in the passenger seat of their unmarked car, pondering the case. They were parked on Mountaintop

Drive, having gotten an early start to look through the house now that the scene-of-crime officers had finished.

"I have an idea," Sandhu ventured.

McNoll grunted.

Encouraged, Sandhu continued, "The Halvises' house is 36033."

"So?"

"Remember 'John 31,' the message on the bottom of the coffee table? Could it be referring to the house next door, 36031?"

McNoll jerked open his door. "Let's find out." Sandhu scrambled after him as he marched up the neighbor's sidewalk.

The door chime was answered by a short, bald, red-bearded man with wire-rimmed glasses.

"John?"

"Yes."

He flashed his badge. "I am Detective McNoll. This is Detective Sandhu. Can we talk with you for a few minutes?"

"Sure."

They sat on the rich blue velvet of the living room furniture, their black shoes resting on the white carpet.

"What is your relationship with Sylvan Halvis?"

"Who?"

"Sylvan Halvis, the woman next door," McNoll demanded.

"The blonde woman?"

"Yes, the blonde woman. What's your relationship with her?"

"No—no relationship," the man stammered. "I think I saw her once in the backyard."

"Then why would she write your name in her own blood on the bottom of her coffee table?"

"Wh–what?"

"You're John, and you live at house number thirty-one. Why else would Sylvan Halvis write 'John 31' on the bottom of her coffee table? You thought you had killed her when you stabbed her. You didn't know she was still able to leave a message identifying her attacker, did you?"

"The woman next door has been stabbed? I–I haven't stabbed anyone."

"Don't waste our time."

"I don't even know the woman," the man insisted.

"Don't know her? How long have you lived here?"

"I–I don't live here. We're just visiting."

"What?"

"Didn't that other policeman tell you?"

"What other policeman?"

"The one who came to see us last night."

"We, uh, haven't had time to read all the reports yet. Why don't you tell us what you told him?"

"My name is John Smyth." Seeing Sandhu's notebook, he added, "That's spelled with a Y. My wife, Ruby, and I are staying here for a couple of weeks . . . We normally live in Winnipeg. We came out for the annual convention of the Grace Evangelical Churches of North America, which was held last weekend at Mountaintop Grace Evangelical Church just down the road. That's why we only saw Mrs. Halvis once."

"When was that?" McNoll asked wearily. He sagged as if all the air or energy had seeped out of him. "When did you see her?"

"Let's see. Last Wednesday night. She was out weeding her garden while we were eating our dinner on the deck."

"Did you talk to her?"

"No."

"Did your wife ever talk to her?"

"I don't think so. We were at the convention all last week, so I don't think she would have had a—"

"Maybe we should ask her. Is she here?"

"No. Sorry. She went for a walk—at Mill Lake."

"Are you two staying here alone?"

"Well, at the moment, yes. We are guests of our friend Dr. John Robinson. He owns—"

"Dr. *John* Robinson?" McNoll asked, his interest reviving.

"Yes. Do you know—?"

"Where is he?"

"He went away."

"Where?"

"I don't really know. He caught a plane Saturday morning."

"When did you say?"

"Saturday morning."

"And he didn't say where he was going?"

"No. I think something must have come up. He hadn't said earlier he was going—just told us Saturday morning as he was leaving."

"A sudden decision?"

"I think. But then, as my wife says, Doctor John doesn't say very much about his personal life."

"When is this John Robinson coming back?"

"I don't know."

"He didn't say?"

"No."

"Didn't you find that odd?"

"Not really. As I said, Doctor John is, well, reticent about his personal life. Ruby . . . uh, we even wondered if he might have gone on purpose, to, uh, give us a second honeymoon. See, his parents lent us their cottage years ago for our first honeymoon—"

"Do you know any way to contact him?"

"No. His parents live in Winnipeg, Peter and Astrid Robinson. They might know where he is."

"Does he have any family here?"

"No. He has no brothers or sisters."

"He's not married?"

"No, not now."

"Why do you call him Doctor John? Is he a medical doctor?"

"People in the denomination call him that. He has a Ph.D. in sociology, I think. He's a professor at Abbotsford College."

McNoll paused and sighed.

Sandhu asked, "Was Dr. Robinson with you the other night when you saw Mrs. Halvis?"

"Yes. He served dinner."

"Did he talk to Mrs. Halvis?"

"No. I don't think he knows her either. Ruby actually asked him that, I think, and he said he had just talked to her husband."

"Did she see the three of you having dinner?"

"Probably. She must have."

"Did she wave or smile or anything?"

"Not that I noticed. Doctor John is a shy man. He doesn't talk to strangers easily. And I got the impression that people in this neighborhood don't talk to their neighbors much."

"Mr. Smyth, would you mind if we sear—"

McNoll cut Sandhu off. "Thank you, Mr. . . . Smyth." He paused. "Here is my card. If you hear from Dr. Robinson, could you let me know right away? And . . . I would appreciate it if you didn't talk to him about this conversation."

Smyth looked puzzled but said nothing. The two detectives rose to leave.

"Wait," Smyth said. "How is Mrs. Halvis? Is she going to be all right?"

"She's dead. Her husband got home from Kelowna Saturday evening and found her body in the living room. She'd been killed late Friday night."

Smyth looked genuinely shocked.

They had just reached the front hall. At that moment a short, round blonde woman started down the stairs.

"I thought you said you were alone?" McNoll demanded of Smyth.

Sandhu, looking up at the descending woman, asked, "Are you Mrs. Smyth?"

John Smyth interjected, "I never said I was alone. You asked if anyone else was *staying* here. As I told you, my wife Ruby is not here. This is Henriette, Dr. Robinson's housekeeper.

"Housekeeper?" McNoll said.

"Yes, she comes in three mornings a week."

Looking at the woman, McNoll asked, "I suppose you have thoroughly cleaned the house this morning?"

"Almost, sir," Henriette said, puzzled. "I still have the third-floor bathrooms to do."

"That went well," Sandhu remarked archly as they got back into the unmarked car.

McNoll let loose with a string of swear words as he slammed the car door. "That was a disaster! You and your half-baked suggestions!"

"You're saying it's my fault?" Sandhu defended himself. "You were the one who rushed in there without checking the reports. And I still think I was on to something. The guy who owns the house is also named John, and his leaving town the morning after the murder is suspicious."

"Of course it's suspicious. That's why I pushed him, trying to catch him off guard."

"You were pushing him before you ever knew about Dr. Robinson," Sandhu shot back.

McNoll blinked, unaccustomed to being confronted by

his partner. He wasn't about to admit error, but he did lower his voice. "Point is, our only chance of surprising him just went down the tubes. Now that other John will tell him about the writing under the table. By the time we find 'im, he'll have a logical explanation."

"But Smyth said he wouldn't tell him—"

McNoll gave an exaggerated, world-weary sigh. "Of course he'll tell him. They're friends. He's staying in his house."

They sat there for a minute in the car, looking over at the yellow tape of the crime scene next door, both a bit unnerved by their unaccustomed argument.

"So you think Robinson will come back?" Sandhu finally asked in a normal tone of voice. "You don't think maybe he's on the run?"

"Could be." McNoll paused, then resumed his normal tone as well. "But we don't have enough evidence for a warrant against him. He can go wherever he wants."

"I was going to ask if we could search his house. That Smyth guy doesn't seem too bright. I think he might have let us search."

"And if we found anything, it would be ruled inadmissible in court because he doesn't have the right to authorize a search. Besides, that housekeeper has probably dusted and vacuumed up all the evidence by now."

"Did you believe Smyth's story about them being at a church convention all week?"

McNoll shrugged. This was Abbotsford, where people were always talking about church. "I suppose we could check it out, but what difference does it make where he was if he isn't a suspect?"

"So what are we going to do?"

"Check out the church-convention thing, I guess. Check

with the airport and see where Dr. Robinson flew to, if he re ally flew anywhere."

"What about the autopsy? That starts in five minutes."

McNoll swore. "After the autopsy." He started the car and put it in gear. The tires squealed as they pulled away from the curb.

Deep in the bowels of Abbotsford's only hospital, the group of men gathered around a stainless-steel table, anonymous in gowns and masks. One of them, a man of medium height, held a bloody scalpel above the naked form of a dead woman laid out on the table. The others held back slightly, watching. Waiting for the pronouncement.

"Well, that's about that." The man with the scalpel placed it with the rest of the instruments laid on a side table and stepped back. "She was a healthy woman—no sign of heart disease or other major problems. She bled out as a result of seven stab wounds to the chest. None of the blows hit the heart or severed any major arteries, but the bleeding was quite severe nonetheless."

"So she died fairly fast?" Darwinder Sandhu questioned, leaning in closer toward the body. Once he'd gotten used to the sights and smells, he had always found postmortem exams intensely interesting.

"Not immediately," the medical examiner replied. "But she probably would have gone into shock fairly quickly, significantly limiting her ability to get up and run, for instance, and death would have come within fifteen minutes, unconsciousness probably sooner."

"There's bruising around the wounds," Sandhu remarked. "Scene-of-crime guys noticed that."

The medical examiner nodded. "The instrument wasn't very sharp or very long, or she would have died more quickly.

See, there are minor defensive wounds on her hands and arms, and there's bruising on the right shoulder and across her neck."

"Which means?" Randy McNoll asked, standing a little farther back. Unlike his partner, he hated this part of the job.

"The killer was probably standing behind her with his left arm across her chest and his left hand gripping her right shoulder. He stabbed her with his right hand. I'd say he was taller than she was and quite strong."

McNoll shook his head, looking down at the defenseless-looking body. "Poor girl. Never had a chance."

Sandhu looked at him in surprise over his surgical mask. He'd never seen this tender side of McNoll before.

Back in the car, Sandhu said, "I guess that lets John Smyth out."

"Why?"

"He's shorter than the victim. Couldn't be much over five feet, in fact."

McNoll scowled. "Smyth isn't a suspect anyway. I wonder how tall Dr. John Robinson is."

"Good question. And should be easy to find out. I'll get on that as soon as we get back to the station."

"I'm not going back to the station—just going to drop you off. You finish checking out Thomas Halvis's story and then start pushing for the forensics results. I'm going to the airport."

"The airport, eh?"

Ignoring Sandhu's knowing grin, McNoll threw the car in reverse and backed out of the parking space.

"I had the most lovely walk! It's about a mile and a half around the lake, and it's a really nice place. There are Canada geese and mallard ducks and some coots and some other birds I don't know the name of. Some of the ducks and geese have babies, a couple of dozen altogether. There was this old man who said that there would be more except they addle the eggs, shake them up, so that the eggs never hatch and there aren't too many geese messing up the lawns. There's also a pair of bald eagles nesting in the park—"

Ruby realized John wasn't listening. "What's wrong?"

He took a deep breath. "Two policemen were here this morning. Do you remember that blonde woman next door who was weeding her garden when we were eating on the deck the other night?"

Ruby nodded.

"The policemen said that she was attacked Friday night."

"Is she going to be all right?"

"She's dead."

"Oh, John." She caught the look on John's face. "What else?"

"I think the police think Doctor John might have done it."

"Why?"

"Mrs. Halvis—that's her name—evidently wrote 'John 31' in her own blood on the underside of a coffee table. This is Doctor John's house, and its number is 36031. When they came here, they thought *I* was Doctor John. And they obviously suspected me—even accused me of stabbing her."

"They did *what?*"

Abbotsford Airport was a former military airport that, until the early 1990s, had been used for little besides an annual air show. Then two things happened. The airport was taken over by the City of Abbotsford with a view to expanding the local economy. And WestJet, a new low-cost regional carrier, began looking for new markets. When the two came together,

Abbotsford Airport quickly became one of the busiest commercial airports in the province, handling forty to fifty flights a day. Parking was cheaper and the terminal far easier to access than the overcrowded Vancouver International Airport. McNoll parked in a designated police stall and strode into the building. Flashing his badge, he walked into the small administrative center of the building. Admitted to the chief administrator's office, McNoll smiled for the first time all morning.

"Morning, Marsha. Paperwork arrive?"

Marsha Freeman smiled back at him. Slender, dark-haired, and very competent, she was also a lovely woman. "Good morning, Detective. Yes, it's here. Now, let's see. You wanted to know if a John Robinson flew out of here Saturday morning, right?"

"Right."

Clicking keys on a computer, Freeman soon found what she was looking for. "Yes, here it is. He was on the eight forty WestJet flight to Winnipeg, stopping in Calgary to change planes. He arrived in Winnipeg at two fifteen."

"When did he book the flight?"

"Saturday morning at five thirty. He booked it online, paid with a credit card."

"Isn't it a bit unusual to book last-minute like that?"

"It's not how most flights are booked, but it's not that uncommon for WestJet. It's a low-cost airline. As long as they have seats available, you can book last-minute and still pay only a reasonable fare."

"Was it one-way or return?"

"It's the same price for WestJet, but yes, he also booked a return flight for this coming Friday."

"Friday," McNoll mused.

"Of course, with WestJet, you can reschedule up until two hours before flight time, so it's easy to change."

"So he could change his mind and fly somewhere else?"

"Sure. He could get a credit and apply it to another flight as long as it is in the country. WestJet flies mostly in Canada."

"Thank you, Marsha. You've been a big help."

Marsha smiled up at him. "Care to stay for coffee?"

"I'd love to, but I'm in the middle of a murder investigation. Can you put a flag on the file and let me know if Robinson changes his booking?"

"Sure," she called after him. "Come back when you can stay longer."

It was late afternoon when Sandhu again approached McNoll's desk. McNoll nodded toward the chair beside the desk, and Sandhu sat down.

"You finish checking out Halvis?" McNoll asked.

"I checked all his credit cards. According to them, he got gas in Kelowna when he arrived on Friday and hasn't bought gas since. He paid the toll on the Coquihalla Highway on the way up to Kelowna Thursday afternoon—also with a credit card—and he paid the toll on the way back at three minutes after five on Saturday afternoon. No other relevant credit-card listings."

"Could've paid cash, but might not be worth checking if the alibi holds otherwise."

"I also checked the Halvis house phone. Other than the call from Kelowna at seven-sixteen that we already know about, there were no other calls that night."

"You check Halvis's cell phone?"

"Yes. He called his office several times on Friday. He didn't make any calls on Saturday."

"Okay. What about the third man Halvis was meeting with?"

"Baker's still not back yet." There was a pause. "How about you?" Sandhu asked with the hint of a smile. "What did you find out at the airport?"

McNoll ignored the implication. "John Robinson booked a flight on the Internet at five thirty Saturday morning, flew out at eight forty to Winnipeg."

"So it was last-minute. Do you think he's running?"

"He has a return flight booked for Friday."

"Oh."

McNoll snorted. "Good way to throw us off. Fly to Winnipeg on a round-trip ticket, but as soon as you get there, rent a car and drive across the U.S. border or fly to Europe. Could be anywhere by now."

"Are you going to have the Winnipeg police look for him?"

"Don't know. Might tip him off that we suspect him. He might come back on his own if he thinks he's in the clear." He paused. "I checked his credit cards, and he hasn't charged anything since the plane ticket."

"Do you think that's suspicious?"

McNoll shrugged. "Who knows? Maybe he just likes to use cash."

"Are there any new forensics reports?"

"Fingerprints still not finished. They're being careful on this one. But I did get a list of the items found on the floor, probably knocked off the table she was found under." He paused and picked up the report he had been reading. "A plant—spider plant, to be exact. Some dirt from the pot. A TV guide. The TV remote control. A lamp. Two books—*The Testament* by John Grisham and *Mere Christianity* by C. S. Lewis. And a business card, which forensics thinks might have been used as a bookmark."

Sandhu pondered this information for a moment. "Whose name is on the business card?" he asked.

"Doesn't say. I think they're still trying to get prints off it and the books."

"Did you read Cooper's reports?"

"Yeah, no one saw or heard anything. Except for Ruby Smyth—John Smyth's wife—sleeping next door, who thought she heard something at some unspecified time in the middle of the night."

He paused. "We haven't talked to her, have we?"

"Who?"

"Ruby Smyth."

"Right. We were going to go out again and try to interview the neighbors we missed the first time. Why don't we start there?"

When the doorbell rang, John and Ruby Smyth were sprawled on John Robinson's powder-blue sofa in the living room, their stockinged feet on a chrome-and-glass coffee table that had cost almost as much as their entire living-room suite. They lowered their feet guiltily when the door chimes sounded. John got up to open the door.

"Good evening, Mr. Smyth," McNoll said. "We're doing some follow-up on the interviews we did earlier. May we ask you a few more questions? Is your wife here?"

"She's here," Smyth said, more cautiously than before. "Come in. Ruby, this is Detective—"

"McNoll of the Abbotsford Police Department." McNoll smiled. "And this is my partner, Detective Sandhu."

Ruby planted a hand on her hip instead of extending it in welcome, her face showing a mix of anxiety and indignation. These were the detectives who'd accused her husband of murder.

When they were all seated uncomfortably in the living room, McNoll asked, "Have you heard from Dr. Robinson?"

"No," John answered. "Do you want me to try to find him for you?"

"No, that's fine," McNoll responded. "Mrs. Smyth, I understand you were awakened on Friday night. Is that correct?"

Ruby seemed startled by the question. "Yes, I think it was a noise that woke me, but I don't know what it was, just that I woke up thinking I had heard a noise. Or half woke up."

"Do you remember what kind of noise?"

Ruby reflected, "Sorry, no. It was just an impression I remembered."

"Did you ever meet the woman next door?" McNoll asked, continuing to look at Ruby.

"No, we only saw her once. She was working in the yard."

"When was that?"

She thought. "It was the first evening we were here. Last Wednesday."

And so it went. The answers were the same as in John's previous interview. The detectives moved on to the next house, where they found no one at home.

Chapter 7

TUESDAY, JULY 13

She must have been about thirty-five, but looked much older —gaunt and gap-toothed, her dirty spaghetti-strapped top hanging loosely from her shoulders. John Smyth, fiddling with the radio dial, heard the door latch click and looked up, startled to see her opening the door and preparing to slide into Ruby's spot beside him.

"Don't get into the car." His voice surprised him with its firmness, when what he was feeling was much closer to panic.

"What?"

"Don't get into the car."

"I thought you were waiting for me."

"No."

Smyth glanced over anxiously at the bank, an old two-story brick structure with no windows. It looked something like a medieval castle, designed to be impregnable rather than aesthetically pleasing. Ruby was inside, getting some cash out of the ATM.

"I need money for food," she said. "Got two kids to feed, and I got no bread."

Smyth doubted that any money he gave her would go for food and doubted even more that any social welfare system, no matter how badly run, would allow this woman to have custody of children. "There's a Grace Evangelical church near here that has a food bank, I think," he said.

"I know, but they won't give me none."

"Why not?"

"'Cause I'm a known prostitute."

Smyth glanced anxiously at the bank again, wanting to get rid of the woman before Ruby reappeared. She wouldn't believe him guilty of anything immoral—she knew him better than that. But the filthy woman repulsed him, and he didn't want her anywhere near his wife.

Reaching into his wallet, he pulled out five dollars and thrust it at her. *Now go away,* he thought but he did not say it out loud. She took the money, grimaced, and shuffled off around the corner of the bank. John Smyth shuddered as Ruby emerged from the building.

He looked around him. Abbotsford had once been two small villages—Abbotsford to the east, and Clearbrook to the west. A developer had built a mall on an empty field halfway between the two hamlets. The population had then filled in the empty space in the middle and was now spreading out in all directions. This was the oldest part of Abbotsford, the site of the original village, with buildings stretched out along the Canadian Pacific Railway tracks. Some were a century old. There were also gas stations, minimalls, bars, boarded-up commercial buildings, vacant lots, run-down houses, and a hydroponics store. Poverty was staring him in the face. He shifted his position uneasily.

"John?" Ruby asked.

"What?" He had not noticed that she was already in the car, waiting for him to start the engine.

"Sorry," he said. "I was thinking about something."

McNoll, Sandhu, and the uniformed officers had knocked on doors on Mountaintop Drive and adjacent streets until almost ten o'clock the past two nights. They had talked to every person in those houses, taking careful notes and going back to double-check with people who had not been home at first. They had found at least one person home in almost every house and had a list of individuals they would go back and try to interview today. Now, at nine thirty in the morning, McNoll and Sandhu sat in the Abbotsford police station reading through the reports the uniformed officers had stayed up half the night writing.

McNoll finished a report and looked up. "Got anything?"

Sandhu took a moment to focus. "Most of the immediate neighbors knew the Halvises by sight, and a few had talked to them, but no one seems to have known them well. They were not known to argue."

"The walls of the rich are soundproof," McNoll observed.

Sandhu didn't know what to make of that statement. "Anyway, nobody so far saw or heard anything Friday night. Was there anything in the reports you read?"

McNoll raised the report he had just finished. "Mrs. Sandy Martino, couple of blocks down the street. Around two or three in the morning, she saw an old red minivan coming up the street—Toyota or something. She didn't think it was domestic. Said it was really beat-up."

Sandhu felt he was expected to say something, but he didn't see much significance to this. "So?"

"Point is, what's an old red minivan doing in that neighborhood at that time of night?"

"Too late for a maid. Babysitter, maybe?"

"Maybe. Could be a son who bought his own wheels rather than waiting for a Jag from his old man. Point is, a hundred Jags or Beamers could've driven up the street that night, and no one would have noticed or remembered. Old red minivan is a crime against good manners. Must be up to no good."

The two men returned to their reading. Ten minutes later, Sandhu cleared his throat. "Here's something."

"What?"

"A man named Nathan Lee got up to go to the bathroom in the middle of the night—"

"The weak bladders of the middle-aged are a policeman's best friend."

"What? How do you know Mr. Lee is middle-aged?"

"How old is he?"

Sandhu consulted the report. "Forty-nine."

McNoll shrugged. He was forty-six.

Sandhu continued. "Mr. Lee got up in the middle of the night—he thinks it was Friday night—and saw a teenager running down the street away from the Halvis house."

"How close?"

"Let's see. Transfer Boulevard. That's about four blocks away."

McNoll said nothing, so Sandhu continued. "The teenager is described as a male—short, thin, blond, and wearing a gray jacket.

McNoll snorted. "Good description. Pale colors. What you see by moonlight. Kid's probably six foot tall, dark-haired, wearing a blue coat—and female."

"Do you think he could be the boy who drove the red minivan, now running away?"

"Then where's the minivan? Same thing. Hundreds of guys in expensive track suits go running in that neighborhood and nobody notices. Casually dressed kid doing the same thing is obviously up to no good."

"So you don't think it is significant?"

"Could be—it's just too early to tell. Collect the pieces before you try to put the puzzle together."

John Smyth was also engaged in conducting interviews, collecting information for his stories. He had dropped Ruby off a few blocks away from the bank at Mill Lake.

"Are you sure you'll be safe walking around the park?"

"Of course. Look at all the people walking here."

"It's not that far from the older part of town." He was still thinking of his encounter with the prostitute, but he wasn't ready to tell Ruby about it.

"John, we live in the older part of Winnipeg, and I walk around there all the time. Besides, this is an entirely different neighborhood."

Still with some misgivings, he left her at the park and drove to the address he'd been given—a four-story white stucco office building in the Clearbrook area of Abbotsford. On the top floor, behind a polished oak door, he discovered an artfully designed waiting area watched over by an elegant blonde receptionist. After waiting the obligatory ten minutes for his nine o'clock appointment, Smyth was ushered into an even more elegantly designed inner office featuring royal blue carpets and gleaming cherrywood furniture.

Calvin Henderson was a tall, erect man with white hair, a bronze tan, and a firm handshake. He wore a tailored charcoal-gray suit with a conservative maroon tie. When the preliminaries were over and Smyth was seated in a comfortable chair across from the gleaming cherry desk, Henderson asked in his deep baritone, "Now, Mr. Smyth, I understand your appointment was made through Pastor Marv Andreason at

Mountaintop Church. What kind of legal problem can I help you with?"

Smyth blinked. "Uh, I don't have a legal problem. I am editor of *Grace* magazine."

Henderson looked blank.

"It is the magazine of the Grace Evangelical churches— it's sent to the home of every member. You are a member of Mountaintop Church, and you do get the magazine, right?"

Henderson looked slightly less blank. "Regular-sized magazine, comes out . . . monthly?"

"Every two weeks, actually."

Henderson seemed to be gaining confidence. "Black-and-white cover?"

"We switched to a two-color cover eight years ago."

Henderson's confidence seemed to be fading again. "Maybe your wife reads it?"

Henderson's face lit up. "Yes, she says some of the articles are very good." He added, "I, uh, don't have time to read much besides professional journals."

Smyth wasn't surprised. Reader surveys showed that in 80 percent of member households, at least one person read a significant portion of *Grace* magazine—and that 60 percent of readers were women.

"So, how can I help you, Mr. Smyth?"

"I am writing an article on Mountaintop Church, and Marv Andreason has arranged for me to interview a number of the church leaders."

Henderson's confidence seemed fully restored. "Yes, of course."

"You don't mind my taping our interview?"

He hesitated, then nodded decisively. "That would be all right."

Smyth nodded, turned on the tape, and consulted his notes. "You are an elder at Mountaintop, I believe?"

"Yes, I have been on the board for twelve years, the last five as chairman. Let me tell you, Mr. Smyth, we are very pleased to have Marv Andreason as our pastor. His sermons are just wonderful. So many churches are just marking time, but under Marv's leadership our church is moving forward. We are making an impact. People in the community know about our church, and they are attracted to it. And these are quality people I am talking about, the kind of people I work with every day."

"I understand you are a lawyer, Mr. Henderson."

"Yes, I deal in corporate law and high-end real estate. My colleagues and clients are the kind of people who live on Mountaintop Drive. They demand quality in everything they do, and Pastor Marv can speak to those people, gain their respect. He puts on a top-quality church service every week, and they value that."

"I thought maybe as a lawyer you would also run into criminals."

"No, not at all. I told you, I do contracts, real-estate transactions, business mergers, and the like. I don't do criminal work. The money's better in the corporate arena, and to tell the truth, I'd rather not spend my time with burglars and dope dealers. But you're not really here to talk about me, are you?"

"Well, in a way I am. I'm trying to get a sense of what the congregation is like."

"Well, that's what I'm trying to tell you. Mountaintop Church is important because it attracts quality people—hardworking people with integrity and intelligence, people who can change society from the top down, not the kind of people who have social problems and commit crimes. The last time the premier of the province was in Abbotsford, he had a private meeting with several of the leading people in town, and Pastor Marv was among those invited to the meeting."

"About time," McNoll growled.

Mangucci had joined McNoll and Sandhu. He smiled. "We're making some progress," he said. "Shall I start with the murder scene?" McNoll said nothing, so he continued, "We have analyzed the stab wounds. The weapon was three-and-a-half inches long, an inch wide at the top, tapering to a point, and an eighth of an inch thick, not particularly sharp on either edge. From the bruising, it was driven in hard, meaning that the murderer was reasonably strong."

"Doesn't sound like a knife," McNoll observed.

"More like a letter opener, something like that."

"Not a kirpan?" Sandhu asked.

Mangucci was puzzled by the question. "No, they have a different shape and are sharper." There was no further comment from the detectives, so he continued. "The fingerprint in the blood on the bottom of the table matches Mrs. Halvis's right index finger. Our assumption, then, is that she wrote the message."

"Could someone else have written it and she touched it afterward?" Sandhu asked.

Mangucci considered. "It's possible, but seems unlikely." He shrugged and continued, "There were lots of prints in the room. We haven't analyzed them all yet, but almost all of them so far belong to the Halvises. There were a couple of unidentified prints, but they were not near the body and could be old."

"What about the items on the floor?" Sandhu asked.

"I'll start with the easy things. There were no usable prints on the TV guide. Newsprint does not hold prints well."

"Whose prints were on the TV remote?" McNoll asked.

"Why, do you think that is significant?" Sandhu said.

"No. Just wondered about the husband-wife relationship, who controlled the remote."

"Both Halvises' prints were on the remote, hers on top."

"Since he was away for the weekend, that probably means he controlled the remote and she only got it when he was away," Sandhu suggested.

McNoll shrugged.

"Or that he watched the television and she read the books," Mangucci said.

"The lamp was turned on, but the bulb was burnt out."

"Could the filament have broken when it was knocked off the table?" Sandhu asked.

"Sure. There's no way to tell."

"So she might have been reading when the killers came in?" Sandhu continued.

"It's possible."

"Pretty late for most people," McNoll grunted. "Maybe she couldn't sleep."

"There were two books on the floor, which were probably knocked off the table in the struggle—*The Testament,* by John Grisham, and *Mere Christianity,* by C. S. Lewis. Her prints were all over the covers of both books, and there were a few of her discernible prints inside. There are also some unidentified prints on the covers of both. One of those prints is on both books. They are probably only from the store clerk or some other shopper who looked at the books before Mrs. Halvis did, but we might get lucky."

"The prints are not Mr. Halvis's?" Sandhu asked.

"No."

"There was also a business card?" McNoll prompted.

"Yes. One of the books had the corner of the page turned over, possibly to mark the place. The other book did not have any pages turned over, so we think the business card might have been used as a bookmark. It was found a few inches from the book."

"She was reading both books at once?" Sandhu asked.

"No way to know that," Mangucci said.

"So, which book had the corner of the page turned over?"

Mangucci consulted his notes. "*Mere Christianity*, page 151."

"Anything significant on that page?"

Mangucci paused. "Well, it's a pretty significant book— I've read it, in fact—but we didn't see anything on that page relevant to the murder. You can read it if you want."

"Did you look at other books in the house?" McNoll asked. "Were there bookmarks or turned-over page corners in other books?"

Mangucci looked somewhat flustered for once. "We, uh, didn't check."

"Do it."

"Something else about the card," Mangucci said tentatively. "Three bloody fingerprints, the tips of the fingers, Mrs. Halvis, right hand."

Sandhu frowned. "She picked up the card after she was stabbed?"

"No. The fingerprints are on the back of the card, which was face down on the floor, and they are just fingertips, as if she put her hand down on the card as she was pushing herself under the table. There are no other prints at all on the card, which seems unusual."

"Whose business card?" McNoll asked.

"You mean the name on the card?" Mangucci consulted his notes. "Some professor at Abbotsford College."

"John Robinson?" McNoll shot back.

"Uh, yes. How did you know?"

"Dr. Robinson lives next door to the Halvises."

"Oh. The card just has his college address."

Byron Masters Enterprises filled a massive three-story brick-and-steel office and warehouse complex in an industrial park at the west end of Abbotsford a few blocks from the airport. Unlike the sedate grandeur of Calvin Henderson's office, the first floor offices of Byron Masters Enterprises were a beehive of whirring office machines and bustling clerical staff. John Smyth watched the activity with fascination, hardly noticing that he had to wait fifteen minutes before a middle-aged secretary in slacks and sensible heels led him through a maze of desks and filing cabinets to an office in a back corner. "Mr. Smyth," she announced, ushering him inside and closing the door behind him.

Byron Masters was of medium height, although at five-ten he still towered above John Smyth. His handshake was firm and meaty. His suit jacket was hung on a hook by the door, his tie was loose, his tailored light-blue shirt failed to hide a spreading middle-aged paunch, and his pants were supported by dark-blue suspenders.

"Mr. Smyth, I can spare you about twenty minutes. Do you want coffee?"

"No, thanks. I quit a few years—"

Masters cut him off. "I understand you want to interview me about Mountaintop Church."

"Yes, I am writing a profile article about the church for *Grace* magazine. I'm the—"

"I know who you are, Mr. Smyth. Read the magazine all the time. Now, do you want to ask me questions, or should I just tell you what I know?"

"Why don't you start with telling me what you know, and then I can ask—"

"Fine. I've only been at the church about ten years. I wasn't there at the beginning. But I've been an elder for the last four years. I'm committed to Mountaintop because it's a church that knows its purpose. My company's purpose is to build and manage buildings. Mountaintop's purpose is to change people. It deals with the real issues that people are dealing with—divorce, alcoholism, raising teenagers. It doesn't get all bogged down in the mushy liberal issues that some churches get into—saving the spotted owl, recycling cans, promoting socialism and women's rights. And it's not anti-business like some churches whose pastors have never had to achieve anything in the real world and who blame all the world's troubles on the people who are building something. Mountaintop knows that the real problem in the world is human sin, and sin exists at all levels of society. And Mountaintop knows what to do about it. We have youth programs that stress abstinence from sex, drugs, and alcohol. We have marriage retreats and seminars that encourage faithfulness in marriage. We have great Bible studies and support groups. I've gotta tell you—I'm at Mountaintop because Mountaintop works."

Smyth, who had barely managed to switch on his tape recorder, had little opportunity to ask his prepared questions or think of additional ones. Before he knew it, he was walking across the busy parking lot back to his car.

McNoll's phone rang, interrupting the moment. A metallic voice at the other end of the line said, "A Thomas Halvis is here to see you."

McNoll did not answer but put his hand over the mouthpiece and looked up at Mangucci. "Halvis is here. Is now a good time to take him up to the house for a walk-through?"

Mangucci said, "Sure. I can give you the rest of my report later."

Into the mouthpiece, McNoll said, "Tell him to wait."
Turning to Sandhu, he said, "Go get him."

Sandhu rose stiffly and went out. When he had gone, Mangucci asked, "It's none of my business, but why do you treat him like that?"

"Who?"

"Darwinder. You treat him like an assistant. A junior partner."

McNoll shrugged. "He is a junior partner."

Sandhu and Halvis were making their way across the floor to McNoll's desk. Halvis wore the same pin-striped suit he had been wearing on Saturday. McNoll rose. "Mr. Halvis," he asked, "how are you?"

"What kind of question is that? My wife has been murdered."

"I understand that, Mr. Halvis. We are trying to find out who murdered her. Please sit down. I only meant to ask what brings you here today."

"What do you think? I want to know how the investigation is going. You haven't told me a thing."

"I think we're making some progress. I'm afraid I don't have any specific information to give you."

"I've been practicing law for over ten years, and I'm well aware of the way you people work. I know you don't like to give out information. I understand that. But I have a right to know what happened to my wife."

McNoll looked at him for a moment, considering. "Mr. Halvis, your wife was grabbed from behind and stabbed several times. Whoever did it seems to have left through the back door."

"Do you have any idea who did it?"

"No. It might have been that she surprised a thief who had broken in, but we don't know."

Halvis was silent a moment. "Was she sexually assaulted?"

McNoll looked at Mangucci, who seemed startled that the question had been referred to him but answered, "No, she was not."

Halvis asked, "Have you learned anything from the knife or whatever she was stabbed with?"

"No murder weapon has been recovered yet," McNoll said. "Now, Mr. Halvis, I'd like to ask some questions if you don't mind."

"Of course I don't mind. I want to help any way I can."

"Thank you. Now, does the phrase 'John 31' mean anything to you?"

Halvis seemed puzzled. "No."

"Could 'John 31' be the beginning of a longer phrase that might mean something?"

"No," Halvis said slowly, "although I did tell you that my wife received a phone call from someone named John."

"Do you have any idea who that could be? Do you have any friends named John?"

"We probably have friends named John, but I have no idea who it could have been. Why are you asking me about this 'John 31' phrase?"

McNoll did not answer. "Mr. Halvis, could you tell me a bit more about your wife—what she did, places she went, people she knew?"

Halvis took a deep breath. "Let's see. She was a homemaker —her choice, not mine. She took care of the house and the yard herself. She spent quite a bit of time at the Bakerview Golf and Country Club and the Right Fit Fitness Centre. We're members at both places and were quite active in the social side of things as well. Most of Sylvan's friends were from there. She was involved in some charities, things like the cancer run. And in the last year or so she started taking courses at Abbotsford

College. Just for interest—she already had a degree."

"How well do you know John Robinson?" McNoll asked.

"John Robinson?"

"Your next-door neighbor."

"We've met once or twice. Maybe Sylvan knew him better. She was the one who was around the house most of the time. Why? Is he a suspect?"

"No, Mr. Halvis. It's just that we have been interviewing all the neighbors to see if they saw anything suspicious. Mr. Robinson seems to have left town, and I was wondering if you knew where he might have gone."

"No." Halvis paused. "Could he be . . . ?"

"Could he be what, Mr. Halvis?"

He shook his head. "Never mind."

"Mr. Halvis, we are not yet finished investigating the house, but I was wondering if you would be willing to accompany us there now and see if you notice anything unusual or out of place."

"Yes, I could do that. I was also going to ask if I could go to the house and pick up some clothes and other things."

"Sure. You can do that at the same time."

"How was your walk?" John Smyth was pleased that Ruby was waiting for him in the parking lot, but he did not raise the issue of her safety again.

"It was great. It really is a very interesting place to walk. I was talking to this older man who said that the eagles sometimes catch ducklings, rabbits, and even cats in the park."

"What eagles?"

"The bald eagles. The ones I told you nest in the park."

"Oh."

"You know, maybe we do tell each other everything—but sometimes you just don't listen."

John didn't say anything. Ruby softened. "How were your interviews?"

"Very interesting." John paused. "Ruby, remember when you were in the bank this morning?"

"Yes."

"A prostitute tried to get into the car."

"Our car? How do you know she was a prostitute?"

"She said she was."

"She walked over to the car and said, 'Hi. I'm a prostitute'?"

"No. She started to open the door, and I said, 'Don't get into the car.' She said she thought I was waiting for her, and then she asked me for money. I told her to go to Shadow Valley Church, but she said they wouldn't give her anything because she was a known prostitute. I finally gave her five dollars to go away." John shuddered. "The whole thing was just . . . creepy."

"And then she went away?"

"Yeah," he said thoughtfully. "She just disappeared."

Even after only four days, the silent house had a musty, deserted feel. A light layer of dust lay on the table in the front hallway.

"Mr. Halvis, if you could start in the living room, we would appreciate it," McNoll said. "Please don't touch anything unnecessarily."

Halvis walked slowly into the room, his eyes methodically sweeping around the walls, furniture, and floor, but always returning to the bloodstains that marked where his wife had lain. He stopped a few feet short of the place and stared.

"Mr. Halvis, is anything missing or out of place?"

"There was a table . . ."

"Yes, Mr. Halvis, we took a table, a lamp, the TV guide, and the television remote. Is anything else missing?"

"No . . . I don't think so."

"There were also a couple of books."

"I don't remember any books."

"The titles were *Mere Christianity* and *The Testament.* Were those your books?"

"No. I don't remember them. They might have been Sylvan's, but they don't sound like the type of books she would read. Maybe they were for one of the courses she was taking. She is—was—the reader in the family. I don't really have time. In my leisure time, I prefer racquetball or golf."

They proceeded in the same manner through the rest of the house. Halvis insisted that nothing significant was out of order. A chair had been moved a foot or two in one spot, and there was a different box on the kitchen counter, but there were no changes Sylvan might not have made herself in the normal course of living. Halvis also carefully checked the desk in his office and Sylvan's jewelry box, but nothing seemed to be missing. When he was finished going through the house, he went to his bedroom and packed some clothes and toiletries in a suitcase under the watchful eye of the detectives.

"I am sorry about this, Mr. Halvis," McNoll said. "I hope we will be able to let you have your home back soon."

When Halvis had gotten into his silver sports car and driven away, McNoll turned to Mangucci. "Well?" he asked.

"I checked the bookshelves in the study and Mrs. Halvis's dressing room. Found some bookmarks and also some books that have had their corners turned under. Anything else you want me to look at, or do you want to go back to the station and get the rest of my report?"

Back at the station, Bobby Storch joined his colleague Mangucci and the two detectives.

"Carpets don't really hold footprints," he explained. "But

there was a lot of blood, and the killers got blood on their shoes."

"Killers?" McNoll demanded. "The medical examination suggests there was only one killer."

"Yeah, but remember there were two sets of footprints leading away from—"

McNoll interrupted. "One killer and one watcher."

"That would be consistent with the evidence, but it's up to you to figure out what the evidence means. The watcher wasn't very close, though. There was no gap in the blood spatter, as there would be if the watcher were standing in front of the victim. Perhaps he was in another room. But both left bloody footprints. Both sets of shoes were flat soled, no clear design, both probably men's shoes. One is a size eleven and the other a size seven. Both sets cross the rug and go out the back door, then turn right across the back porch and down the outside stairs. They go around the corner of the house to the side yard, leaving the walkway and moving onto the grass. As I told you before, there is blood on the hedge as if one of the killers tried to wipe some of the blood off his body there. We think that may have been the actual killer. From that point on, the trail gets less distinct. There are traces of blood all the way down the side yard past the driveway and across the sidewalk to the road. The traces are fairly far apart and unevenly spaced, indicating the killers may have been running. The last trace was on the storm drain at the edge of the road. We assume the killers got into a car there."

"Two killers," McNoll said thoughtfully. "No trace on the road? Both killers got into the same door of the car?"

Storch shrugged. "The evidence doesn't tell us. Maybe they both got into the backseat and a third person was driving. Maybe they both got into the passenger side of the front seat and one slid over to the driver's side. Or the blood could have worn off the shoes of one of the killers by then and so he left no trace on the road. Or, since there has been a fair amount of traffic on the road, the blood traces could have been lost."

"Two killers," McNoll repeated.

"At least," Sandhu added. "Or three if there was a third person driving."

"Gang related?" McNoll suggested. "Drugs?"

"I think I'm going to take the rest of the day off," John Smyth said. "What do you want to do with the rest of our holiday, Ruby?"

McNoll and Sandhu had no such luxury. They spent the afternoon and part of the evening back on Mountaintop Drive, trying to connect with the neighbors that they hadn't found home the evening before.

Chapter 8
WEDNESDAY, JULY 14

A walk around Mill Lake had become a much-anticipated daily ritual for Ruby. And today, especially, was turning out to be a beautiful morning. The sun glinted off the water and turned distant Mount Baker a dusky rose color. Children scrambled over play structures under the watch of their mothers, and seniors strode, strolled, rolled, or hobbled around the paved walkway. The air was fresh and cool, and Ruby walked swinging her arms, enjoying the scene along with the exercise. She even pushed it a little, walking briskly until she was puffing, then slowed to catch her breath as she neared her favorite bench.

That was another thing she liked about the park. Benches dedicated to the memory of a previous generation of walkers were scattered all around it. This particular bench nestled fifteen feet off the path, in a grove of trees. Ruby liked the seclusion, the sense of being all alone in her private place.

Today, though, a dark-haired woman was sitting there.

Ruby hesitated, wondering about walking another circuit and seeing if the bench would be free then. But something about the woman's posture, the way she hunched forward, made her stop. She approached cautiously and sat down carefully on the other end of the bench. The other woman did not move.

"Hello. My name's Ruby."

The other woman jerked to life and turned frightened eyes toward Ruby.

"I'm sorry. I didn't mean to startle you."

The woman rose quickly and unsteadily to her feet, head hanging, and started to slide away around the corner of the bench.

"Don't go," Ruby pleaded. "We can share the bench."

The woman hesitated, then sank back down to the bench and looked at Ruby from the corner of her eye. Then she turned her head to face the lake in front of them. Ruby did not think she would speak, wondered if she *could* speak, and thus was startled by the mumbled words. "Name's Mary." Her long hair was straggly, her jeans faded, and her shoes badly worn at the heel. She was about Ruby's age.

"This is such a peaceful spot, don't you think?" Ruby said.

McNoll was in a sour mood. The afternoon and evening before they had spent trudging up and down Mountaintop Drive knocking on doors and looking for people they hadn't interviewed yet. They had found fifteen people they had not talked to before, not one of whom had seen or heard anything that seemed useful to their investigation.

"The biggest problem in investigation today," McNoll observed over coffee the next morning, "is empty porches." Sandhu said nothing, just raised his eyebrows, so McNoll continued. "Front porches used to be the eyes and ears of the police. Old ladies used to sit out and watch everything that happened in the neighborhood. Now they're all inside watching television or at work. Nobody sees anything, and nobody knows anyone. Did we find anyone in that neighborhood who actually knew Sylvan Halvis?"

"Nobody who knew her well," Sandhu conceded. There was another long silence before Sandhu asked, "What next?"

"Don't know. We have a dead woman with no enemies and no clues to her killers' motives or identity. Ruby Smyth heard something in the middle of the night, and there was a teenaged blond kid and a beat-up minivan in the neighborhood—none of which might have any bearing on the case. You want to interview all the neighbors again and ask if they saw a blond kid or a red minivan?"

"Not really."

"Might come to that."

"What about the books?"

"No price sticker. Suppose we could try to find the store they were bought in, but they might have nothing to do with the murder anyway."

"And the business card?"

McNoll pondered that. "A business card used as a bookmark? Might mean nothing. But I still want to talk to John Robinson—if he comes back."

"You're late."

"My walk was very enjoyable, thank you. And how was your morning?"

John Smyth gulped. "Sorry. I was starting to worry about you. Your walk didn't take this long before. It's almost lunchtime, and we wanted to get to the restaurant before the rush."

"Then we'd better get going." She climbed into the passenger seat and slammed the door shut.

John Smyth had always liked Ruby's red hair, and most of the time he liked the feistiness that went with it. But he wasn't always sure when Ruby was really angry with him and when she was only teasing.

Constable Richard Brown had been patrolling the downtown area for six years, and he knew all the regulars by name. He also had developed a nose for trouble. So when he saw Harry Cider duck into the alley behind the bank, he cruised on by, hit the gas, made two right turns, and pulled into a parking space. As a result of this maneuver, he was standing tight against the brick storefront when Harry slithered out of the alley. Brown's hand shot out and grabbed Cider by the back of his sweatshirt before the man saw him coming. Cider yelped in surprise and tried to twist away.

"Good morning, Harry."

At the sound of Brown's voice, Cider stopped squirming, but he sank a little lower in the policeman's grasp.

"What were you doing skulking around behind the bank, Harry?"

"I wasn't doin' nothin'."

Brown's grip tightened. "What were you doing, Harry?"

"Nothing. Nothing. Just checking out the dumpsters. Wednesdays the bank people have doughnuts for coffee break, and sometimes they don't eat 'em all."

"That's a nice sweat suit, Harry. Looks new. Where'd you get it?"

"It's not that new."

"Where'd you get it, Harry?"

"I found it."

"Where?"

"In a dumpster, couple of days ago."

"It's a new sweat suit, Harry. Nobody would throw out a new sweat suit like that."

"But they did. I found it in a dumpster, honest. It's got paint on it—see. That's why they threw it out."

Brown took a closer look at the brown stains on the sleeve. "Looks more like blood to me, Harry. What did you do, mug somebody and steal his clothes?"

"No, no. I found it in a dumpster couple of days ago in a bag, with some other stuff. I wouldn't lie to you."

"How about you show me the dumpster, and then we'll go down to the station and see what those stains are. Shall we do that, Harry?"

Cider said nothing as Brown shoved him, still squirming, into the backseat of the cruiser.

McNoll and Sandhu were still plowing their way through various reports.

"That was helpful," Sandhu said, tossing a forensics report on top of the pile on the desk in front of him. "We have fibers, lots of fingerprints, shoe impressions—but no suspects to match them against.

"I wouldn't say that."

"Why?"

"The papers that we took from the filing cabinet in Mrs. Halvis's dressing room."

"Yes, what about them?"

"She took several courses at Abbotsford College."

"So?"

McNoll picked up a sheaf of papers. "Here's an essay she wrote—'Collateral Social Guilt in Complex Human Societies.' Course, Sociology 306. Professor, John Robinson." He tossed the papers onto the desk so Sandhu could see them.

The phone rang.

"McNoll." He sat up straighter. "Yes." He was leaning forward in the chair now. "When?"

"Doctor John is back."

"How do you know?" Ruby asked.

"The blind on one of the front windows is open."

The two of them remained seated in their old gray car. "Are you sure one of us didn't open it?"

"Yes. I looked back when I left, and the blinds were all closed as usual."

"Maybe Henriette opened them."

"No. She left early today, just before I came to pick you up."

A worried look came over Ruby's face. "How do you know Doctor John opened the blind? What if someone broke in?"

John glanced at the house next door. "If someone broke in, they would be more likely to close the blinds, not open them."

"Did you remember to turn on the burglar alarm when you left?"

John nodded but pulled out the remote control. "I guess I should make sure it's off just in case Doctor John came home and then left again."

"Don't bother. He's there at the window."

John looked up. John Robinson was standing in the window looking out at them.

"I guess we should probably go in," Ruby said.

"You don't sound glad that he's back."

Ruby smiled. "Well, it was nice to have the house all to ourselves."

John smiled back. "Yes, it was. Are you envious? Do you wish our house looked like his?"

Ruby thought a minute. "Not really. Can you imagine what the kids would do to that white carpet and those glass tables? It's just not practical for us. And I'd rather have the kids than nice furniture." She paused. "But a house like this is sure fun to visit. And I wouldn't mind borrowing Henriette every now and then."

John Robinson was still standing by the living-room window when the Smyths walked through the doorway into the front hall. "Welcome back," Smyth told him.

Robinson offered a brief, distracted smile that didn't seem to go beyond his lips. "It's usually the person inside the house who does the welcoming."

"Did you have a good trip?"

"Yes," Robinson said noncommittally, still not moving from the window. After a moment, he walked past John and Ruby and opened the front door, which they had just closed. A tall, erect man with white hair and a deep tan was striding up the sidewalk. He wore a tailored black suit with a dark-blue tie.

"Hello, Calvin," Robinson said, extending his hand. "Thank you for coming." After a firm handshake, Robinson turned to the Smyths. "John, Ruby, this is Calvin Henderson."

John Smyth in turn shook hands. "Hello, Mr. Henderson. Good to see you again."

Henderson looked blank for a moment. "Ah, yes. The writer."

Turning to Ruby, Smyth explained, "I interviewed Mr. Henderson yesterday morning. He is chair of the elders' board at Mountaintop Church." To Henderson he said, "This is my wife, Ruby."

Ruby also shook hands with the white-haired man. "How do you do?"

After the introductions, there was an awkward silence. "Would you like me to get some cold drinks?" Ruby asked. "I was thinking about having one."

"No, thank you," Robinson said. "Calvin and I have some business to discuss." Turning to Henderson, he said, "Why don't we go to my study?"

John Robinson's study was down the hall to the left, just behind the double garage. John Smyth had seen it. At five hundred square feet, it was as large as Smyth's home office and his work office combined.

Looking at her husband, Ruby asked, "Would you like some iced tea or something?"

"No, thanks. I think I should get back to my writing."

"I'm going to have some anyway."

Ruby had reached the kitchen, Robinson and Henderson had closed the office door behind them, and Smyth was halfway up the stairs to their bedroom when the Westminster chimes echoed through the house. Smyth reached the door first.

"Detective McNoll," Smyth said in surprise.

"And Detective Sandhu," Sandhu added pointedly.

"Come in."

"We would actually like to talk with Dr. Robinson," McNoll said. "I understand he flew back here today. Is he in?"

"I'm John Robinson," a voice answered behind Smyth's back. Smyth turned to see both Robinson and Henderson coming down the hall.

"Detective McNoll from the Abbotsford Police Department." McNoll gestured toward his partner. "Detective Sandhu."

Robinson shook hands with both men. "How can I help you?"

"We would just like to ask you a few questions regarding a recent incident in your neighborhood."

"All right." Robinson inclined his head. "Why don't we go into the living room?"

"We would prefer to talk to you privately, Mr. Robinson," McNoll said.

106

"This is Calvin Henderson," Robinson replied. "He is my lawyer."

Henderson smiled and shook hands with the two detectives.

"And John and Ruby Smyth are my friends," Robinson continued. "I don't mind having them present. I have no secrets."

"All right," McNoll said after a moment's hesitation.

When they were all seated uncomfortably in the living room, McNoll turned to Robinson and asked, "You have been away. Where did you go?"

"I was in Winnipeg."

"Why?"

"I went to see my parents and to do some research at the university there."

"What kind of research?"

"Among other things, archival research. I am writing a book on the social aspects of prohibition, and certain records pertaining to prohibition in Manitoba are only available in Winnipeg."

"Detective," Henderson intervened, "is Dr. Robinson under investigation? Of what possible interest to you is Dr. Robinson's personal and professional life?"

Without taking his eyes from Robinson, McNoll responded, "I just want to establish Dr. Robinson's recent whereabouts in order to see if he might be a useful witness to us in an investigation. Now, when did you leave, Dr. Robinson?"

"I left Saturday morning."

"Was this a planned trip? When did you make the decision to go?"

Robinson hesitated. "I had known for some time that I would have to go to Winnipeg, but I didn't actually decide to go until Friday night."

"Why so sudden?"

"I had reached a point in my research where I realized I could go no further until I had gone to Winnipeg."

"Isn't it pretty expensive to book a flight last-minute like that?"

"Not that expensive if you book with WestJet. I can afford it."

Sandhu surreptitiously looked around the living room. There was no doubt that Robinson could afford it.

"When exactly did you decide to go?" McNoll continued. "Friday evening or after midnight?"

"Detective," Henderson intervened again, "what possible difference does it—"

"Was it before or after Sylvan Halvis was murdered?" McNoll overrode the interruption in a loud voice.

"Detective, are you accusing my client—"

"I decided late Friday night shortly before midnight," Robinson said in a calm, quiet voice. "I don't know when Mrs. Halvis was murdered."

"Detective," Henderson said more loudly and firmly. "If you are accusing my client of the murder of Mrs. Halvis, then I am going to insist that he answer no more questions."

"I am not accusing Dr. Robinson of anything," McNoll insisted. "I am just trying to question him as a possible witness since he lived next door to the murdered woman. Now, Dr. Robinson, you did not seem surprised when I said that Mrs. Halvis had been murdered. How did you know about it?"

"I heard about it Monday afternoon."

"Did Mr. Smyth phone and tell you?"

"No. I had not talked to Mr. Smyth from the time I left Saturday morning until I returned home a few minutes ago."

"That's true," John Smyth contributed.

"Then how did you find out about it?"

"I heard about it on the radio."

"But you were in Winnipeg."

"They have radio stations in Winnipeg. I believe it was a national news broadcast."

"How well did you know Mrs. Halvis?"

"She was a neighbor. We had talked a few times."

"What did you talk about?"

"Detective, asking questions about private conversations between my client and Mrs. Halvis is an unwarranted invasion of privacy. Those conversations can have no relevance to your investigation." Henderson had spoken, and Robinson had remained silent. Watching, Sandhu wondered if Robinson was giving Henderson a signal instructing him to interrupt whenever he didn't want to answer a question.

"Dr. Robinson, to your knowledge, did Mrs. Halvis have any enemies? Did she mention anyone who might have wanted to kill her?"

Robinson hesitated, then said, "No, not as far as I know."

"Did you hear or see anything unusual Friday night?"

"No."

"Dr. Robinson, did you ever give a business card to Mrs. Halvis?"

"No, I don't believe so."

"Did she ever take a course from you at the college?"

Again Robinson hesitated. "Yes, I believe she took one course from me. Last year."

"Do you know the books *Mere Christianity* and *The Testament?*"

"Yes, they are both good books, though very different. I would recommend them."

"Did you recommend them to Mrs. Halvis?"

Henderson interrupted again. "What possible relevance can this have to your murder investigation? You have no grounds for this kind of intrusion into Dr. Robinson's personal and professional life."

"Dr. Robinson," McNoll suddenly became tense. "Why would Mrs. Halvis write your name in her blood as she was dying?!"

Robinson froze. "I have no idea," he said at last, then added after a pause, "Are you sure it was my name?"

"Dr. Robinson, when was the last time you saw Mrs. Halvis?"

Henderson interrupted. "I think you have asked enough questions, Detective. I am advising my client not to answer any more."

"I hate lawyers." McNoll pounded the steering wheel with his hand.

"Do you think he did it?" Sandhu asked.

"That's the problem. With a lawyer keeping his answers vague and correct, there's no way to tell. If he had lied outright, we could've caught him in it. But since he didn't say anything, we can't tell if he's hiding anything or not. He only told us what his lawyer figured we might already know."

"But you do think he did it?"

McNoll reflected. "Don't know. Certainly still a suspect." Turning to look at Sandhu, he added, "Never let your convictions get ahead of the facts. Thinking about who you want it to be is a dangerous habit you don't want to get into."

Sandhu sighed, tired of being lectured. "Storch said there were two sets of footprints. My impression of Dr. Robinson is that he is a loner. Who would his accomplice have been?"

"John Smyth?"

Sandhu considered. "That could be. One of the sets of footprints was quite a bit smaller than the other."

"What are you thinking?" she asked.

"That the rich are different from you and me."

Ruby gave a small laugh. "I know that. But what made you think of it?"

"Doctor John knew he was going to be interrogated by the police. That's why he invited Calvin Henderson to come here, so they could talk strategy for the interrogation. Maybe he even knew when the police would show up and arranged for Henderson to be present at the time."

"How could he do that?"

"I don't know exactly. I just know that when people like you and me, the poor and the middle class, are interviewed by the police, we just tell the truth or think up the best lies we can on the spur of the moment. We don't have a regular lawyer and wouldn't think to call one—at least, not until we've been charged with something. But the first thought of a wealthy man is to call a lawyer who can devise a strategy for the interview ahead of time. The lawyer doesn't care what is true, just what the safest answer is. The poor have no such protection."

"John . . ." Ruby got up from her seat on the bed and walked over to the window where he was standing. "You don't think Doctor John could have . . . done it . . . do you? Murdered that woman, I mean?"

John looked into her eyes and thought about it. "You know we believe that all human beings, even Christians, are sinful."

"Yes," Ruby said quietly.

"That means that every one of us is capable of murder, given the right circumstances. Some are more likely than others, of course, and I would say that Doctor John is not one of the likely ones. He's a friend and a Christian, but . . ."

"But what?"

"Well, he has always been well-off, used to getting whatever he wants, and you yourself said he is too reserved—you never know what he is thinking."

"Oh, John! That means we could be sleeping in the same house as a murderer!"

"Ruby, any of the people we talk to or work with every day could be guilty of all kinds of things. Everywhere we go, the world is full of sinful people. We have no reason to think Doctor John is any worse, or any better, than anyone else. And we are in no more or less danger than we were a week ago."

Ruby turned away. "That's not very reassuring," she said.

Dinner that evening was a strained affair. Doctor John had prepared a stir-fry. Ruby wondered whether she should offer to take over cleanup duties but did not have much enthusiasm for doing so. John Smyth was preoccupied. Robinson seemed tense but made an effort to keep a conversation going by asking the Smyths questions about how the convention had gone, what they had been doing since then, and how they were enjoying their time in the Bible Belt.

Chapter 9

THURSDAY, JULY 15

With no outside windows, the room was lit only by imitation candles on the tables and by tiny white Christmas lights scattered across the black-painted vaulted ceiling in imitation of stars. The effect was cozy and intimate, and John Smyth found himself sinking down gratefully into the comfortable upholstery of the corner booth.

Capable of seating a couple of hundred people, the Starlight Café was a permanent coffee shop located on the top floor of Mountaintop Grace Evangelical Church, above the foyer. John had known it was there but had not visited it; the main meals for the convention had been served in a double gymnasium on the floor beneath the foyer and main auditorium. It was seven in the morning, and John Smyth and Marv Andreason were just two of twenty-five people scattered at tables and booths around the room.

"So how are the interviews going?" Andreason asked when they had given their breakfast order.

"Quite well. I think I am starting to understand what Mountaintop Church is all about."

"By the way, isn't this a great spot?" Andreason asked. "It has become one of my favorite places for talking to people. In the original plans for this building, this space was designated for storage, but one of the youth pastors came up with the idea of putting in a café."

"But is it worth the expense?" Smyth asked. "Couldn't you use regular restaurants or your office?"

Andreason stared at Smyth for a few moments. The two of them had met at various denominational events, but this was their first in-depth conversation. "You ask hard questions," he said.

"Yes," Smyth said. "I'm not out to make you look bad, but I've learned to ask the real questions other people may be asking. That way, you can answer them. If I don't ask the questions, they will continue to exist unanswered in people's minds."

"Fair enough," Andreason said, and then continued after a pause. "Any expense is worth it if it helps even one person become a Christian. Even though we pay some of the café staff and we let some people eat for free—anybody we are counseling for instance—the café actually makes a profit. This is quieter than most restaurants, and people feel more comfortable here than in an office."

"I wasn't just thinking of the café," Smyth said, adjusting the volume on his tape recorder.

"Let me begin with explaining the vision for our church. We didn't call it Mountaintop Church just because it's on Mountaintop Drive. The motto for this church is 'Meeting Jesus on the Mountain.' We wanted to create not just a place where Christians could worship, but a place where other people can come and get to know Jesus. That motto is on our church sign, and I preach on it at the start of every year. Periodically we go out into the foyer and ask the people if they know what the motto of the church is. If 75 percent can't tell us right away, we do some more teaching on it. We have to keep the motto front and center, or this church won't achieve what it was established for—to convince more people in our society to become Christians." Andreason had recited this technical explanation with practiced ease.

"But did you really need to build such a beautiful building in order for people to meet Jesus? This building must have cost something like twenty million dollars."

"A little over twelve million actually. And we had a lot of material and labor donated, so it's worth about twice that. But you have to remember that we put four thousand people in here on a Sunday. It's probably better value for the money than a church of two hundred and fifty people with a million-dollar building. There are a lot of those."

"You have a lot of extras here that other churches don't have. That multistory parking garage, for instance."

"Parking is key. We're trying to attract people who are not yet committed to Jesus. If they have to park on the street and walk a few blocks or look for a parking space, they won't come. You also have to remember that land is very expensive here in the Fraser Valley, and it would cost as much to buy more land as it did to build the car park. And because of the natural depression in the land, very little excavation was required."

"It's also a very beautiful building, with the wood paneling, padded pews, sound systems—"

"But God loves beauty," Andreason spoke emphatically. "Just look at a sunset or mountains. Besides, this building may look luxurious to you, but look at the houses in this neighborhood. The people here are used to luxury. They drive

Jaguars and Mercedes-Benzes. They have five-thousand-square-foot houses, big-screen TVs, and designer clothes. A cheap building would be a barrier for these people. It would say to them that Jesus really isn't that important, that he doesn't have anything to offer them. We are trying to change people, and we can't begin to do that if they won't come. Does that make sense?"

"I can see your point," Smyth answered noncommittally. He reached to switch off the recorder. "Listen, there's something else I wanted to ask you—off the record. How well do you know Doctor John?"

"John Robinson?" Andreason looked thoughtful. "He is a member of Mountaintop, but I can't say I know him very well. When Deirdre died, I conducted the funeral, you know, and I talked to him a few times then. He was—"Andreason paused. "I was trying to offer him comfort, but I don't think I understood how to go about it because he would never open up and tell me what he was thinking and feeling. Why do you ask?"

It was Smyth's turn to pause. "No specific reason I can explain to you. I was just trying to understand."

Darwinder Sandhu hated those moments in an investigation when they had finished one task and needed to embark on the next one. Those were the times when McNoll's attitude annoyed him the most.

At the moment, for example, they were at the station once more, reports and interviews stacked neatly on McNoll's desk next to two foam cups of poisonous coffee and the remains of a spectacularly unhealthy fast-food breakfast. McNoll sat without speaking, tapping a pencil rhythmically against the desk.

"Well, we've finished the interviews," Sandhu said. "I'm thinking we might want to check with the burglar-alarm company—see if they have any way of tracing when it was switched off."

McNoll didn't even look up. "Not now," he said. "Do it later maybe. Won't tell us much."

Sandhu sighed. "So what do you think we should do next?"

McNoll kept tapping. "Wouldn't mind getting a search warrant for John Robinson's house."

"Do we have enough evidence for a warrant?"

"No."

"So we don't have enough evidence to arrest him because we can't search his house, and we can't search his house because we don't have enough evidence to get a warrant."

"Precisely. And every day, more of whatever evidence might be there gets lost or covered up. Lesson for you. Be rich. Robinson can afford a good lawyer, and that makes it a lot harder to get evidence against him."

"So what are we going to do?"

"Get more evidence."

"How?"

"Go by the book."

"What do you mean?"

"Just what I said." A corner of McNoll's mouth twitched. "Go—buy—the—book."

Tim Horton's doughnut shops are as Canadian as beavers and the RCMP—the Royal Canadian Mounted Police. Named after a famous hockey player, now deceased, they are one of Canada's largest fast-food chains and one of the few that didn't originate in the United States. Abbotsford has more than half a dozen of them, and it was in the back corner of one of these that John Smyth sat, soaking up the midmorning sunshine, with a middle-aged man of medium height. A few strands of black hair lay across the man's otherwise balding head, and his smile revealed a gold front tooth.

"I'm sorry Alice couldn't come," he was saying. "She works at Wal-Mart and was supposed to have the day off, but got called in."

"That's all right, Mr. Hearne," Smyth replied.

"Call me Ralph."

"Sure. Thank you for agreeing to meet me. Do you know who I am?"

"Of course. Don't you?"

"I mean, you know I'm the editor of *Grace* magazine, right?"

"Yeah."

"Sorry. It's just that one of the other people I talked to didn't seem to know who I was, and . . ." Smyth was aware that he was rambling.

Hearne smiled. "I know. Some people don't seem to read. I read the magazine regular. It's actually pretty good sometimes. I think you're doing a good job. Your editorials are interesting."

"And you always agree with them, right?"

"No. Not always."

"That's okay. I've never met anyone who has said yes to that question." Smyth took a sip of his hot chocolate and explained about his tape recorder. "I'm here because I'm writing an article about Mountaintop Church. You and Alice are members there, right?"

"Yes. For about eleven years now. It's a good church."

"Pardon me for asking. The church arranged these interviews and hasn't told me much about the people I am meeting. Are you a member of the elders' board?"

"No. Alice and I are just members."

"May I ask what you do for a living?"

"Sure. I'm a correctional officer."

Smyth looked blank. "A what?"

"A prison guard, at Matsqui Institution."

"Oh."

"Is there anything wrong with that?"

"No, no. It just surprised me. I thought that since the Shadow Valley Church has such a strong prison ministry and you are a prison guard, you might go to that church. You don't live on the top of Sumas Mountain, I suppose?"

Hearne snorted. "Not even close. But I don't live in old Abbotsford either. We have a new house in west Clearbrook."

"I'm sorry, Mr. Hearne, uh, Ralph. I seem to be saying the wrong things. I am just trying to understand, that's all. Can you tell me why you chose Mountaintop?"

"Alice and I became Christians about twelve years ago through a marriage seminar Mountaintop sponsored. We were—well, we were having some problems, and a friend invited us." Anticipating a further question, he added, "The friend is Alf Jones. He's a guard at Matsqui too. Look, there are only two Grace Evangelical churches in town, Mountaintop and Shadow Valley. And a lot of middle-class people go to Mountaintop. It is not just for lawyers and millionaires. There aren't that many lawyers and millionaires in Abbotsford, anyway."

"I see what you mean. But what keeps you and Alice at Mountaintop?"

Hearne considered. "Well, it's a good church with a lot of good programs. We have three teenaged girls, and they like the youth group, like the music. We like the music too. And frankly, I don't want my daughters hanging around some of the people who go to Shadow Valley."

"What do you mean?"

"Well, Shadow Valley does all that work with troubled

people —homeless people, prostitutes, prisoners. Besides, I'm a prison guard. To a lot of the people who go to Shadow Valley, I'm the enemy. They don't want me there. If I went there, some of them maybe wouldn't go."

"But you are in agreement with Shadow Valley's ministry?"

Hearne was quiet for a few moments. "Look. Don't get me wrong. I think Shadow Valley is doing something good for a lot of people who really need help." He hesitated again.

"But?"

"Well, sometimes I think the Shadow Valley people are naïve. They're too ready to believe every sob story that comes along." He gestured with half a doughnut. "Look, I work with federal prisoners. And they're almost all of them con men, practiced liars. If they haven't learned to lie before they get to prison, they learn to do it once they get inside. And if you listen to them, every last one of 'em is innocent. They didn't do it. Or they had a good reason for doing it. Or it was someone else's fault. Us guards are used to it. We learn not to trust them. But the Shadow Valley people come along—really nice people, by the way—and it doesn't take the prisoners long to figure out what they want to hear. They lie, and the Shadow Valley people believe 'em."

He shook his head. "The thing is, I don't think that helps. Most of these guys've had someone making excuses for them all their lives, and that's part of the problem. They need to be forced to face up to what they've done wrong, held to account."

"You're talking about tough love?" Smyth asked.

"Absolutely. Look, half the people in prison were arrested. The other half were, well, rescued. For a lot of 'em, going to prison was the only way they could sober up and get clean. It's like being forced to go to a detox center for a few months. If they hadn't been arrested, they would have overdosed by now or been shot in a drug deal that went bad. By putting 'em away, we saved their lives for a few more months, but we haven't changed 'em. And chances are, as soon as they get out of prison, they'll be right back at it."

Smyth thought a moment. "So you don't believe the conversion stories?"

Hearne thought in turn. "God can change people. I absolutely believe that. He changed me. But I think it's tough for a con man to change because he's so used to lying, even to himself."

He drained his coffee and started gathering up the trash on the table. "What I think is that some of the conversions probably are genuine. But not all of them. Maybe not even most of them."

Ruby was sitting beside Mary on the bench again. A blue heron stood motionless among the lily pads about seventy feet away, looking like a hunched old woman, his scruffy feathers sticking out in all directions in the sunlight, his bill poised like a knife to murder the next fish that should happen to come within reach.

McNoll and Sandhu stood patiently in line at the large chain bookstore in Abbotsford's central mall. McNoll let his gaze wander distractedly over a rack of new releases while the two clerks finished with the customers ahead of them. When his turn came, McNoll stepped forward toward the stocky, auburn-haired clerk on the left. He discreetly showed his badge without attracting the attention of the customer beside him.

"Detective McNoll with the Abbotsford police," he said quietly. "I am interested in two books, *The Testament* by John Grisham and *Mere Christianity* by C. S. Lewis." He handed the clerk a piece of paper with the names written on it.

The clerk busied herself with the computer. "We don't

have either book in stock. We mostly sell Grisham's more recent books. We can get both books, but it will take a few weeks for the Lewis one."

"Can you tell me if you have sold either book recently?"

The clerk checked the computer again. "It doesn't look like we've stocked either book all year. It would take a while to check the back records, and I couldn't do that without a court order."

"Thanks anyway," McNoll said. "Are there any other bookstores in town?"

"I don't think so," the clerk replied, "except for some small specialty stores."

"It's probably a waste of time anyway," Sandhu said quietly to McNoll. "A man like Robinson would probably buy his books on the Internet. A lot of people do. I suppose we could check to see if there is a bookstore at Abbotsford College, though."

McNoll, who had been turning away from the clerk, turned back. "Are those religious books?" he asked.

"Well, John Grisham writes novels, but the other book sounds religious, doesn't it? I don't really know it."

"Is there a religious bookstore in town?"

"Yes, I think so. In a converted car dealership building just off South Fraser Way."

"Thank you."

Out in the mall, McNoll growled, "I'm tired of messing around. It'll save time if we get a court order before we go to that store."

John Smyth drummed his fingers impatiently on the steering wheel. From the parking lot, he had a clear view of the blue waters of Mill Lake, with Mount Baker rising majestically behind it. But he was not looking at the lake. Instead, he stared anxiously at the pathway.

At last, emerging from behind a group of seniors, he discerned a head of red hair. Getting out of the car, he went to meet her.

"I was getting worried. It seems to take you longer to walk around the lake every time. Are you sure it isn't too far?"

Ruby smiled. "No. I was just taking my time, enjoying myself. I'm on holiday, remember?"

"Well I'm not . . . um, not exactly. I've got to get to that lunch meeting. Are you sure you don't want to come?"

"Have lunch with a bunch of lawyers? I don't think so. Why don't you drop me off at the house?"

John Smyth didn't know what to say. He was glad Ruby seemed so happy and relaxed. But somehow the more relaxed she seemed, the less relaxed he felt.

The Corporate Room at the Bakerview Golf and Country Club was a sea of maroon tablecloths and white napkins bounded by mahogany paneling and granite molding. Three dozen men and five women in expertly tailored suits clustered in groups of three or four. John Smyth, standing in the doorway, glanced down at his own best suit, bought at a Boxing Day sale at Sears.

"Can I help you?" a black-clad maître d' asked.

"Is this the Abbotsford lawyers' luncheon? I was invited by Marv Andreason."

The frown on the face of the maître d' deepened.

A bronzed, white-haired man detached himself from a knot of lawyers. He was dressed today in an immaculate blue pin-striped suit. "It's all right, Trevor," he said. "Mr. Smyth, isn't it? Marv told me he'd invited you."

"Good afternoon, Mr. Henderson," Smyth said, a little too formally and feeling like an idiot.

"Come, sit at our table," Henderson continued, gesturing toward a front table. "We will start in a moment. Excuse me." He walked to the front of the room and stood beside the fireplace. Smyth noticed he had a lawyer's ability to speak effortlessly in a controlled voice that could be heard clearly in the back corners: "Please sit down. Court is now in session."

The announcement was met by a flurry of subdued laughter, and the lawyers broke out of their groups and settled around the tables. Smyth found himself at a table with Marv Andreason, three other men, and a vacant chair.

"Welcome to the monthly meeting of the Abbotsford Legal Association," Henderson continued from the front of the room. "We have a special guest with us today, but let's eat first, and we will do the talking later."

"I thought you said this was a gathering of lawyers," someone called. "Don't you know we prefer talking to eating?"

Amid further laughter and talk, Henderson sat down in the vacant chair at Smyth's table as Marv Andreason explained, "Calvin is president of the Abbotsford Legal Association."

In a moment, however, Henderson was on his feet again. He strode over to the doorway where a tall, brown-haired man in an identical dark-blue pin-striped suit had entered the room. Several other lawyers had also risen, but Henderson got there first. "Tom, I am so sorry about Sylvan," he said. "How are you doing?"

Smyth could not hear the answer through the crush of lawyers gathered around the newcomer. After a minute or two, Halvis seated himself at a table near the door, and the other lawyers returned to their tables.

Conversation at the table revolved around golf scores, upcoming vacations, expensive cars, and proposed changes in certain provincial laws. Fortunately, Smyth did not seem to be expected to contribute to the conversation. For the most part he simply enjoyed the dishes that were served one after the other by a red-coated waiter, although he couldn't always put a name to the things he was eating.

After dessert and coffee had been served, Henderson again moved to the front of the room and stood on a raised stone platform beside the fireplace. He quickly and efficiently conducted the business portion of the meeting, then moved to introduce the "special guest," Andreason. "One of the most successful pastors in the history of Canada, Marv is a man who understands what it takes to reach and maintain a standard of excellence, a man of substance who understands and values the achievements of those who take the lead in building our Canadian society. Marv?"

Andreason rose to polite applause and replaced Henderson on the platform. Smyth noted that he seemed as comfortable here in this gathering of lawyers as he did in front of his church.

"There was a young couple," Andreason began, "who looked forward to being married. Unfortunately, just a week before their wedding, they were involved in a serious automobile accident and were killed. When they reached the gates of heaven, the prospective groom approached St. Peter.

"'We were really looking forward to getting married,' he said. 'Do you think we could get married up here?'

"'I don't know,' replied St. Peter, 'but I will see what I can do.'

"After about a week, St. Peter found the couple and announced, 'I have good news. You can get married.'

"But the groom replied, 'We have been doing some further thinking, and eternity is a very long time, and marriage such a major commitment What if later on, after a few centuries or so, we decide we don't want to be married anymore? Do you think it would be possible for us to get divorced?'

"'Oh, no,' replied St. Peter. 'It took me a week to find a minister up here. I'll never find a lawyer.'"

The room erupted into laughter.

"Well, that's a lawyer joke," Andreason continued. "But I'm here to assure you that the legal profession is anything but a joke in our society. The legal profession is charged with the task of maintaining justice, with making sure that society operates justly. When injustices take place, the legal profession has the responsibility to restore justice. To do this, the legal profession makes use of a series of tools called laws. Unfortunately, the legal profession has sometimes become so focused on maintaining laws that it has failed to provide justice. It has been sidetracked into mistaking the means for the end, maintaining law rather than justice."

The room had become quiet.

"In the same way," Andreason continued, "the church also has an important role to play in society. The church's main purpose is to help put people in touch with God. In order to do its job, the church makes use of a number of tools called institutions and religious rites. Unfortunately, the church has also sometimes mistaken the end for the means. Sometimes the church has been so busy maintaining its tools, its institutions and the trappings of religion, that it has lost touch with God and failed to help other people get in touch with God.

"Christianity was never meant to be a religion, a series of ceremonies or activities for people to participate in. Jesus Christ, the Son of God, came to earth not to establish a religion, but to establish a relationship between individual human beings and himself, between individual human beings and God. He died on the cross—paid the penalty the legal system required for the things we all have done wrong—so that we can be forgiven and go free."

Andreason's talk was simple, direct, brief, and pointed. After another ten minutes, he finished with the words: "Jesus Christ would like to have a personal relationship with each of you. If you would like to talk to me about any of this, please call my office, and my secretary will set up an appointment—my business cards are there on the table—or come to church some Sunday morning."

Andreason sat down to polite applause. Smyth noticed that some of the faces in the room seemed open and interested, others annoyed. He suspected that the lawyers in this organization were unaccustomed to this particular kind of presentation.

Henderson stood and thanked Andreason, then dismissed the meeting.

John Smyth rose from the table, nodded to those he had shared the meal with, and began heading toward the door. Marv Andreason, moving effortlessly through the crowd and greeting individuals here and there, reached the door before him. He went up to Thomas Halvis and put his hand on his shoulder.

"Mr. Halvis, I was very sorry to hear about your wife's death."

Halvis turned to face Andreason. "Thank you. It has been very difficult. I suppose I shouldn't have come to this meeting, but I needed to go out and do something normal, get my mind off . . . what is happening."

"That's perfectly understandable. It is a wise and healthy thing to think about other things. If you would like to talk anytime or if there is anything else I can do, please let me know."

"As a matter of fact," Halvis said, "there is one thing.

Sylvan and I weren't particularly religious. We didn't go to church, and I don't know any other ministers. The police will probably be releasing Sylvan's body in a few days, and I would like to give her a good funeral. Would you be willing to officiate?"

"Of course," said Andreason. "Here is my card. Give me a call when you get the word that your wife's body is being released, and we'll sit down together and plan the service. Our whole church will be available to serve you."

John Smyth marveled again at Andreason's grace in difficult situations, his ability to put Halvis at ease and to connect on a personal level with a stranger.

The room had once been an automobile showroom with big glass windows, but it now made an attractive bookstore. McNoll and Sandhu stood just inside the door and looked around. It was larger than the chain store in the mall, with more books and more customers, separate sections for cards, music, and knickknacks, and even a coffee shop.

"Can I help you?" a clerk asked.

"Yes, I would like to see the manager," McNoll said, "on police business."

They were led up a back stairs to a cluttered office where a middle-aged woman in slacks greeted them. "I am Betsy Wallace, the assistant manager," she said. "How can I help you?"

"Detective McNoll of the Abbotsford Police Department," McNoll said. "And Detective Sandhu. We have a warrant to examine your sales records."

"Oh." Betsy Wallace collapsed back into her chair. "Wh-what do you think we . . . ? We, um . . ."

"Relax, Ms. Wallace. We don't suspect you of doing anything wrong. Some books were found at a crime scene. We just want to see whether they might have been bought in this store and, if so, who bought them. This doesn't mean the person who bought them did anything wrong either. That person might be an innocent bystander or even a witness."

"Oh." The middle-aged woman continued to sit and stare at the policemen, her mouth open slightly.

"The two books are *The Testament* by John Grisham and *Mere Christianity* by C. S. Lewis. Can you tell me if you have sold those books recently?"

"Oh, of course," Betsy said. "It's just that we have never been investigated . . . uh . . . had policemen here like this . . ."

"The books?"

Betsy consulted the computer in front of her. "Yes, we have sold five copies of *Mere Christianity* and one copy of *The Testament*. It's not a book we normally stock, so it must have been special ordered."

"Can you tell us who ordered it?"

"Probably. We have a frequent-customers reward system. When customers have spent a certain amount of money, they get a discount on their next purchase, and to do that we have to keep track of what those customers buy. Let me see here . . ."

"Do you have it?"

"Wait. Oh, here it is. A man named John Robinson. He's one of our regular customers."

"Did he also buy one of the other books, the one by C. S. Lewis?"

"Yes, he did."

"Do you have his address?"

"36031 Mountaintop Drive."

"Thank you. You have been very helpful. Could you print out a copy of those transaction records?"

Back in the car, Sandhu asked, "Does this give us enough evidence to get a search warrant?"

"I think so," McNoll said with satisfaction.

They were silent a moment. "I've been thinking," Sandhu said. "Remember that Storch said one of the killers rubbed blood off on the hedge?"

"Yeah. So?"

"What if he wasn't trying to rub the blood off but was pushing through the hedge to go home?"

"Robinson?"

"Yes. And if he left the blood trace on the hedge, he probably left some kind of evidence over there."

McNoll looked at Sandhu for a long moment. He offered no commendation of Sandhu's thinking, saying only, "That would definitely help with the search warrant."

As the station wagon wound its way up Sumas Mountain, John Smyth became aware of a string of vehicles spread out behind him, led by a big white van. "I am not going that slowly," he muttered, annoyed. As they rounded a curve, he noticed there were two police cars directly behind the van. And as he pulled to a stop in front of John Robinson's house, the van and police cars pulled in behind him.

Now what did I do? he wondered. He slowly got out, walked around the front of the car, and stood mesmerized on the sidewalk. Armed police were scrambling out of four vehicles and rushing to surround the house next door—not the one where the murder had taken place, but the one on the other side, where the Korean or Japanese people lived and the blinds were always pulled down.

Two uniformed officers were on the front porch, ringing the doorbell and pounding on the door. Two men in suits were walking quickly around the outside of the house, examining it. When they had gotten back around to the front, they nodded to the officers on the front porch, who smashed open the front door with some kind of small, handheld battering ram, then went inside, guns drawn. A minute or so later, Smyth heard three loud reports. More officers rushed inside.

Five minutes later, nothing more seemed to be happening, so Smyth walked up the driveway toward Robinson's house.

Ruby had heard the door and was halfway down the stairs. "Did you hear something?" she asked.

John opened the window blinds, and for a while they sat in John Robinson's elegant living room and watched. After about fifteen minutes, an officer backed the van up into the driveway next door, and other officers began carrying out large plastic garbage bags and piling them in the van. The Smyths did not notice that Robinson had come into the room until he had been standing behind them for about five minutes.

"Must have been a grow-op," he said.

"What?" John asked.

"Marijuana. I'll tell you about it at dinner." With that, Robinson turned and walked back into his office.

Detective Jeff Stantzky was standing on the front lawn supervising the loading when the car pulled up. He was of medium height with a rumpled suit, dark shirt, no tie. His thinning blond-red hair went with his florid face and slightly spreading midsection. And his back was to the road, so he didn't see them coming until McNoll stepped in front of him, his livid face staring down into Stantzky's.

"What do you think you're doing?!" he said through clenched teeth, his voice barely restrained from shouting.

"My job," Stantzky said evenly. "Conducting a raid."

"Don't you know there was a murder committed two doors down last weekend? You're interfering with my investigation."

"I'll let you know if we find anything relevant to your investigation."

"And how will you know what's relevant unless you talk to me about it? We're supposed to work together on these things. How am I supposed to get a search warrant for the house next door when you just got one for this house? Judges are going to think we're on a fishing expedition in this block."

Stantzky looked up fully into McNoll's face. "Next time," he said, "we'll put an ad in the paper, so everybody knows we're coming."

"You suggesting I can't be trusted with prior information?"

"Somebody's tipping these guys off."

"It certainly wasn't me . . . since I didn't know a thing." He backed up a half-step, his professional curiosity catching up with his anger. "You catch anybody this time?"

"Nobody home except a couple of dogs, a pit bull and a Rottweiler."

"What did you do with them?"

"They came after us. They won't do it again."

"Okay, look. That house two doors down is still a crime scene—nobody's gonna be home. And when you canvass the other neighbors, don't go to the house next door. Got it?"

Stantzky was about to speak, but McNoll cut him off. "If you need to talk to them, call me, and we'll do it together." He turned to go but said over his shoulder, "And don't leak any of the information I just gave you."

They sat on the second-floor deck as before, eating barbecued stuffed salmon and wild rice.

"Tell us about the marijuana," Ruby said.

Robinson put down his fork. "There are thousands of grow-ops in the Lower Mainland, undoubtedly the highest concentration in the country. This is for a variety of reasons, including our proximity to the U.S. market, particularly California. I think it also has something to do with the West Coast of North America having a frontier mentality. Most of the marijuana is grown in houses now because such operations are less visible than open fields and more productive as well —there's perfect climate control and a year-round growing season."

"But why use houses?" Ruby asked. "And why here?"

"Homes are cheaper to rent and less suspicious than warehouses, and the more expensive the house, the less suspicion. Who would think someone would use an expensive house like the one next door to grow marijuana? But it's simple economics. That house rents for two thousand, maybe twenty-five hundred dollars a month. But it can hold hundreds of plants, with each plant yielding about seven hundred dollars' worth of marijuana, and growers can produce three crops a year. That's easily a million dollars a year, tax-free. Compared to the profit, the rent is inconsequential. You would have to be crazy—or moral—not to do it. And believe me, a lot of people do it."

"But what if they get caught?"

"In the first place, most of the people doing this don't get caught. The police don't have enough resources to raid all the grow-ops. And another thing—did you actually see anyone arrested next door?"

"Uh, no."

"The people who rent houses for grow-ops usually don't live there. They just visit to check the crop. They probably rented the place under an assumed name. But even if they used their real names, their address is listed as the grow-op house, so nobody knows where to look for them. The landlord can't legally inspect the place without the tenants' permission, and he can't get their permission because he can never find them home to ask them. So the tenants can do whatever they want inside without much fear of being caught."

"I think someone was inside, though," John Smyth said. "I heard shots fired."

"Did they carry out body bags, or did an ambulance come?"

"No, I don't think so."

"Then the shots might have been the police shooting a dog—a pit bull or something like that. The growers often have guard dogs in the place to deter intruders. If the police shoot the dog and the growers are caught, the growers can complain that the animal was a family pet and portray themselves as the victims of police brutality."

"But," Ruby said, "won't the dogs make a . . . mess in the house?"

"Of course. But the people growing marijuana don't care about the house anyway. They often knock holes in the walls and put in heat lamps, heating ducts, and watering systems. If nothing else, the humidity rots the walls and grows mold. So the house will not be fit for human habitation, anyway, unless it is totally gutted inside. They need huge amounts of electricity, which is expensive, and consumption is monitored by B.C. Hydro. So to avoid detection, growers usually bypass the meter and the fuse box, which means that there is a greatly increased risk of fire. In fact, many grow-ops are discovered because the house catches fire."

"Which endangers the other houses on the street," Ruby mused.

"That's not the only danger. Sometimes the growers booby-trap the house with bombs or guns. The traps are for the police, of course, but also for other criminals. Growing marijuana is easy money, but it is even easier money to let someone else grow the marijuana and then steal it. And of course the growers can't get insurance or complain to the police."

"So the criminals steal from each other—"

Robinson nodded. "Then we get feuds and killings between various gangs of drug dealers, all of which directly endanger the public. There have been quite a few cases where armed thieves have broken into a house looking for marijuana and terrorized an innocent family."

They ate in silence for a few moments, thinking about the implications.

"But surely some of the growers are arrested?" Ruby said.

"Of course, some are, but for various reasons most of the charges get dropped before the cases come to court. The growers can afford good lawyers. And if a grower is convicted, do you know what the penalty is?"

"A prison sentence?" Ruby guessed.

"In Canada, the punishment for a first-time offense is usually a fine of a few hundred or even a few thousand dollars. The punishment for a subsequent offense is often not much higher. For many, that is simply a license to do business. The government does have legal authority to confiscate the proceeds of crime, but that requires another lengthy and expensive legal process. And remember that the growers use rented buildings, so there are often no assets for the government to seize. It often happens that a specific house has several tenants in a row who grow marijuana. In those cases, of course, the police suspect that the owner knows what is going on and deliberately rents the house to growers in return for a cut of the profits—something like sharecropping. But there is no direct link to the owner, and the police can't prove anything, so the landlord remains in business."

"Why doesn't the government do something to stop all this?"

"That's the real question. The answer is presumably because our governments don't want to. I am currently writing a book on prohibition in the first half of the twentieth century, when various nations, including Canada, outlawed alcohol."

"But prohibition didn't really work, did it?"

"That's a common misconception. Prohibition actually had some very positive effects. Crime rates for assault, robbery, murder, and domestic abuse all dropped significantly. But prohibition ultimately failed because it could not be enforced. One of the things I discovered is that a government cannot enforce a law if a significant minority of people is determined to break it and if the government is not committed to enforcing it."

"Are you saying our government is corrupt?" Ruby asked.

"I'm saying our society is corrupt. The people making and enforcing the laws now—the politicians, lawyers, and judges —all went to university twenty or thirty or forty years ago, and a lot of them smoked marijuana. They aren't going to get very serious about stamping out something they did themselves. There is also the fact that marijuana is a huge cash crop. All the money the criminals spend boosts the economy, and that spending is taxable. And since a lot of the marijuana is sold into the U.S., it brings a lot of wealth across the border—it may even boost employment. Since the marijuana trade is considered a victimless crime, the government isn't really committed to eradicating it."

"But is it really a victimless crime?"

"Of course not. That's another misconception. It's true that smoking marijuana doesn't seem to do a lot of physical harm. But a lot of the marijuana grown here is sold into the U.S. and often traded for guns and harder drugs such as cocaine. Drug dealers and drug addicts are responsible for the majority of the murders, petty thefts, stolen cars, and break-and-enters in the Lower Mainland. The users are almost always addicted and have to keep committing crimes to get their next fix. The growers and dealers are addicted in another way—to easy money. We don't put any of these people in prison for any length of time, so the crimes continue, and the rest of us continue to suffer."

"You must have spent a lot of time studying this."

"Well, yes, for my prohibition paper. But what I have told you I got from the newspapers. It is public knowledge. Aside from the other costs, think of the corroding effect this has on public morality. Our acceptance of these practices and our dishonesty in admitting what is going on is corrupting our society."

John Smyth spoke for the first time in several minutes. "We underestimate the corrupting power of evil. I was thinking of the resolution the convention passed a week ago, stating that some actions are simply wrong and condemned by God. It struck me that much of our society doesn't have any such concept."

Robinson smiled. "People now don't talk about sin or guilt. They tend to say they made a mistake or did something inappropriate. Saying two and two makes five is a mistake. Deliberately hurting someone else for your own benefit—or allowing someone to be hurt because you simply don't care— that's not a mistake. It is morally wrong. I would go so far as to say it is evil. The drug trade is often considered harmless to the people who aren't involved in it, but the drug trade is an extreme form of selfishness and antisocial behavior.

"Consider the example of the people next door," he added. "They may have been growing marijuana for two or three years and made a couple of million dollars. They pay no taxes. Sometimes such people even collect welfare because they have no reportable income. The rest of us pay higher taxes because they don't. We also have to pay the extra policing and fire costs, and we pay for the electricity they use free of charge. That new house next door, worth probably half a million dollars, is now unfit for human habitation. That's one less house for people to live in, the deliberate destruction of a significant social asset, and that in turn makes houses relatively scarce and thus more expensive for all of us."

"Doesn't it make you angry," asked Ruby, "having your beautiful neighborhood invaded by all this crime?"

Robinson seemed shocked, as if he had been suddenly snapped back to reality. He stammered over his next words: "Oh no," he said. "It saddens me. It's all such . . . a terrible, terrible waste." At the end, he seemed to have been talking more to himself than to the Smyths.

The meal was over, and they got up to go in. It had been another of Doctor John's lectures. But they were glad to have had something else to think about, so they could avoid thinking and talking about what might have happened the previous weekend in the house on the other side of John Robinson's home.

Chapter 10

I've been working too hard," announced John Smyth the next morning as Ruby dressed for her morning walk. "And I haven't been spending enough time with you. Would you like me to go with you to Mill Lake this morning?"

Ruby hesitated. "Maybe not today. Why don't you work on finishing your articles today, and then we can do something together tomorrow?"

"Oh."

Seeing John's reaction, Ruby added, "Maybe we could go out to lunch. I find it a bit creepy staying in this house and making polite conversation with a murder suspect."

McNoll had been standing in front of Stantzky's desk for several long moments, but the other detective had not looked up. "How's your investigation going?" McNoll finally asked.

Unable to ignore him any longer, Stantzky looked up from the report he was reading. He stared at McNoll for a while, then shrugged. "We found three hundred and fifty plants and a few bags from the previous crop."

"Big one," McNoll observed.

"Yeah. The house was a mess. This was obviously not the first crop grown there. The meter had been bypassed, and no one was living there other than the two dogs."

"Renters?" McNoll asked.

"Apparently."

"Who owns the house?"

"A holding company. We're now checking who owns the holding company."

"Didn't you do that before the raid?"

"No. It leads to leaks. Somebody might tip them off. Listen, what're you getting at?"

McNoll answered with another question. "You'll trace the renters through the owner?"

Stantzky sighed. "We'll try, but the company will probably say they know nothing about the renters, and they thought the renters were living in the place."

"What else do you try? Fingerprints?"

"Sometimes."

"Did you do that this time?"

"Yeah, we looked for fingerprints on the grow-op equipment and a few other places, but we don't have the budget to dust the whole place like you guys can for a murder investigation."

"Any results?"

"We're at the end of the line on that one too. The lab sometimes takes weeks to process our prints and check for matches."

McNoll nodded. "Want me to see if I can hurry it up?"

Stantzky shrugged. "If you want. It might speed up this case, but it won't do anything for my other fifty cases."

"How did you find out about this grow-op?"

"It was an anonymous phone tip."

"From one of the neighbors?"

"From a phone booth in downtown Abbotsford."

"Could've still been a neighbor."

"Could've been. Could've been a rival gang using us to drive out the competition."

"Is that common?"

"Anonymous phone tips? Sure. It's one of the ways we find out about grow-ops."

"Did you dust the phone booth for prints?"

Stantzky rolled his eyes. "Do I look like I've got the resources to dust public phone booths for prints? What's the point? I don't have enough resources to catch the growers. Why would I waste time and money trying to catch a tipster?"

McNoll shrugged that off and asked casually, "Any sign of a break-in?"

"At the house, you mean? There was a broken basement window, but there were bars on the inside."

"So somebody could have tried to break in but was stopped by the bars?"

"It's possible. Or a kid could have thrown a rock, or a lawn mower might have thrown something."

"Did you dust the window for prints?"

Stantzky sighed again in exasperation. "Probably not."

"Would your search warrant cover it if I had it dusted?"

Stantzky considered. "Maybe. Why are you so interested in my case?"

McNoll shrugged.

"You think somebody tried to break into my grow-op and broke into your murder victim's house by mistake?"

McNoll shrugged again. "It's a possibility."

"I'll help you with that. If we could put away a drug dealer on a murder rap, It sure beats another thousand-dollar fine." He paused. "The search warrant is good for a couple more days."

"I'll have the fingerprinting done tomorrow."

"We're going to be interviewing neighbors of the grow-op this afternoon and tonight. You wanted me to hold off on visiting the house next door. Is there a suspect there?"

"Could be," answered McNoll. "I'm going there first thing Saturday morning. If you want to come along, you can ask your questions then."

Stantzky nodded.

"I think I will take you somewhere completely different tonight."

"John, you know we're going to Bob Young's house."

"Yes, Ruby, and that will be completely different from where we have been staying the last few days. I'm sure of it."

At five o'clock, the Smyths' station wagon pulled up in front of a bungalow on Shadow Street in old Abbotsford. A couple of blocks farther on, the street led between two arms of Lower Sumas Mountain, a feature which gave the whole area the name Shadow Valley. The bungalow was finished in gray stucco above six rows of peeling lime-green wooden siding. An ancient Toyota minivan sat in the driveway next to a portable basketball net. In a few patches, the brown summer lawn had been worn down to bare dirt.

"Well, this feels familiar," Ruby said.

John smiled.

A teenaged boy in a white tee-shirt and blue jeans stopped shooting hoops in the driveway and walked over to the car. He grinned. "Are you the Smyths?" he asked.

"Yes, we are," John replied and held out his hand.

The boy shook it. "I'm Barry. Dad and Mom said to tell you to go right in."

The boy led the way up the driveway, along the sidewalk, up three steps, and through the front door. "They're here!" he called.

The Smyths found themselves on a small landing that seemed to hover between two stories. Seven carpeted steps led down to a basement, and seven carpeted steps led up. A round face appeared over a half-wall at the top of the steps. "Come in, come in," Bob Young said. Balding and a little on the heavy side, he wore a casual sports shirt and slacks. Beside him appeared a short, thin woman with sharp features and long, curly dark-brown hair. She wore a black print top and black slacks and was stirring something in a bowl.

"Welcome here," Bob Young said, coming down to meet them. "This is Brenda."

The woman wiped her hand on her slacks and shook hands with the Smyths. "It's good to meet you."

"Can I help you with dinner?" Ruby asked.

"No," Brenda answered, "but you can come into the kitchen and talk."

John Smyth followed the pastor into the living room and sat on a brown couch. It was a clean but plain room with just enough disorder to make it seem lived-in. A large square fan hummed in a corner, stirring the air. Sheer drapes had been pulled across the picture window to keep out some of the sun. Barry had apparently returned to his basketball game, and John found himself alone with Bob.

"Thanks for inviting us to dinner," John said.

"No problem," Bob said. "We usually have someone extra for dinner, and it's a good way to get to know people."

"Bob, I wanted to do a formal interview with you about Shadow Valley Church. Can we do that now? Do you mind if I record our conversation?"

"No, go ahead. This is probably our best chance to talk without being interrupted."

"The church was started about fifteen years ago, right?"

"Not exactly." Bob had an energetic way of talking that John found both intimidating and infectious. "There was a Grace Evangelical church started here in Abbotsford about fifty years ago, but it struggled. Their building was inadequate, and they couldn't afford to keep it up, so they eventually sold it. The congregation was quite small, and when Mountaintop Church started twenty years ago, four or five families switched over. At that point the first congregation dwindled to a house church, about twenty people meeting once a week in different people's homes. They met Sunday nights, and some of them also went to various other churches Sunday mornings. But they never lost their concern for this part of town, and they dreamed of becoming a full church again."

"Which they obviously did," observed Smyth.

Young nodded. "About that time, a small factory and warehouse on Shadow Street closed down. Nobody seemed interested in starting a new business there, so the owner of the property approached the congregation to see if they might be interested in leasing the office part of the building. And about the same time, the denominational headquarters had received a bequest from a former Abbotsford resident and was looking for an appropriate project to spend the money on, so they offered funding for a year and asked me to come and try to get something going."

"And *that* was about fifteen years ago?"

"Right. It was pretty hard at first, but we started by making friends in the neighborhood—people down here really need friends. There was a man who had played in a rock band—he was an alcoholic, but he became a Christian and got sober, and he offered to help with our music. A lot of people in the neighborhood knew him, and pretty soon we had about fifty people attending. One thing led to another, and now we've taken over the whole building. In fact, we bought it a few years ago for a good price."

"Would you say that Shadow Valley Church has a well-rounded ministry?"

"Yes, I think so. People around here tend to have a lot of problems, and we try to help them in whatever ways we can. We try to be proactive; it's a big thing with us that God not only forbids evil actions but commands good ones. So early on, we began having AA meetings, and we set up a counseling and referral service to help people get government assistance and things like that. At that point, we were renting only the office. After a year or so, we took over the cafeteria too and began offering soup lunches a couple of times a week. We've expanded that now to seven days a week, and we even managed to secure a government grant to train people as cooks."

"So when did you take over the whole building?"

"That was shortly after we got the grant. The owner couldn't find any other tenants or buyers, so he let us have it cheap—with the understanding that we would move out if he found a tenant who could pay more. He never did, so we started using the main part of the building for our worship services. We also put in some basketball hoops and started a youth drop-in center. And we started the thrift store, which actually makes money because it is staffed by volunteers."

"Like me." A teenaged girl had stuck her head around the corner from the hallway. She had chiseled features and carefully straightened shoulder-length hair. "Hi," she said, "I'm Brianne."

"Our oldest," explained Bob. "Brianne is seventeen, and yes, she does work in our thrift store some weekends. Bri, this is John Smyth, and he's interviewing me for a magazine article."

"Hey, cool," she said. "So I guess I need to stop bothering you, huh?"

"You're not bother—" Smyth started, then saw she was not in the least offended. She gave them a grin and a little wave and disappeared into the kitchen.

"Brianne, as you might notice, is not the least bit shy," her father offered. "But let's move on—I think dinner will be ready soon. Any more questions?"

"Umm." Smyth checked his notebook. "What's the slogan of your church?"

"Slogan?"

"The motto, the purpose statement, the vision."

"Oh . . . um . . . we don't have one. We never had time to work on anything like that. We just try to do what needs doing and preach the Bible."

"Since you took over a factory, I suppose there's adequate parking?"

The pastor shrugged. "Well, sure, but parking isn't really an issue. A lot of the people who come don't have cars. It's more important that we're within walking distance of where most of our people live in old Abbotsford, and we're on a bus route."

"I would also like to talk to some of your members. When I was working on the story about Mountaintop Church, Marv Andreason had his secretary set up lunch and coffee appointments with representative members of his congregation."

"I don't have a secretary. Well, we have various volunteers who help out, but they are pretty busy as it is. And the truth is, some of our members don't have phones, and some of them aren't very good with appointments. They'd forget to show up or would be too intimidated to be interviewed by the editor of a magazine. Their experience with the media has often been negative. Look, why don't you show up on Sunday morning, I'll introduce you as a friend of mine, and you can talk to people after the service? We serve a light lunch, and people are never in a hurry to leave."

"Okay. That sounds good. Now, tell me about your prison ministry."

"We got into that quite naturally. Families of people in prison are often poor, and those are the people we work with. Almost right away, some of the families asked us to visit their relatives in prison. Eventually we organized regular one-on-one visitation, where we match church members to specific prisoners. The church member visits the prisoner, escorts him when he gets a pass or is out on day parole, and eventually helps him get settled when he is released— you know, find a job, a place to live, and so on. We've learned that the months after release are often more crucial than the time in prison. The recidivism—or relapse—rate is pretty high—over 50 per-cent according to some calculations, but it's much lower for prisoners who've been through our program."

"And you're involved with this ministry personally, right? You're also matched with a prisoner?"

"Yes, several prisoners actually. A pastor can't ask his people to do something he isn't willing to do himself. The most recent ones are David Black and Kurt Hallbach. I took over relating to Kurt after Allen Walker died."

"They're the ones who spoke at the convention last weekend?"

"Yes. They got weekend passes and stayed here in the house that weekend, in the boys' room in the basement. The boys slept up here."

"Are they here this weekend? I had wondered about inter-viewing them."

"No. They don't get passes every weekend. I suppose you could go over to Ferndale and interview them, but I am not sure a magazine interview would be the best thing for them. They're pretty fragile people, and the burden of being celebrities might create stress they can't handle. I thought about it for a long time before I agreed to let them tell their stories at the convention."

"How does your family feel about them staying here? Do you feel safe with convicts sleeping in your basement?"

"Would I feel any safer if those same convicts were wandering the streets? The reality is that convicts do get released from prison. We can either help them change or let them keep on committing crimes. I happen to believe we're all a lot safer because of programs like Shadow Valley's."

"Do you ever get conned? I mean, are there convicts who pretend to have changed their lives but are really just using you to get whatever they can get?"

"Oh, sure. Sometimes we are conned. Sometimes the convicts are also lying to themselves; they think they've changed, but they haven't. And sometimes they really try to change, but they lose their temper and hit somebody, or they give in to a sudden temptation to steal. A lot of prisoners fail us—and themselves. But at least we've given them an opportunity to succeed. And a lot of them don't—"

"Hey Daddy, Mommy says—"

A ten-year-old in blonde pigtails and white shorts bounced into the room and stopped short when she saw Smyth.

"Hi, honey." Bob Young gave the girl a squeeze. "Can you say hello to Mr. Smyth? John, this is my youngest daughter, Britanny."

John solemnly shook hands with the girl. "You have how many kids, Bob?"

"Four. Brianne, Barry, Benny—you haven't met him yet—and Britanny here."

"All *B*s," John observed.

"Yes," Bob deadpanned. "We think it is important to . . . B. Young." He grinned at John's good-natured groan. "Now, Brittany, what did Mommy say?"

"She said it's time to eat spaghetti."

A few minutes later, they were all seated around a table in the cramped dining space that formed an ell at one end of the living room. Everyone was busy helping themselves from heaping bowls of pasta, garlic bread, and Caesar salad in the middle of the table. The children were chattering, and for a time the Smyths remained quiet and listened.

"May I ask your children some questions?" John finally asked.

"Sure," Bob said.

"Daddy said you might ask us questions and not to say anything that would embarrass him," Britanny chimed in.

"Like what specifically?" John asked, and everybody laughed. "What do you think about living in this neighborhood, in the old part of Abbotsford?" he continued.

The children looked at each other and shrugged. "It's where we live," Barry said.

"Do you feel safe here?"

"I guess," Barry said. "We don't go wandering around the neighborhood alone, but Dad says no neighborhood is completely safe."

"How do you feel about your dad's church? Do you like it that he is the pastor there instead of at some other church?"

"It's our church too," Barry said. "Besides, we get to help out, which we probably wouldn't get to do in another church."

"Do you mean do we feel safe with the people there?" Brianne asked. "Most of them are very nice, even some of the ones who have serious problems."

"Daddy says our church is there for people who need

help," Brittanny contributed, "and that means that the church will help *us* if we ever need it."

"We have friends there too, the kids we go to school with," Benny, a freckled boy of about twelve, added.

"There are people we don't trust at church, but there are people we don't trust at school either," Barry said. "Dad says there are people you can't trust in big churches too, and everywhere else. This way we get used to dealing with it."

"There are precautions we take," Bob said. "We make sure we drive the kids places after dark, we keep the doors locked, and we leave the outside lights on at night."

"But that's mostly for Dean," Britanny chirped.

"Who's Dean?"

The chatter and movement came to an abrupt halt.

Bob's face became serious. "Dean is a sad case. We got to know him because he went to school with Brianne."

"And he's got exactly the same birthday as me," Brianne offered, "September third. But he's had this really tough life, and he's got lots of problems now. His dad went to prison when Dean was just a baby."

"He lives in Vancouver now, we think," Brenda added. "The dad I mean, not Dean. After he got out of prison, he never had much to do with the family."

Bob took up the story again. "At any rate, Dean's mother found a new boyfriend who didn't want Dean around, so she dumped Dean with his grandmother, who lives in a tiny one-bedroom house by the railway tracks. I think she loves Dean, but she doesn't know much about raising children—didn't do that well raising her own. So Dean grew up without parents, without a television, without books, sometimes without food, more or less without rules."

"Not a good combination," observed Ruby, and John nodded.

"It was so sad," Brianne said. "I mean, he wasn't a bad guy. But the other kids made fun of him in school, so he dropped out—that was in grade nine. He was hanging around with a bunch of losers and users—you know, druggies. So of course he started using, and then he started stealing stuff and begging and conning people out of money."

"We tried to help him," said Bob. "I would pick him up for youth group nights if he happened to be home. We'd invite him over here for dinner or basketball or just to talk, but we had to watch him all the time. He would go down the hall to the bathroom and then sneak into the bedrooms and steal jewelry or money."

"He took Brianne's CD player," broke in Benny, "and one time he took all of my Christmas money. And then—"

"Benny, that's enough," said Brenda. "We don't need the details. The point is, Dean was a very troubled boy, and things were getting worse even before his grandmother got sick."

"It was a heart attack," said Bob. "A mild one, thank goodness, but she was in the hospital for a couple of weeks. We tried to have Dean stay in church members' homes or at least provide him with meals, but he would steal something or run away. Then when his grandmother got out of the hospital, she found out that Dean had sold most of her furniture for drug money. The police made the secondhand dealer give most of it back, but the grandmother had finally had enough, and she kicked Dean out of the house. He had just turned sixteen then; he's almost eighteen now. And he's been living on the streets ever since—stealing, begging, and dealing. He won't let us near him to help him."

"That boy has such a bruised and broken soul," added Brenda softly. "The way he's going, he won't live to twenty-one."

"I think we all feel a special burden for him," said Bob. "I don't know why exactly, since there are so many other needy kids in this neighborhood. But we leave a light on for him every night, and I don't know whether it's to stop him from robbing us or to welcome him if he ever admits he needs help."

As they were getting ready for bed, Ruby said, "I really liked the Youngs. I felt at home there. Their family was so . . . so . . ."

"Lively?" John suggested.

"I was going to say their family—not their house but their home—seemed so much richer than Marv Andreason's home."

"We've never been invited to Marv Andreason's home."

"Oh, that's right." There was a pause. "John?"

"Yes."

"We should call the kids tomorrow."

"We just called them yesterday."

"I know, but we should call them tomorrow too."

Chapter 11

SATURDAY, JULY 17

John and Ruby were still asleep when Robinson knocked on their bedroom door. Smyth muttered something that was unintelligible even to himself.

Robinson called through the door, "Could you both get dressed and come downstairs right away, please?"

Smyth muttered, "Okay. What time is it?"

"Eight o'clock."

"Okay." After a moment, he turned to Ruby and asked, "What now?"

Ten minutes later, they descended the stairs to find several men standing in the front hall. Robinson was impeccably dressed and shaved. The smell of coffee wafted from the kitchen. John Smyth also recognized Detectives McNoll and Sandhu.

"Shall we sit in the living room?" McNoll said.

The Smyths followed him and Robinson into the room.

"This is Detective Stantzky," said McNoll when they were

seated. "He would like to ask you all what you know about the house next door. The one to the west—number 36029."

There was silence for a moment. "We have never seen anybody there," John Smyth said. "We saw the raid on Thursday. It was a grow-op, right?"

"The Smyths are, of course, just guests here," McNoll said. "Dr. Robinson, what do you know about the people in the house next door?"

"I don't know much," Robinson replied. "I have never talked to them, and I have only seen them in passing a very few times. I think they are Korean or Chinese. The people who first owned the house, the Blanchards, lived there about three years and then moved to North Vancouver. He was a medical researcher. The house was vacant for a few months. The Korean or Chinese people took possession of the house about eighteen months ago, about the beginning of January."

"You remember the time that specifically?" Stantzky had taken over the interrogation.

"It occurred about the same time as another . . . event in my life. Otherwise I wouldn't remember."

"What was the other event?"

Robinson was silent, and his jaw tightened. John and Ruby exchanged glances.

Robinson finally said, "It was personal, and it has absolutely nothing to do with your investigation."

Stantzky did not push it. "You must have talked to the tenants a few times. What did you learn about them?"

"I told you. I have never talked to them."

"How many of them were there?"

"I saw a middle-aged man and woman. They had a grey minivan, I think. There was also a younger man, about twenty, who came in a sports car. I only saw him once or twice, so I doubt he was living there."

"Were the man and woman living there?"

"I don't know. I didn't pay much attention. They moved a lot of boxes into the house when they first arrived. After that, their drapes were always closed. I saw the man mowing the lawn a few times, I think, but I honestly didn't pay much attention. I spend a lot of time here in my office and in my office at work. I don't spend a lot of time looking out the windows."

"Did you suspect they were growing marijuana there?"

"I never thought about it. There are a lot of houses on this street where people could be growing marijuana. People rarely see their neighbors and don't get to know them very well even if they do."

Stantzky nodded. "Do you sit on your sundeck?"

"Sometimes. That's when I saw him mowing the lawn."

"Do you think you would recognize him if you saw him again?"

"I don't think so. I only saw him at a distance, and I didn't pay much attention."

"But you paid more attention to the neighbors on the other side, didn't you, Dr. Robinson?" McNoll suddenly intruded into the interrogation.

Robinson turned a cold stare on McNoll. "I told you I will not talk about the Halvises without my lawyer present."

McNoll turned to the Smyths. "Mr. and Mrs. Smyth, perhaps you would be willing to speak without your lawyer. Have you remembered or discovered anything about what happened next door?"

Ruby sat rigidly silent. John Smyth held his hands out openly, opened his mouth, and shook his head.

"Well?" McNoll asked.

"We don't know anything we haven't told you," John said.

McNoll continued, "We have a warrant to search this house. Do you have any objections to that?"

"John, you and Ruby were planning to go to Vancouver to see Stanley Park and some other things," Robinson said suddenly. "Perhaps today would be a good day to do that."

"Could we do that?" Smyth asked McNoll.

"Sure, but we will search you when you leave the house. And we'll need your fingerprints, for elimination purposes."

Smyth turned to his friend. "John, are you sure you don't want us to stay?"

"No, I would prefer that you go," Robinson said. "Calvin Henderson will be here shortly, and he will give me any help I need."

Fifteen minutes later, as the Smyths were walking down the driveway to their car, they encountered Calvin Henderson coming up the driveway. "Good morning, Mr. Smyth, Mrs. Smyth," he said.

John stepped in front of the lawyer to stop him. "They're going to search Doctor John's house," he said.

The lawyer looked Smyth up and down. "If their search warrant is in order, as it probably is, yes, they are going to search the house."

"Does that mean they suspect Doctor John of killing Mrs. Halvis?"

"It means that they are investigating all possibilities."

"Are they going to arrest Doctor John?"

"Certainly not today. After that, it will all depend on whether they find anything in the house." Seeing the look on the Smyths' faces, he put his hand on John's shoulder. "Don't worry. I will take care of Dr. Robinson." With that, he brushed past John and walked into the house.

John and Ruby stared after him.

"Did you notice," said Ruby, "he never said that Doctor John is innocent?"

While the Smyths spent an interesting day seeing the sights of Vancouver and trying not to worry, Darwinder Sandhu spent an absolutely mind-numbing day at 36031 Mountaintop Drive. McNoll had gone home for the day and left Sandhu to keep an eye on Robinson while the police conducted a search of his house. Robinson spent the day reading in the living room. Henderson spent the day reading and writing briefs using his briefcase as a desk and stepping outside from time to time to make calls on his cell phone. Sandhu just sat, bored out of his skull.

McNoll walked into the living room about four o'clock. "Where's Mangucci?" he asked.

"In Robinson's office," Sandhu replied. "Storch is there too. He says he has some things to show you."

"Has he shown them to you?" McNoll asked sharply.

Sandhu shook his head. "I said I would wait for you."

The two detectives walked to the door of Robinson's office, where Mangucci, Storch, and two other scene-of-crime officers were methodically going through papers on the desk and bookshelves.

"We'll be done in about half an hour," Mangucci said without greeting. Turning to the thin man kneeling in front of a bookcase, he said, "Bobby, why don't you show them what you found outside."

Bobby Storch carefully replaced the books he had been looking at and stood up. He led them down the hall, out through the front door, and around the side of the house adjacent to the Halvis property.

"Remember I showed you the bloodstains on the hedge

about there, as if one of the killers had tried to rub the blood off before going down to the road?"

The detectives nodded.

"It turns out the blood trail comes through the hedge and straight across to the back corner of Robinson's house."

"That was our idea," McNoll said. "Why didn't you discover it sooner?"

Storch sighed. "You're right. I should have checked it, but there were no broken branches or any other evidence of someone pushing all the way through the hedge, and I was fooled by the rest of the blood trail that led out to the road. In any case, the trail leads directly to the back corner of the house, where the garden hose is. I even found a partial shoeprint in the softer ground just this side of the hedge. It seems consistent with the larger of the two shoeprints coming from the Halvis house, although I'm doubtful there will be enough detail to declare an exact match. There are traces of blood on the hose, the tap, the side of the house, and the sidewalk."

"So he came over here and used the hose to wash the blood off?" McNoll asked.

"Looks like it," Storch continued. "There are no fingerprints in the area, however, so he either wore gloves or the water washed them away. There is a garbage pail right here, so we thought he might have put his bloody clothes in the pail, but there is no evidence of blood in it. There are traces of blood on the steps up to the second-floor deck, on the railing, and around the handle and frame of the door leading into the house, but no bloody fingerprints. There are other fingerprints, of course."

"That's pretty good evidence," Sandhu said.

"What's the bad news?" McNoll asked.

"There is no trace of blood inside—on the floors, walls, washing machine, clothes, sink traps, anything."

"Who says you can't get good help these days? Rich man like Robinson can afford one very efficient housekeeper. She's had several days to make the house spotless."

"That would be an exceptional housekeeper not to leave even a trace of blood."

"Yeah," McNoll agreed.

"The other thing we found is a pair of shoes, size eleven, sitting right there beside the door, with significant traces of blood on them. The soles appear similar to the prints at the murder scene."

"It gets better and better," Sandhu said.

McNoll just frowned. "What did Robinson say about the shoes?"

"We haven't asked him. We're leaving that to you guys."

"Anything else?" McNoll asked.

"You asked us to dust the broken window at the grow-op house. I found good prints and maybe a trace of blood on the glass and frame and some trace evidence on the bars, not yet identified. Can you use that evidence in this investigation?"

"Let me worry about that," McNoll said. "Let's go and see what Mangucci's found."

"Not much conclusive," Mangucci said when they asked him. "There are fewer fingerprints than you would normally expect to find in a house, but Robinson lives alone, he is very neat, and he has a very efficient and thorough housekeeper. We have not yet matched any of the prints, of course. We have collected all the tools, knives, and other instruments that we think could even remotely be suspected of being the murder weapon. We will check them all for blood stains and for a match to the wounds. We have also taken some of Robinson's financial records. He is quite well-off, has investments and income far beyond his professor's salary."

"I think it's family money. Anything else?"

"One thing. Notice the desk supplies, the distinctive leather-and-gold design of the desk blotter, pen holder, desk clock, and trays—not real gold, by the way. There is a space for a letter opener, but this is the letter opener that was there." Mangucci held up a stainless-steel utensil that seemed cheap and ugly in comparison to the rest of the desk accessories.

McNoll thought for a moment. "You are ready to wrap up?" he asked Mangucci. "You fingerprinted Robinson?"

"Yup. The houseguests too. We'll still have to get the housekeeper's prints. Other than that, we're done."

"Okay. You have the list of the items you are taking for analysis?" Mangucci nodded. "Bring the letter opener and the shoes, too, but don't show them to him."

"What are you going to do?" Sandhu asked suspiciously.

McNoll raised an eyebrow. "Watch and learn."

McNoll, Sandhu, Mangucci, and Storch went into the living room where Robinson and Henderson were sitting.

"Ah," Henderson said, pulling his papers together and putting them away in his briefcase. "You are finally ready to let Dr. Robinson have his house back? I trust you have not done too much damage?"

McNoll smiled. He knew how to be gracious when he wanted to be. "Yes, Dr. Robinson can have his house back. I was wondering, Dr. Robinson, if you have anything else you would like to tell us, anything about your relationship with Sylvan Halvis or about her death?"

Robinson did not move or speak. Henderson said, "Dr. Robinson has already told you everything he has to say on the matter. He has been fully cooperative and has answered your questions as far as they are relevant to your investigation."

McNoll said, "Well, we appreciate it."

After a while, Henderson asked, "I take it you have found

no evidence linking Dr. Robinson to the unfortunate events next door—and you no longer consider him a suspect?"

"On the contrary," McNoll answered, "we have found a considerable number of items which we are taking for further analysis." He held up the list of items that Mangucci had drawn up.

"I would like to see that list," Henderson said, holding out his hand.

"In a moment." McNoll nodded at Mangucci, who handed him a plastic evidence bag containing the shoes. "Do you recognize these?" he demanded, flourishing them dramatically in front of Robinson's face.

Robinson looked intently at the shoes. "They look like the shoes I use for gardening. I leave them sitting on the back deck."

"And can you explain why they have Mrs. Halvis's blood on them?"

"He doesn't have to answer that," Henderson intervened. "It calls for conjecture."

"I have no idea," Robinson said calmly.

"I have some ideas," McNoll pressed, and Sandhu shot him a questioning look.

"Wait a minute," Henderson said. "When did you find those shoes?"

"Today," McNoll said.

"Then you wouldn't have had time to test them for DNA to know whose blood it is. That means you must have taken those shoes earlier, and it also means you obtained them without a search warrant. If you ever try to use those shoes as evidence against my client, I will move to have it declared inadmissible. You should know better than to try a stunt like that."

McNoll said nothing, just gave a minute shrug and stared at Robinson. "We found the shoes today," Mangucci said, "and we haven't tested them yet. We are just assuming the blood is Mrs. Halvis's because there is a trail of blood leading from Mrs. Halvis's body to these shoes."

Henderson smiled and said nothing more.

McNoll held out his hand toward Mangucci, who handed McNoll the second bag. "Can you identify this, Dr. Robinson?"

Robinson peered at it. "It looks like my letter opener."

"Can you tell me why you are using this letter opener rather than the one that matches your desk set?"

Robinson smiled. "The other one disappeared awhile ago, and I was using this one as a replacement until I found the other one."

"When did it disappear?"

"I don't know. About a month ago."

"What happened to it?"

"I suspect it got put into a file by mistake or fell into the wastepaper basket and was thrown out, but I really don't know. I was actually hoping you might find it in your search."

The momentum had been lost, but McNoll pushed on. "Was this before or after you used it to murder Mrs. Halvis?"

The response in the room was obviously not what he had wanted. Henderson raised an unbelieving eyebrow. Sandhu exchanged worried glances with Mangucci. Robinson looked at him evenly for a moment. "I did not murder Mrs. Halvis."

"That is quite enough, Detective McNoll," Henderson said. "If you are going to make wild, unfounded allegations, I am going to advise my client not to answer any more questions. Now, if you have no more rabbits to pull out of your hat, I would like to see that list of items you have taken from Dr. Robinson."

McNoll handed the list over without a word, and Henderson gave it a cursory glance. "This is nothing but a fishing expedition, an unwarranted intrusion into the personal life of my client. You have no justification to take most of these items."

"Nevertheless, we are taking them," McNoll said quietly. "You can argue about it later in court."

Out in the driveway, Sandhu knew better than to question McNoll's judgment in confronting Robinson without all the evidence he needed. Part of him was furious with his partner for making the case more difficult. But he also had to admire McNoll's nerve. The older detective had seen an outside chance to blow the case wide open and taken it, even though he must have known it was risky. The man had never backed down, even against that smooth-talking lawyer.

"Misplaced his letter opener!" McNoll growled. "There isn't a single item out of place in the whole house. I'll bet that man never loses anything. Have you ever seen a neater house than that one?"

"No," Sandhu answered, "and I don't think I have ever seen anyone as tense as Dr. John Robinson. Did you see how tight the muscles were in his face and neck?"

McNoll grunted.

"On the other hand," Sandhu continued, "Dr. Robinson is a religious man. Is he the kind of man who would murder his neighbor's wife?"

"Religion just makes some men more violent," McNoll observed. "Otherwise," he added with a sidewise glance at his partner, "why would Sikhs carry kirpans?"

It was well after ten that evening when the Smyths got back from Vancouver, and the house was quiet. But there was a light on in the front hall, and another light was showing under Doctor John's bedroom door.

"Well," Ruby said, "he's still here."

Chapter 12

SUNDAY, JULY 18

John and Ruby had overslept. Rushing downstairs, they found the table set for two, some bacon on a plate by the toaster, and a note from Doctor John saying he hoped they enjoyed their visit to Shadow Valley Church.

"Too bad he's already left," John said. "I wanted to ask him about what happened yesterday."

Ruby took a bite of bacon. "Maybe that's why he left early," she said.

Shadow Valley Grace Evangelical Church sat on a lesser-traveled street in the heart of old Abbotsford between one of Abbotsford's hills and the railway tracks—a two-story building of weathered brick. A rusty chain-link fence surrounded three sides of the property but had been removed from the front. The driveway, of uneven gravel with small patches of pavement here and there like vestiges of a former glory, ran down one side of the building. A small, empty executive parking lot sat in front of the building, but the Smyths drove through to the back of the building where the work was done. They parked next to the building between two sets of metal industrial doors, which stood open to welcome an assortment of people who were straggling down the driveway.

Inside, the cement floor had been painted gray and the brick walls white. The roof girders were open to view, but the large two-story room was surprisingly bright, thanks largely to the row of ten-foot, multipaned windows that circled three sides of the room.

"It took us two months to scrape the paint off all those windows," a fat man in blue jeans and a clean yellow tee-shirt said. "Welcome here. I'm Isaac Fellows."

"John and Ruby Smyth," John said.

"Are you new here?"

"We're visiting," John said. "I'm the editor of *Grace* magazine in Winnipeg. I'm here to write an article about Shadow Valley Church."

"Then you should talk to Pastor Bob."

"I have already talked to Pastor Bob. We were at his house for dinner on Friday night."

"Pastor Bob invites a lot of people over."

"Do you go to this church regularly?"

"Sure, I've been here about twelve years. You might not believe it to look at me now, but I used to be an alcoholic. Then the Lord saved me. Have you been saved?"

"Uh, yes," John replied. "*Grace* magazine is the denominational periodical for all of the Grace Evangelical churches across North America. Do you ever read it?"

"I don't read much."

The big man turned to welcome another couple into the building. John and Ruby passed on into the room, which was about 125 feet square. Five hundred plain padded chairs had been set out in rows, but most people in the room were still standing about. As at Mountaintop Church, the dress ranged from suits and dresses to blue jeans and shorts, but here the suits and dresses were definitely in the minority and clearly less expensive.

"There's Brianne Young," Ruby whispered to John. He looked and saw the pastor's daughter in animated conversation with a girl her age and a shabbily dressed middle-aged woman.

Music began to play, and people started drifting to the middle, eventually filling about four hundred of the five hundred chairs. The music came from a band on a raised platform at one end of the room—a drummer, a couple of guitarists, and a pianist pounding on an old upright. Four singers stood on the front edge of the platform, one in frayed jeans. The drummer had unnaturally red hair and looked bored and unhappy.

"Ow," whispered Ruby as the pianist took a brief solo turn, "that thing really needs to be tuned."

John, who was no musician, merely shrugged.

On a cue from the musicians, the congregation stood and began singing words handwritten on a plastic sheet and projected onto a screen from an overhead projector. John Smyth smiled to see that one line of the words read: "All of our days, we're going to sing your prays." Some things don't change, he reflected, no matter where you are.

Most of the congregation sang enthusiastically, if not harmoniously. A few sat on their chairs or stood silently, arms folded, refusing to sing. One big swarthy man wandered up and down the aisles, either looking for a place to sit or trying to remember what he was there for.

After about fifteen minutes, Bob Young stepped onto the stage, took a microphone from one of the singers, and said,

"Good morning! Welcome to Shadow Valley Grace Evangelical Church. If you are walking in shadows this morning, I pray that you will experience God's grace before you leave here today." He went on to give several announcements, mostly about things like AA meetings, soup-kitchen hours, and the need for various volunteers, then said a prayer and asked the ushers to collect the morning offering. The band resumed playing and singing almost immediately while deep buckets were passed down the rows to collect the offering.

After another fifteen minutes, the band members laid down their instruments and put their microphones back onto stands, and Bob Young returned to the stage. He laid his Bible and some notes on one of the music stands and pushed it over in front of one of the microphones. He said another short prayer, then picked up his Bible. "Today I am going to talk about two roads that lead to death from the first two chapters of Proverbs. If you have a Bible, Proverbs is just past the middle of the book, after Psalms."

For the next half hour, he talked of two temptations mentioned in Proverbs—the temptation to commit crimes and the temptation to engage in sex outside marriage. Both temptations, he said, promise something for nothing, easy pleasure with no cost. But in both cases, looking for the easy way rather than waiting for God's way results in death.

"You know this is true," Pastor Bob said quietly. "Those who break the law eventually end up dead or in jail. They live in fear, and they almost always end up poorer rather than richer. And those who go after easy sex often end up with sexually transmitted diseases as well as divorce problems, loneliness, and despair."

"But there's a better way," Pastor Bob told his congregation. He spoke in simple, straightforward terms and urged the congregation to follow God's harder but better way of working to earn a living and enjoying sex only within marriage, stating that through Jesus Christ members of the congregation could be forgiven for their crimes and sexual sins and find the strength to live godly lives. "God's way," he said, "is the only way to find a fulfilling life." He then asked anyone who wanted to "accept Jesus" or who wanted help fighting temptations to talk to him after the service. He reminded the congregation of the lunch that would be served after the service and said another short prayer.

People immediately stood up and began talking among themselves. Smyth noticed that two young men approached Pastor Bob. He led them through a door toward the front of the building. Several men and a couple of women began picking up collapsible tables from the back wall of the room and setting them up in the middle of the room, arranging the chairs around them. Two wooden shutters were opened in the front wall of the room, revealing a counter where plates of food would soon be served.

"John Smyth?"

Smyth turned to see a tall, thin, older man with wispy hair and spectacles. "Yes?"

"I'm Ira Williams." He held out a long, bony hand. "I am one of the council members here. Pastor Bob asked me to answer any questions you might have and to make sure you know you are welcome to stay for lunch. It's five dollars a person, twelve for a family of three or more—although obviously that doesn't apply to you. Anyway, the five dollars covers the costs. You can pay more if you like—or less. It all depends on what you can afford. Some people pay as little as a dollar."

"What about the very poor who don't even have a dollar?"

"Occasionally we make an exception, but we encourage people to save and contribute to the cost of their own food. Poor people are usually poor in many ways, and it is as important to feed their sense of worth as their stomachs. Of course, the majority of our congregation can pay the five dollars. Many of them are middle-class. I am a retired teacher, for instance."

"I noticed nobody handed us a church bulletin with the order of service and announcements in it when we came in. Isn't that sort of unusual?"

"Probably so. Actually, we used to have a bulletin, but we dropped it to save money. Most of the programs are ongoing anyway, and a lot of people here are not paper-oriented. They might remember things that are important to them, but they rarely write anything down or consult anything that is written down for them."

"That's not good news for a writer," Smyth said.

"Oh, many of us read *Grace* magazine and get a lot out of it. For the rest—well, theirs is an oral culture."

The Smyths lined up for food with the others and sat at a table with Ira Williams and his wife, Gladys; a single mother with three young children living on welfare; an unemployed twenty-year-old man who admitted he was sleeping outside in the good weather; two young women who said they were social-work students at Abbotsford College; and two ex-convicts aged forty or fifty who now worked as laborers on a Byron Masters construction site. John learned as much as he could about the church through the informal conversation without tape-recording anything, taking notes, or asking too many pointed questions.

"Ruby, my love, why don't we go for a walk around Mill Lake, and you can show me this park you enjoy so much?"

They were in the car, driving back from Shadow Valley Church.

"I think that would be wonderful," said Ruby. "You'll love it."

They joined hundreds of Abbotsford residents strolling the paved path around Mill Lake. John saw the bald eagles' nest, the blue heron hunting at the edge of some bulrushes, a contingent of cormorants and turtles sunning themselves on logs, and dozens of geese and ducks swimming on the lake and grazing on the grass.

Once they were stopped by two older couples who recognized John Smyth from his editor's photo in *Grace* magazine. As they were walking away, one muttered, "He always looked taller in his picture."

But even though they took their time, walking hand in hand and enjoying their time together, they completed the circuit in less than an hour instead of the two or three hours Ruby usually took.

"Hi, Mom! Camp was great! We went swimming and rode on the banana boats and . . ."

Ruby smiled. It was five minutes before nine-year-old Elizabeth slowed down enough for Ruby to get a word in. "That's great, honey. I told you you would enjoy camp."

"Mom, when are you coming home?"

"We'll be home in a week."

"A week? That's a long time."

"Elizabeth, we told you we would be gone three weeks."

"I know, but I miss you."

After Ruby had enjoyed equally enthusiastic conversations with eleven-year-old Matthew and six-year-old Anne, another voice came on the line.

"Hello."

"Hi, Mike. How are you doing?"

"Okay."

"How's summer vacation going?"

"Boring."

"Well, you're the one who decided you didn't want to go to camp this year. Are you being helpful to your grandparents?"

"I guess. Sometimes."

"Mike, you know we are counting on you to set a good example for your brother and sisters."

"I know. I have to be good or Dad will lose his job."

"You know that's not it, Michael."

"Why doesn't he want to talk to me?"

"He does, but last time he phoned, you didn't want to talk to him."

"Whatever."

After this up-and-down phone call, John and Ruby took a nap, ate a light supper, did some reading. They did not see John Robinson until the next day.

Chapter 13

MONDAY, JULY 19

On Monday morning, John and Ruby Smyth headed east for some sightseeing, planning to visit Minter Gardens, Bridal Falls, and Harrison Hot Springs. McNoll and Sandhu, however, were not on holiday. They had taken Sunday off but were hard at work early Monday morning.

Over coffee that morning, Mangucci briefed them on what the scene-of-crime officers had found so far. The DNA tests on the blood were not complete yet. None of the utensils found in John Robinson's house matched the wounds in Sylvan Halvis's body, but some of the fingerprints on the two books found on her floor belonged to John Robinson.

"That's scarcely news," McNoll said. "Or at least it only confirms what we already know."

"We're still working on matching fingerprints, but so far none in the Halvis house belong to Robinson, and none in the Robinson house belong to Mrs. Halvis."

"The Halvises can afford good help too, and Robinson is not a stupid man," McNoll observed. "Anything else?"

"We have matched the prints on the broken window at the drug house to a Dean Carpenter, a young offender suspected in a number of drug, theft, and break-and-enter cases. He has had only one conviction, on a petty theft charge, and was given a suspended sentence, although some other files are still active. He has no fixed address, so it may take awhile to track him down. If he's still in town, that is."

"Doesn't sound relevant to our case," McNoll said. "Tell Stantzky."

"I have."

At nine thirty, Thomas Halvis was shown in to see McNoll.

"Good morning, Mr. Halvis," McNoll said, rising.

Halvis ignored the greeting. His square jaw was quivering slightly. He blurted out, "Have you found out who murdered her yet?"

"We are making good progress, Mr. Halvis. We have a lot of evidence already, and we are checking very carefully to make sure we don't miss anything and don't make any mistakes so that we can get a conviction." Halvis was a lawyer, and McNoll was taking advantage of the opportunity to convince a lawyer of the police force's thoroughness and professionalism. "You said that you wondered if your wife might be having an affair with a man named John. Have you thought any more about who John might be?"

Halvis thought a moment. "I don't know. I suppose it must be someone close by, someone she met at the country club, in the neighborhood, or in her college courses. Actually, the college makes sense. Sylvan was a very intelligent woman, and I think she would only be attracted to someone who was also intelligent."

"Could it be, I don't know, somebody like your next-door neighbor John Robinson, for instance? He's a professor at Abbotsford College."

"Robinson? I've never actually talked to him. But now that you mention it, I think Sylvan may have mentioned his last name was Robinson. Could she have taken courses from him at the college?"

"We will certainly check out that possibility, Mr. Halvis. But you think she might be attracted to somebody like that?"

"Yes. A professor would certainly be the kind of person that would attract her. Do you suspect—"

"Thank you, Mr. Halvis. I am sorry this is taking so long, but the investigation is really proceeding quite rapidly in comparison to many other cases. I will let you know when we find out anything definite. I think we should be able to release your wife's body by the end of the week."

"Thank you," Halvis said through a catch in his throat.

"This may be his second!" It was ten thirty, and Sandhu had rushed excitedly to McNoll's desk.

"Whose second?"

"Robinson. I think he may have committed another murder before this one."

"Who?"

"His wife."

"Sit down and tell me what you're talking about."

"I was going through the financial papers we took from Robinson's house. A year and a half ago, he collected a half-million-dollar life insurance policy on his wife."

"A dead wife makes a rich husband. How did she die?"

"Her car went off Mountaintop Drive and over the edge of the mountain. It slid a couple of hundred feet down the slope, bouncing off trees. She wasn't wearing a seat belt and was pronounced dead at the scene."

"I think I remember that accident, but I didn't remember the name. Was there any suspicion of foul play?"

"I don't know. Ron Tracy was the investigating officer. I've asked him to come in and talk to us."

McNoll nodded but did not comment, which was about as close as he was ever likely to come to paying his junior partner a compliment.

"Thanks for the fingerprint," Stantzky said. "It won't do us much good, but thanks anyway."

"Why won't it do you much good?" McNoll asked.

"It belongs to a teenaged punk, a small-time addict. He was probably trying to rip off the grow-op but was deterred by the dogs. Mangucci has identified a substance on the bars inside the window as dog saliva."

Sandhu had been sitting on the edge of a desk in the background, again watching the interaction between the two senior detectives. "May I ask what the teenaged punk looks like?"

"Sure. Dean Carpenter is about five-six—a skinny blond kid, must be seventeen or eighteen."

"Can you tell how recent the fingerprints on the window are?"

"Not very exactly Mangucci said. They were probably put there in the last month, since the last heavy rainfall. The window is exposed, so a heavy rain would have obliterated or at least smudged the prints. Why do you ask?"

"One of the neighbors said they saw a skinny blond teenager running down the street on the night of the murder."

"If he was trying to break into the grow-op house," McNoll said, "it's doubtful he would have broken into the Halvis house too."

"But he might have seen whoever did," Sandhu insisted.

"We'll have to ask him," Stantzky offered. "If we ever find him."

There was silence for a moment. "Did you catch the guys who set up the grow-op yet?" McNoll asked.

"No. The place is owned by FOI Properties, a management company, which is in turn owned by FOI Investments, a holding company, which is owned by—"

"Skip the chain. Have you got to the top?"

"We think it is ultimately owned by a guy named Charles Baker, who keeps cropping up in a lot of our investigations. Far as evidence goes, he's a completely legitimate businessman. In other words, we've got our suspicions, but we've never been able to make anything stick. Anyway, it's pretty clear that Charles Baker will have no knowledge of these specific tenants and maybe won't even remember that he owns this particular house. FOI Properties says the tenants are James and Louise Hui, who paid their rent in cash and whose only address is the house on Mountaintop Drive. The staff at FOI Properties say they think they checked past references for the Huis, but they didn't keep a copy. They say it's hard to find tenants, so they have to take whoever they can get. Apparently the Huis paid cash and were never late with their payments."

"And since they paid cash, you have no idea how much they actually paid."

"More than the official rent, you mean?" He smiled. "You have a suspicious mind."

"True. Requirement for the job."

"The Huis rented the place in January of last year, so they may have harvested four or five crops before we raided them."

"So the bottom line is the Huis have a million dollars or more from selling the stuff, FOI Investments has unspecified rental profits, and you have nothing but a marijuana crop that will cost you money to dispose of?"

"That's about it. Pretty standard scenario."

"So why did you raid the house in the first place?"

"Beats me." Stantzky shrugged. "It's a job."

"I mean how did you find out about the grow-op?"

"I already told you. An anonymous phone tip. Again, that's quite typical."

"Any idea now who gave the tip?"

"It could be a rival gang or an unhappy customer or just a neighbor. It could have been the teenaged punk. But if it was, he'd be playing a pretty dangerous game. These guys play for keeps."

"Well, I don't envy you your job. Give me a good murder case any day. But thanks for keeping me informed. Doesn't sound like any of this will have anything to do with our case."

Ron Tracy was a square-shouldered, square-jawed career officer with a pockmarked face and close-cropped salt-and-pepper hair. He looked like a drill sergeant.

"Suspicious?" he said when Sandhu asked him about Deirdre Robinson. "Sure it looked suspicious, especially when we found out about the insurance policy. We did a very thorough investigation. But there was no evidence the car had been tampered with. There was freezing rain falling and ice on the roads."

"It was an accident, then."

"Looked like it on the surface, and we never could get below the surface. Robinson's fingerprints were on the car and steering wheel, but we couldn't make anything of that because both of them were known to drive the car at times. The accident occurred around midnight, and we never did figure out why she was driving down the mountain at midnight in an ice storm. And Robinson was not a very cooperative witness. Didn't actually refuse to answer questions, but he lawyered up pretty quick, and his lawyer said he was too upset to talk much about the accident. He certainly seemed upset, but that could have been guilt—or acting. In the end, we couldn't make a case for anything but an accident, so I signed off on it, and he collected the insurance. Why are you asking?"

"We think he may have done it again," Sandhu answered.

"The Halvis woman?"

"He lives next door."

Tracy whistled.

At twelve thirty, Mangucci found McNoll and Sandhu eating lunch at their desks. "We just got the preliminary DNA results on the Robinson search," he said. "The blood on the house and the shoes belongs to Mrs. Halvis. Now, if there is nothing further you need today, I have been working all weekend, and I'm going home."

"Go ahead, Tony. Thanks."

"Do we have enough evidence now?" Sandhu asked.

"Not enough to arrest him, but certainly enough to interrogate him again. And I think this time we'll have him come in here."

It was four thirty before Calvin Henderson and John Robinson appeared at Abbotsford police headquarters. Henderson explained that he had had a lunch meeting and then had to track down Robinson after he returned. McNoll suspected they had also taken time to plan their strategy for the meeting. And lawyers always seemed to think they gained some kind of tactical and psychological advantage by making the police wait as long as possible.

"Dr. Robinson—"

"Before we begin," Henderson interrupted, "I want to know if my client is being charged with anything."

"Not at the moment."

"Then why did you drag him in here? My client is a busy man, and this is nothing less than police harassment."

"Your client is not being charged at the moment, but that may change depending on what he has to tell us. I will warn you that anything your client says can and will be used against him."

Henderson waited a moment. "My client is eager to cooperate with the police, but I will not allow you to unjustly implicate him in a crime which he did not commit."

"Let's try this question. Dr. Robinson, why didn't you tell us that you bought the two books that were found on the floor beside Mrs. Halvis's body? Your fingerprints are all over them."

"I never denied I bought the books for Mrs. Halvis. She is my neighbor."

"Why did you buy her the books?"

"They are excellent books. I thought they would help her."

"Help her how?"

"I mean I thought she would enjoy reading them."

"How many other neighbors did you buy presents for?"

"That is an irrelevant question," Henderson intervened. "We have stated that my client bought the books for Mrs. Halvis. That is not a crime. You must stop trying to make something out of nothing."

"Okay. Dr. Robinson, how well did you know Mrs. Halvis?"

"We were neighbors. She took a course from me at Abbotsford College."

"Can you explain why there is a trail of Mrs. Halvis's blood from her body to your back door—and why whoever killed Mrs. Halvis was wearing your shoes?"

Robinson said nothing. Henderson said, "You know my client will not answer a question like that."

"Is that why you killed your wife—because she found out you were having an affair with Sylvan Halvis?"

Something snapped in Robinson's face. His lips compressed into a tight line, and fire sprang into his eyes. He said nothing.

"We have tried to be cooperative, Detective McNoll, but if you are going to make ridiculous accusations, I am advising my client not to answer any more questions."

"Why didn't you arrest him?" Sandhu asked. "We've easily got enough evidence to make an arrest."

"Enough for an arrest. Not enough for a conviction."

"The blood trail leads right back to Robinson's door and Robinson's shoes."

"Then who made the other shoe prints?"

"John Smyth?"

"They're such good friends he helped his friend kill his mistress?"

"Maybe. Maybe that's what woke Ruby, Smyth coming back to bed. That's not a bad case."

"Yes, it is. Won't hold up."

"So what else do you want?"

"I want the murder weapon. I want Dr. Robinson's letter opener." There was silence for a long while, and then he asked, "Is Mangucci still here?"

Robinson was still cleaning up the dishes from his late supper when John and Ruby walked into the house at nine thirty that night.

"Would you like some herbal tea before bed?" he asked.

"Sure," Smyth said.

"How was your day?"

"Wonderful. It's fun to be a tourist—and great not to be working for a change. What about your day?"

"Uneventful. I would also like to know what you thought of Bob Young's church."

"I was actually quite impressed. They seem to know what they are doing, and they seem to be doing a lot of good. It's certainly a lot different from Mountaintop Church. And Bob Young is quite different from Marv Andreason."

"He's a lot shorter, for one thing," Ruby said.

"Ah, of course," Robinson said. "And did you notice a lot of other short people at Shadow Valley?"

"I don't think I noticed," Smyth said. "Why?"

"Sociological research says that taller people tend to make more money and get better jobs than shorter people."

"That explains a lot," Ruby said, looking at her husband.

"There are differing interpretations as to why this is true," Robinson continued. "One argument is that the causality is reversed. That is, those who are richer and more competent can afford better food and medical care, and so over the generations they grow taller. The other side of the argument is that being tall is itself an advantage. Tall people look impressive; they look like leaders, and so they tend to get more than their fair share of executive jobs. It is harder for shorter people to get noticed or to be taken seriously."

"Are you saying that if Bob Young was tall and Marv Andreason was short, Bob would be making more money for pastoring Shadow Valley Church than Marv Andreason would make for pastoring Mountaintop?" Ruby asked.

"No, it's more likely that if Bob Young were taller, he might be pastoring Mountaintop, and if Marv Andreason were shorter, he might be the pastor at Shadow Valley."

"I don't think Bob Young wants to pastor Mountaintop,"

Smyth said. "I think he has a heart for the people at Shadow Valley. Bob is suited to Shadow Valley, not Mountaintop, and in more ways than height."

"That's probably true. I'm talking about general tendencies. Height is only one factor, and in itself, being tall does not guarantee success."

"What is success anyway?" John said. "In some ways, I think Bob should be paid more because his job is harder."

"Sure, but on the other hand, you can make the argument that Marv Andreason needs to be paid well so he can dress well enough to be heard by the people he is working with. And if Bob was paid more, he might have trouble relating to the people he works with. They might not accept him as their pastor if he was rich."

"Okay, but it still seems unfair."

"It probably is. But there is a downside to being tall, and that probably isn't fair either. Tall people don't live as long as short people. One study suggests that, on average, people die ten months younger for every inch they grow over six feet."

"Then John could live forever," Ruby said, laughing.

"You're one to talk," he told her. "You're only an inch taller than me."

"Speaking of Bob Young," Robinson said. "He phoned earlier today and left a message. He wants to know if you would like to go to prison with him tomorrow."

"Oh, yes, I do," Smyth said. He thought a moment. "I had forgotten he said he might call today. I suppose if Bob Young were taller, he might get Mondays off like Marv Andreason does."

"I hope you didn't mind having tea with Doctor John tonight," Smyth said when he and Ruby had gone up to their bedroom. "I had a feeling he wanted to talk to somebody."

"Then why didn't he?" Ruby asked. "Lecturing on sociological theories is not talking. And telling two short people that tall people are the natural elite is just plain rude."

Chapter 14

TUESDAY, JULY 20

Bob Young's minivan, with John Smyth sitting in the passenger seat, wound its way down the side of Sumas Mountain. Halfway down, it passed a police van and an unmarked police car going the other way.

The van and car stopped in front of Robinson's house. McNoll and Sandhu got out of the car, and Mangucci and Storch emerged from the van. They walked to the end of Thomas Halvis's driveway and stopped at the drain grate. Mangucci, using a flashlight, peered down into the gloom, then picked up a crowbar. He and Storch pried the grate off the top of the drain. Then Mangucci walked back to the van and pulled out a mechanical arm like those used by maintenance workers to pick up litter. He inserted it down into the drain and a moment later pulled up a gold-colored letter opener with an embossed leather handle. He held it up to the light and examined the brown residue encrusting the blade and handle before dropping the letter opener into a plastic evidence bag.

"Looks like there might even be a fingerprint in the blood on the handle. Is that what you wanted?" Mangucci asked.

"It is," McNoll answered. He glanced up toward Robinson's house and noticed the living-room blinds were open. Robinson stood at the window watching them. Ruby Smyth stood at his elbow.

"Are we going to arrest him?" Sandhu asked.

"Not until the letter opener has been processed."

"What made you think to look in the grate?" Mangucci asked.

"Logic," McNoll answered. "If Robinson and his friend Smyth committed the murder, why did a trail of blood lead down to the road? It wasn't so they could get into a getaway car—they were right next door—so it must have been to dispose of the weapon. Lucky for us they're amateurs. It was dark, and they probably didn't realize they were leaving a blood trail. Probably thought that if they hosed themselves down outside, there would be no evidence to connect them to the murder."

"It's also lucky it hasn't rained since the murder, or the letter opener would have been washed down the mountain by now," Mangucci said.

"Are you going to clean out the rest of the debris in the drain?" Sandhu asked.

"Oh, yeah. You never know what else we might find."

What they found appeared to be just a collection of dirt and garbage, but it was all bagged for later analysis. They were packing their tools and the evidence bags into the van when Ruby Smyth came out of the house. The four men stopped what they were doing and watched as she got into the old gray station wagon, backed down the driveway, and drove away.

Matsqui Institution is a reinforced concrete fortress surrounded by a double chain-link fence topped with razor wire.

It sits just off King Road on the southern edge of urban Abbotsford and is reached by a winding paved lane that leads across a rolling green field and down the side of a hill.

"Matsqui is what they call a medium-security prison," Young said as they reached the outer fence.

"I wouldn't have guessed that," Smyth answered grimly, staring nervously at the cement and barbed-wire walls.

Young and Smyth were searched thoroughly—another nerve-racking experience for Smyth—and passed through a series of locked doors and gates.

"Good morning, Bob, Mr. Smyth," the last guard said.

Smyth, who had seen only a uniform, looked more closely at the man wearing it. "Good morning, Ralph. It's good to see you again."

Ralph Hearne chuckled. "Always remember the guards' names," he said, "if you want them to let you out again."

Young and Smyth passed through the last door into a sealed room. A series of glassed and barred wickets ran along one wall, each with a chair in front of it. Young and Smyth pulled up an extra chair and sat in front of one of the stations. After a few minutes, a man was let into the sealed room on the other side of the wickets. After looking around, he moved forward and sat opposite Young and Smyth.

"Good morning, Gerry," Young said. "I brought a friend today—John Smyth, a writer from Winnipeg."

Gerry, a big man with a barrel chest and an even bigger stomach, nodded warily in Smyth's direction. He was about fifty, with scraggly black hair, a scarred face, and massive tattooed arms. One of his eyes stared straight ahead, not moving when the other one did.

"How are you today, Gerry?"

"The same as I am every other day in this God-forsaken place," the big man growled irritably.

"That's not true, Gerry," Young said. "If God had forsaken this place, I wouldn't be here visiting you. Have you read any of the things I left for you last week?"

Gerry shifted his bulk uncomfortably in the flimsy plastic chair. "Uh, I'm not much of a reader."

"Have you been talking to anyone else? Has anyone else come to see you?"

"You don't talk in here. No one came."

The conversation continued in this painful, halting way for forty minutes. Young continued to ask questions and talked about the weather, his family, the news, sports, books he had read, movies he had seen. Gerry responded with grunts and short, grudging answers.

"It's been good to talk with you again, Gerry," Young concluded. "Hang in there. I hope God gives you a good week. I'll see you next week."

Gerry shrugged and nodded, then sat watching as Young and Smyth were let out of the sealed room through a steel door.

Back in the car, Young and Smyth sat for a few moments, staring at the steel and concrete wall in front of them.

"What's wrong with his eye?" Smyth asked at last.

"That's a prosthetic eye. He had the eye gouged out in a bar fight. Gerry claims he won the fight. He beat the other man to death."

"Why did you ask if anyone has come to see him?"

"He has no friends that I know of. He has a wife and three grown kids who were in Calgary the last he heard of them. They refuse to have anything to do with him. He has been inside for ten years now."

"You didn't talk to him very much about God."

"No. I've only started seeing Gerry recently, and with prisoners you have to start off slowly. It's hard to know what to talk about, so I talk about a lot of things, hoping to find a topic that will interest them. I talk openly to them about my life, hoping that will encourage them to talk about their lives. Even when there seems to be no response, it's important to keep going week after week. It takes a long time to get past their walls of distrust and pain. Sometimes it is months or years before they are convinced you aren't going to give up on them like everyone else in their lives has."

"It seems like a tough ministry. I'm not sure I could do it."

"I'm not always sure I can, either. In fact, I really didn't want to take on another prisoner. But Gerry needs someone badly, and there were no volunteers willing to visit him—for obvious reasons. The two men you heard at the convention may be paroled sometime soon, so that may free up some more time for me to visit Gerry."

"Was it a problem for me to be there? Maybe he would have talked more openly if I hadn't been there."

"Maybe, but he doesn't talk much at the best of times. And I want him to get used to other people, to see that a person can have more than one friend."

"I wondered if you weren't coming no more," she said.

"I told you I wouldn't be here Saturday and Sunday," Ruby answered, taking a French fry from the bag between them, "but then we changed our plans and went away yesterday too." Ruby pushed the bag toward the other woman in offering.

"I thought you decided you didn't want to waste time talking to me again." Mary paused. "Why did you talk to me the first day?"

Ruby was silent for a moment. "I think I was supposed to talk to you." After another pause, she added, "Why did you listen and talk to me?"

"I don't know. I guess I was supposed to too." Tentatively

she reached into the bag for a French fry. "I don't talk to women much."

McNoll was sitting at his desk, drumming his fingers when Mangucci approached.

"Got something?" he asked. "I thought it would take longer."

"The DNA testing will take awhile, so we thought we'd start with the fingerprints. We got two clear prints off the letter opener."

"Good, but we will wait for the DNA testing before we arrest Robinson."

"You might have to hold off on the arrest even longer than that. The prints aren't Robinson's."

"What?! Whose are they?"

"You'd never guess."

When Bob Young dropped Smyth off at John Robinson's house, Smyth was surprised to find no one there. Ruby was probably taking her walk, but where was Robinson?

Smyth managed to turn off the burglar alarm, then climbed the stairs to their bedroom, pulled out his laptop computer, and began pounding away on his articles. He was in a hurry to get them finished. Despite his promises to Ruby, the vacation had been far more work than play.

"What do you want?" McNoll's case had hit a snag, and he wasn't happy about it.

"I'm still doing some of the routine work on the Halvis case," Sandhu ventured.

"Good for you. We'll hand out the citations next week."

Sandhu pressed on. "Remember that I was supposed to talk to all the people at the meeting Thomas Halvis had in Kelowna, and I was having trouble tracking down the last one?"

"So?" McNoll said irritably.

"I tried again today. He's the businessman from Abbotsford, and he finally came back to town. I've got an appointment to see him in an hour. But as I was looking up the phone number, I remembered I had heard the name in another context. Charles Baker—that's the name of the man Stantzky says owns the grow-op house two doors down from the Halvis house."

McNoll sat up straight.

"We wondered if the killers might have been looking for the grow-op and broke into the Halvis house by mistake," Sandhu said. "Maybe that's really what happened."

"Maybe. And maybe Halvis phoned in the tip on the grow-op in revenge for them killing his wife. Or maybe there's some other connection we haven't thought of. I'll come with you when you go to see Baker."

"Should we invite Stantzky too?"

McNoll considered. "Maybe. It might confuse Baker about why we are really there. Confused witnesses make mistakes."

FOI Holdings had its offices in a two-story red brick building on a side street just off South Fraser Way, the central east-west corridor running through Abbotsford. A young Indo-Canadian woman with long dark hair, expertly applied makeup, and fashionable clothes led them down a hall of offices and knocked on an oak door at the end. She ushered McNoll, Sandhu, and Stantzky inside and closed the door behind them.

Charles Baker was an overweight fifty-something man with a dark mustache, a bald head, and an expensive black suit. He stood behind a massive oak desk in a stark white room with three large wildlife prints on the walls. He reached over the desk to shake hands with the three detectives.

"Good day, gentlemen. What can I do for you?" He showed no sign of discomfort with their visit.

"Just some routine questions," McNoll said, consulting a small notebook. "I understand you have just returned from Kelowna. Can you tell me when you went there?"

Baker consulted his planner. "I went up on the morning of Thursday, July 8, and got back this Sunday evening, July 18."

"You went for business?"

"Yes. What is this all about?"

"As I said, just a routine inquiry. I understand you were involved in negotiations regarding some land, and Thomas Halvis was also part of those negotiations. I wonder if you could tell us when you were with Mr. Halvis?"

"Are you investigating Thomas Halvis?"

"Just answer the question."

Baker shrugged. "Let's see. We began negotiations Thursday evening, but that was a relatively short meeting. We finished around nine. I talked to Tom till about ten thirty; then we went to our rooms. Or I went to my room and I assume he did the same. We were in meetings the next day from about nine in the morning until ten or ten thirty that night, and then we started again around eight thirty on Saturday morning and kept going till about two or two thirty."

"Thank you, Mr. Baker," McNoll said, closing his notebook. "We just needed to confirm Mr. Halvis's whereabouts as part of our investigation into the murder of his wife, Sylvan. Did you know about that?"

"I heard about it, yes. It was on the news. It's a terrible thing."

"Do you know who might have wanted to kill Mrs. Halvis?"

"Me? No. I don't think I've ever met her. I have used Mr. Halvis as legal counsel on several of my real-estate deals, but I don't see him socially."

"Then why did you buy a house two doors from his house?"

"Did I? I'm not sure I even know where Mr. Halvis lives."

"You do own the house at 36029 Mountaintop Drive?"

Baker rubbed the back of his neck. "I may. Look, I own about thirty houses in Abbotsford, as investments and revenue homes that I rent out. I have a management company that oversees that work. I think the list includes one on Mountaintop Drive, but I don't remember the details offhand."

"You should remember this one." Stantzky spoke for the first time. "We raided a marijuana grow-operation in it a couple of days ago."

Baker looked as if a light had gone on inside his head. "Oh, that's what this is about," he said. "Look, if one of the tenants in a house I own grows marijuana, you will have to take that up with the tenant. I don't grow marijuana, and I take a dim view of anyone using one of my houses to do so. I hope you have arrested the tenant."

"The tenant seems to have disappeared," Stantzky said.

"I presume you have talked to my holding company about who the tenants were?" When the detectives did not reply, Baker continued. "Look, I'm the victim here, not the criminal. The laws you enforce won't allow me access to the houses I rent out. A tenant has apparently used my property for illegal activity, probably ruining my house in the process and costing me thousands of dollars. Find the tenant, and I will be glad to help you prosecute him. But you can't blame me for something my tenant did."

"You had no knowledge of the grow-op?"

"Of course not. I barely remembered I even owned the house. Now, if you gentlemen don't have anything more useful to discuss, I have a lot of work to do."

On their way out, the three detectives passed a paunchy

middle-aged man with a scraggly goatee, the lone occupant in Baker's waiting room.

"That went real well," McNoll observed when they were out in the hall.

"The man's smooth," Stantzky agreed. "That's why we haven't been able to get anything on him."

"I don't suppose, since the man owns thirty houses, he might be telling the truth?" Sandhu said. "Maybe it's just a co-incidence that some of his tenants grow marijuana."

"Not a chance," Stantzky shot back. "A man like Baker squeezes every last dime he can out of his rental properties. There is no way he would be careless enough to let some minor hood make hundreds of thousands of dollars without him getting his hooks into most of it."

Dinner that evening consisted of salads and cold meats served from a table in the kitchen and eaten out on the second-floor deck.

"I have a faculty barbecue to attend tomorrow evening," Robinson said, "so this may be our last real chance to talk. What do you think of the Bible Belt now that you have been here awhile?"

"Bible Belt?" Smyth answered. "A murder was committed in the house on one side of you, and illegal drugs were being grown in the house on the other side of you. Since I've been here I've visited a prison and met convicts, prostitutes, and alcoholics. Are you sure this is the Bible Belt?"

"Absolutely. But it's not heaven, and even in paradise there was a snake. That's true here. It's almost as if there are two Abbotsfords. We've got one of the highest rates of church attendance in Canada and one of the highest rates of charitable giving, but also one of the highest murder rates. Christians, because of their numbers, have been able to exercise considerable influence over public policy—restricting casinos and bars, for instance. But that power has generated considerable resentment among the population that *wants* bars and casinos. The existence of any power naturally breeds resentment among those who do not share in that power. So the local newspapers here are full of bitter, nasty debates between devout Christians and non-Christians about issues such as abortion and homosexuality. And every time a church wants zoning permission to build a new building, angry neighbors show up at the public hearings and complain about the increased traffic and noise. They raise every conceivable objection except perhaps the underlying reason—that they don't want to listen to the church's message. Christianity preaches forgiveness, but forgiveness implies morality, that people do wrong things and need to be forgiven, and people don't want to hear that. The Bible Belt is a very divided society. The battle between good and evil occurs in all societies, the best as well as the worst."

"Yes," Smyth said thoughtfully, "and the battle between good and evil occurs in all people too, in the best as well as the worst of us."

Robinson did not answer.

Chapter 15

WEDNESDAY, JULY 21

Bob Young's old red minivan was bouncing down Highway 11 toward the little community of Mission.

"Can I ask you about something, Bob?" John Smyth asked.

"Sure."

"Last week, Ruby and I went down to a bank in Abbotsford to get some cash. Ruby went in while I waited for her in the car. A prostitute came over and tried to get into the car. She said that she thought I was waiting for her."

"She probably saw Ruby go into the bank and knew you weren't waiting for her. She probably just thought that if she annoyed you enough you would give her money to go away."

"Oh."

"How much did you give her?"

"Five bucks."

"That's probably below her usual fee, but maybe not by much. How do you know she was a prostitute?"

"She told me. She also said she needed food, so I

suggested she go to Shadow Valley Church. But she said you wouldn't give her any food because she is a known prostitute. She was medium height and skinny, was missing some teeth, and was probably in her thirties, although she looked twenty years older than that."

"That could be any one of several women we deal with. They come for food, not for Jesus. But if it weren't for Jesus, we wouldn't be operating a food bank or soup kitchen in the first place. We try to treat each individual according to her particular needs or circumstances, and occasionally we do refuse food as a way to get them to think about their life. But we don't do it often, so the woman may have been lying to you. Giving these people food gives us a connection, a reason for them to listen to us, but it only treats the symptoms and doesn't cure the disease. We try to treat both symptoms and the disease, offer them salvation as well as food."

"I think you showed her more love in refusing food than I did in giving money. Afterward, I kept thinking I should have done more for her, but I didn't know what. I certainly didn't want to let her into the car."

"No, it's good you didn't do that. With all the stories about sexual misconduct by church leaders, it could have destroyed your ministry."

"Afterward, I wondered if I should have said something to her—told her to repent or told her that Jesus loves her or something."

"Maybe. I've done that sometimes. But it probably wouldn't have done much good in your situation. Because you're a man, she would see you only as a customer, someone who would use her, and someone she could use to get money. If you had mentioned God, she would probably have thought you meant you wanted kinky sex with crucifixes or something."

"Then what was I supposed to do?"

"Well, you could have referred her to Shadow Valley."

"I did that."

"You could have waited till Ruby came out of the bank and then walked with the woman to the nearest grocery store or fast-food restaurant. If you were lucky, she might even have thanked you. And then, if you did that often enough, one day she might trust you enough to actually talk to you."

"I had an appoint—" Smyth stopped.

Young continued, "People like the woman at the bank need far more love than five dollars' worth and far more time than five minutes' worth. Don't feel bad about it. Giving her five dollars was not an unreasonable thing to do in the circumstances. It might even do some good. If she really did use it for food, it would keep her alive one more day, and as long as she is alive, she has a chance to get some real help."

Smyth nodded. "I think the thing that bothers me the most is that I usually think I identify more with poor people than with upper-class people, but when I saw that woman, she repulsed me. Compared to her, I'm a rich man, and I just sent her away."

Ferndale Institution looks like a country village, a collection of buildings on a spacious lawn behind a cedar hedge. It is located in the hills above Mission, a town on the north shore of the Fraser River directly opposite Abbotsford.

"You will notice some differences between this and Matsqui Institution," Bob Young said as he turned the minivan through a gap in the hedge. "Matsqui Institution is a medium-security prison. This is a minimum-security one."

"It doesn't look like a prison at all. You mean the prisoners live in those buildings? They could walk away at any time."

"Yes. Maximum- and medium-security prisons are designed to punish prisoners and keep them from getting out. Prisoners come to minimum-security prisons like Ferndale near the end of their sentences. They are designed to prepare prisoners to leave prison. The prisoners could walk away at any time, but if they do, they get sent back to one of the tougher facilities. Ferndale forces them to make the decision every day to stay within the boundaries by their own free will. It has been criticized as being too lenient—there is a golf course here, not so much for the prisoners to play on as for them to learn the trade of groundskeeping—but the success rate for prisoners leaving here is better than for prisoners going directly from a place like Matsqui to the street."

Mary sat on the bench staring across the placid water of Mill Lake. A bag of fast food was sitting untouched beside her. "I've reached the end," she said. "I've done horrible things just trying to survive, and now I don't care anymore. There is nothing left. I give up."

Ruby sat quietly, watching an eagle soar over the lake. "The end is not such a bad place to be," she said.

If not for the total absence of personal touches such as photographs, the lounge could have been a living room. John Smyth and Bob Young sat in two of the upholstered chairs. David Michael Black and Kurt Hallbach occupied the couch across from them. Both wore jeans and tee-shirts.

"Thank you for agreeing to talk to me," Smyth was saying. "I would like to put your stories in *Grace* magazine."

The two seemed less confident and animated than they had a few days earlier, when they spoke to the large crowd at the convention. "The people you should write the story about are Bob and his church," Black said.

"Oh, I am writing a story about the church, but I would like something about you as well, to go along with that story."

Over the next fifteen minutes, the two prisoners told their stories again, while Smyth checked details. "What does it mean to have people like Bob's family let you sleep in their home?" he asked.

At first the two didn't answer. Hallbach looked over at Black, who looked down at his shoes. "It's hard to explain," Black finally said. "It gives you an extra reason not to want to mess up."

"Excuse me for interrupting," Young said. "I want to know how your parole hearings went."

The two men hung their heads. "We didn't have them," Black answered. "Our lawyer said he had to go away for the weekend and wouldn't meet with us to prepare, and then he didn't show up for the hearing, so it was canceled. If the lawyer don't make a special appeal to get it rescheduled, we might have to wait a whole year for another hearing."

"Some of those guys don't give a—don't care about guys like us," Hallbach added. "The lawyer gets rich, and we rot in prison another year. It ain't fair. Mike and me can't seem to catch a break."

"I'm sorry to hear that, guys," Young said. "If you like, I could talk to the warden or maybe your lawyer and see if anything can be done. Don't give up. Jesus never promised life would be easy once you accept him. Your faith is being tested, and you have to hang in. Keep holding onto Jesus. Why don't John and I pray for you right now?"

They had bowed their heads and were about to pray when the door opened and seven men walked into the room. Startled, John Smyth recognized detectives McNoll and Sandhu. There were also two uniformed police officers, two uniformed prison guards, and another man in a suit. For an instant, Smyth wondered whether they had come to arrest him.

"David Michael Black? Kurt Hallbach?" McNoll said. "You are under arrest. You have the right to remain silent . . ."

The two men sat on the couch in shocked silence, looking like small animals caught in the headlights of an oncoming truck. The two uniformed officers, burly men, walked over to the couch, pulled Hallbach to his feet, and cuffed his wrists behind his back. Then they pulled Black up and handcuffed him.

"Officer," Bob Young said, rising to his feet and addressing McNoll. "What are these men being charged with?"

McNoll turned to Young. "Who are you?"

"Bob Young, pastor of Shadow Valley Grace Evangelical Church."

McNoll nodded. "They are being arrested on suspicion for now. They will eventually be charged with the murder of Sylvan Halvis. We found Mr. Black's fingerprints on the murder weapon, which we pulled from the drain in front of the Halvis house."

"Hey," Hallbach protested, "we didn't do no murder. You can't pin that on us."

Black, who had been standing with head bowed, then raised it and said, "I'm sorry, Bob."

Young laid a hand on his shoulder. "I'll get in touch with your lawyer if you like. Who's your lawyer?"

The two prisoners stared mutely straight ahead. "Thomas Halvis," Black said at last in a small voice.

Bob Young's minivan was bouncing back down the highway toward Abbotsford. The two men were silent, deep in thought.

"Are you disappointed?" Smyth asked.

"Very. Am I surprised? No. At least, no more than usual. For men like Kurt and David, the temptation to commit crime is very strong, and you can never assume they can never fall again. Crime can be as addictive as drugs or alcohol. In prison work, you have to be prepared to encounter setbacks. But there are a lot of victories as well, so we also keep hoping."

"They said they didn't kill Sylvan Halvis. Do you believe them?"

"I don't know what to believe, to tell the truth. But I'm pretty sure they did something."

John and Ruby Smyth ate lunch in silence, both of them brooding over the defeats and victories of the day and trying to put their trip into perspective.

"I'm glad we came," Ruby said. "It has been a good holiday for me."

"I'm not sure I am," John said. "On the whole, I think it has been more tiring than relaxing."

She cocked her head and shot him a mischievous grin. "I told you we should have gone east."

"I'll get it."

Benny Young ran to answer the knock at the family's door. Peering through the peephole as he had been taught, he saw several unfamiliar men on the doorstep carrying large cases. "Dad!" he called.

Bob Young appeared at the top of the stairs and hurried down to answer the door. "Oh, Detective McNoll," he said, opening the door and holding out his hand. "What can I do for you?"

McNoll shook the hand awkwardly. "We understand that David Michael Black and Kurt Hallbach were staying in your house the weekend that Mrs. Halvis was murdered. I have a warrant to search your house."

"There was no need for that," Young said. "I would have given permission. We're working to help reform prisoners, not to help them escape justice. Our work is based on facing the truth, no matter how unwelcome it is. David and Kurt were indeed sleeping downstairs in the basement."

"I am afraid we are going to have to search the whole house."

"Oh, of course. Do you mind if we finish eating supper first?"

"No, you can do that, but it might be a good idea for you and your family to stay somewhere else overnight if that's possible."

"I think we can manage that. We'll have to make some phone calls. Anything else?"

"I'm afraid we'll also have to search what you take with you, just in case Black and Hallbach might have hidden something among your possessions."

"We understand."

Young showed the officers the room where the two convicts had slept and the drawers where he allowed them to store some of their possessions between visits. The scene-of-crime officers began their search in the basement rooms. McNoll and Sandhu stood in the living room, staring through the front window at the dead brown lawn and waiting for the Youngs to finish their now-silent meal.

Unexpectedly, Sandhu snapped his fingers. "Old red minivan," he said, looking at the Youngs' ancient vehicle in the driveway. "Remember how we were wondering how Black and Hallbach got from here all the way up to the Halvis house and were assuming they stole a car?"

"Two cars were reported stolen in this area that night."

"But remember, when we did the house-to-house searches, one of the neighbors reported seeing an old red minivan."

"Right." McNoll rubbed his chin. "Okay, you drive the

family where they're going using our car, and I'll have to see about extending the search warrant to the car."

"The warrant covers the house and property, right? Wouldn't that include a vehicle parked in the driveway?"

"Maybe, depending on how a judge decides to interpret it."

"Then why don't you just ask him?"

McNoll and Sandhu had been standing in front of the picture window, talking in lowered voices. McNoll turned to see that Bob Young had come into the room.

"We've finished eating," Young said. "We're just putting away the dishes."

"Thank you," McNoll answered. "Officer Scranton will accompany your wife and daughters to collect the things they'll need for the night. Detective Sandhu and I will accompany you and your sons to collect what they need."

Young nodded.

"Mr. Young," McNoll continued, "the red minivan in the driveway—I assume that's yours?"

"Yes."

"Is it your only vehicle?"

"Yes, at the moment. We are hoping to get a second car in the next little while."

"Where do you keep the keys?"

"When we're home, on a wooden key rack just inside the front door. Barry made it at school."

"Is it possible that Black and Hallbach could have picked up the keys and driven off in your vehicle in the middle of the night without your being aware of it?"

"I guess so. We all sleep in bedrooms up here when they are in the basement."

"Did any of you hear or see anything the night Mrs. Halvis was murdered?"

"I didn't. You can ask the others."

"We will do that before they leave. Mr. Young, would you be willing to give us written permission to search the minivan?"

"Yes. But if you do that, how will I be able to drive my family to where we're staying tonight?"

"Detective Sandhu will drive you," McNoll said. "In the unmarked police car. No sense in terrifying your friends."

"Thank you." Then Young added, "But we probably won't all fit."

"We'll make two trips."

"Okay. If you could take Brenda and the kids now, I'll go later."

"Mr. Young, you seem to be concerned for the welfare of your family."

"Yes."

"Then I've got to ask—why do you endanger them by inviting convicts to live in your basement?"

"The truth is, Detective, we live in a dangerous world. My children and I are as likely to be killed by someone breaking in from outside as by someone sleeping in the basement. We believe all people are sinful, which means we are in danger from people who have never broken the law as well as from people who have already been caught. I suppose in one sense my family is in a little more danger because of the work we do, but that is a risk we have all agreed to take. And society as a whole is safer because people like us try to do something to change the criminals in our midst and keep them from committing further crimes."

McNoll looked skeptical. "It doesn't seem to have worked in this case."

It was after midnight, but the street lamps threw anemic pools of light down the street. McNoll and Sandhu stood in the shadows outside the Youngs' house, next to the driveway. Bob Young was with them.

"Mr. Young," McNoll said, "thank you for staying around to answer our questions. You've been very helpful, but I think it's time we took you to where you're staying tonight."

"You're not finished with the house yet?"

"We have finished examining the minivan, but the scene-of-crime officers will likely be working on the house all night. That's why we ask you to leave. Our people do a very thorough job, checking for hiding places and fingerprints and traces of fibers and chemicals. You might be surprised to find out where Black and Hallbach have been in your house."

"Have you found anything?"

"Well, it's early yet." Seeing a hopeful look on Young's face, he hurried to add, "But I think we've found enough to remove all doubt. There's blood in the minivan, for instance. I'm surprised you hadn't noticed."

Young shrugged. "It's twelve years old, and I have four kids, not to mention the wide assortment of other interesting individuals we've given rides to. There are stains all over it. I'm afraid a few more wouldn't be noticed."

"I—"

McNoll broke off. In the still night air, they could hear the sound of running feet pounding down the sidewalk. The policemen stiffened to attention. The pounding grew louder and then deadened as a thin gray figure burst around the corner of the hedge and cut across the Youngs' brown lawn, heading for the front door. Then all other sounds were drowned out by the roar of an engine as a black Oldsmobile popped into view past the hedge, a figure leaning from the passenger side window. The running figure paused in midstride, arched his back, raised his arms in a victory stance, and fell face-first onto the front steps, the echoes of several staccato explosions still reverberating in the stillness.

Instinctively, McNoll and Sandhu slipped their guns from their holsters and then returned fire, running down the driveway toward the street. A black object fell from the passenger window and bounced on the sidewalk. The car veered briefly toward the two detectives, who were still shooting, then veered back. It continued down the road another few car lengths, shedding glass fragments and paint chips, then swerved violently across the road and crashed head-on into a utility pole.

McNoll and Sandhu converged quickly but cautiously on the vehicle, guns at the ready. But all was still, the broken pole slanting awkwardly across the windshield and roof. After a cursory check of the occupants, McNoll left Sandhu to stand watch and returned to the unmarked police car to call for backup and ambulances.

He glanced toward the house. Young sat on the steps cradling the thin gray figure, his shoulders heaving. McNoll walked briskly over and checked a limp wrist for a pulse. The eyes were sightless. Tears washed down Young's face, and he was sobbing. "Poor kid never had a chance," he said. "What a terrible, terrible waste."

McNoll walked back to the smashed car.

"These two are both dead, aren't they?" Sandhu asked in a hushed voice. "How's the other one?"

McNoll shook his head. "Thin blond boy in his teens. He's dead too."

Sandhu nodded. "The shooter," he said, indicating the man slumped in the passenger seat. "It took me a minute to place him. I think he was sitting in the waiting room when we were leaving Baker's office. I remember that pitiful goatee."

McNoll nodded and turned back toward the unmarked

police car. "I'm going to call Stantzky. He'll probably want to be in on this."

"Funny thing," Sandhu called after him in a shaky voice. "We spend weeks or months trying to solve some murder cases. We solved this one in ten seconds." His hands began to shake.

McNoll turned back toward him, took the gun from his hands, and put a hand on his shoulder. "First time?" he asked.

Sandhu nodded.

Sirens came blaring down the street.

McNoll, Sandhu, and Stantzky sat on the curb in front of the Youngs' house, looking bleakly out at the street. A Royal Canadian Mounted Police team, called in routinely as neutral investigators because Abbotsford police had been involved in a shooting, were busy measuring tire tracks and collecting shell casings. They had taken McNoll's and Sandhu's guns for analysis.

"That was Aaron Mueller in the passenger seat," Stantzky was saying. "He's on an FOI payroll as a maintenance worker."

"What about the driver?"

"I don't recognize him. He could be new, or maybe we just didn't know about him. I wouldn't be surprised if he's on the FOI payroll someplace too."

"So you might be able to tie Baker to this?" McNoll asked.

"Not a chance. Baker will deny everything, and he makes sure there is no evidence linking him to any of the nasty stuff. He's a perfectly respectable businessman who happens to be repeatedly victimized by the criminal element."

"What about the kid?" McNoll asked.

"It's Dean Carpenter. He probably tried to rip off the grow-op and maybe tipped us off in revenge when he didn't get anything, so they eliminated him." The three men looked toward the doorstep of the house, where Bob Young still sat in his bloodstained clothes The body had been taken away, and Young looked forlorn and alone.

"The next time somebody tells you the drug trade is a victimless crime," Stantzky said, "remember that picture."

Chapter 16

THURSDAY, JULY 22

It was nine thirty in the morning. John Smyth was typing away furiously, trying to complete his Abbotsford articles before he returned to the accumulated chaos in his Winnipeg office, when Robinson called up the stairs to say that the phone was for him. He picked up the guest-room extension.

"John Smyth."

"Marv Andreason here. I understand you called me yesterday on my sermon preparation day."

"Yes, I had forgotten you had set aside Wednesdays for sermon preparation. What's the sermon on this week?"

"I'm preaching on Philippians four and Proverbs thirty—verses about riches and poverty . . . and the temptations of each."

"Sounds interesting." But Smyth wondered how different the sermon would be if it were preached in Shadow Valley Church rather than Mountaintop.

"You wanted something?" Andreason prompted.

"Oh, yes," Smyth said. "We're leaving this afternoon. I just wanted to thank you for all your help in writing the story about Mountaintop. It was a good experience. I will send you a copy of the article next week."

"So I can make changes?"

"Well, you can suggest corrections and changes, but you know I won't give you veto power over the article. I'll only make the changes if I feel they are justified."

There was silence on the other end of the phone.

"We're committed to reporting the truth in *Grace* magazine," Smyth continued, "even if the truth doesn't always show us in a good light. In this case, I don't think you need to worry. I didn't find very much that was wrong with Mountaintop. I think you're doing a lot of great things."

"Black-forest cake?" Mary asked. "I ain't had anything like that in a long time."

"Well, I wanted to have a last meal with you, and I wanted it to be special," Ruby said. Then she laughed. "My husband is going to want to know why I take so many walks and still gain weight."

Mary tried to suppress a giggle and failed.

"I'm going to miss our talks," Ruby said. "I'm sorry I have to leave today."

"I've got a preliminary report from the RCMP," Abbotsford police chief Peter Rawlings was saying. He was a white-haired, ramrod-straight career policeman who had been appointed chief three years earlier. "The evidence so far corroborates your statements. Two men in a black car, one with a history of drug dealing, use an automatic gun to shoot down an unarmed teenager. They never left the scene. We've got the guns. The tire tracks confirm the driver tried to run you down. And Bob Young, the only civilian witness there, backs up your statements. The investigation will continue, but I don't see any reason to suspend you pending the outcome. You are in the midst of another investigation, and I don't want to delay that. However, I am assigning Detective Stantzky here to supervise you on that case, just so there can be no questions later. Keep doing your work as before, but if any questions arise, Stantzky can verify that everything was aboveboard. Okay?"

McNoll, Sandhu, and Stantzky, sitting in front of the chief's desk like schoolboys in the principal's office, nodded wearily. They had been up all night and were exhausted.

"You can go," Rawlings said. When they reached the door, he added, "You did some good work last night."

By eleven thirty, Smyth was starting to hope he might actually finish the last article before lunch. Then Robinson again called up the stairs to say he had a phone call. Reluctantly he saved his data, laid the computer on the bed, and picked up the phone.

"John, it's Bob Young."

"Oh, hi, Bob. How are you doing?"

Bob sounded shaken. "Well, it's been a tough week."

"Have you talked to David and Kurt?"

"I haven't been able to connect with Kurt. He is either refusing to see me or is being interrogated by the police. The police just tell me that he is unavailable. I did get to see David, but only for a few minutes, and he didn't say much. He just kept saying, 'I'm sorry, Bob. I let you down.'"

"Did he give any reason why they did it?"

"It's what they were telling us when we were talking to them at Ferndale. Thomas Halvis was their lawyer, but he went off to work on some other legal matter and neglected

213

Kurt's and David's parole hearings. That happens all the time. The poor don't get the same kind of legal help as the well-to-do. Kurt and David knew Mr. Halvis was going to be out of town because he told them, and they either didn't know he was married or assumed he would take his wife with him. So they decided to break into his house and steal some things and break some other things just to get even. It wasn't very bright, but convicts often act on their anger without thinking about the consequences. That's what landed them in prison in the first place."

"But Kurt claimed they didn't actually do the murder. What does David say?"

"Well, at one point, David tried to tell me Mrs. Halvis was already dead when they got there and that he tripped over her body in the dark and then just got out of there fast. I told him to stop trying to excuse it or deny it. He needs to face up to the fact that he has committed another crime. That's the only way he can be forgiven."

"You don't think there's any chance he really didn't kill her?"

"It was either him or Kurt. Had to be. And when I told him to stop lying, he didn't deny it or argue about it. He just stopped talking, hung his head, and said, 'I'm sorry, Bob' again."

He sighed. "It's not the first time he's lied to me, and it probably won't be the last. We work very hard with prisoners. We advocate for them and look for ways to rehabilitate them. But it doesn't mean we're stupid. We know we're working with liars and con artists. Most of them didn't get into prison by accident, and even the ones wrongfully convicted are often guilty of something else."

"I'm sorry this has been so hard on you. It must be very discouraging," Smyth said.

Young did not answer.

"Bob?"

"That's not the worst." The words came out strangled and thin.

"Bob? What else happened?"

"Remember Dean Carpenter, the young man we knew from Brianne's school, the boy who has been stealing and doing drugs?"

"Yes. You said you leave the light on for him."

"Well, he finally came home to us last night, ran right up to our front door just after midnight."

"That's good news."

"There were a couple of drug dealers right behind him in a car. They shot him in the back. He died on the front steps."

"Oh, Bob, I'm so sorry."

"He finally came home . . ." Bob was sobbing now. "And it was too late."

Kurt Hallbach sat in an interrogation room facing McNoll, Sandhu, and Stantzky. McNoll smiled, thinking about the satisfactions of the good-cop/bad-cop routine.

"All right, Kurt," Sandhu said gently. "Why don't you tell us what happened?" Definitely good cop.

"I want a lawyer," Hallbach said.

"Sure. You can have a lawyer," McNoll said fiercely, working his way into the bad-cop role. "Won't make any difference, though. You and Black are looking at first-degree murder. Couple of losers like you, that'll mean life. We've already found Mrs. Halvis's blood on the basement window where the two of you sneaked out of the Youngs' house and then back in again, and more of her blood in the Youngs' car, which you borrowed."

Hallbach appeared to be thinking hard. "Okay," he said, "I hate to rat out a friend, but I'm not taking the rap for Mike."

"Mike? You mean David?"

"Mike, David, whatever. David is his first name. Mike is his inside name—what he's called in prison."

"You were saying you don't want to take the rap for Mike," Sandhu prompted.

"Yeah. It was Friday night. Me and Mike are sleeping in the basement. Around two in the morning, I hear something and wake up. And I see Mike crawling out the window. Prison rules—if something's going down, you roll over and don't watch. Safer to stay out of it. Besides, I don't think anything of it. I figured maybe he was just getting antsy being in the basement and wanted to get out into the open air. Anyway, I must have fallen asleep again. An hour later I wake up, and there he is, crawling back in through the window, all covered in blood. He was really ticked off with Halvis for blowing his parole hearing, but I never figured he would go and murder the guy's wife."

McNoll set his jaw and pushed his face into Hallbach's. "Good story. Doesn't wash though."

"You can't tie this to me," Hallbach said. "Mike's the one that done her. He's the one got the blood all over him. You didn't find none on me."

"That's right, Kurt. Blood on Mike, none on you. But if Mike did it alone, perhaps you would like to explain why the blood from Mike's clothes is on the passenger seat of the Youngs' minivan, not on the driver's seat. You're taller than Bob Young too, aren't you, Kurt?"

"So? Who ain't?"

"Did you adjust the seat when you got in?" McNoll smiled.

"I ain't talking no more till I get a lawyer."

Ruby came back just after noon to find a lunch of sandwiches and salads waiting on the table. She wasn't particularly hungry, but she sat down with her husband and host and nibbled while they ate. Neither she nor Robinson felt like talking, so John Smyth told them in detail what he had learned from Bob Young. The story imposed a somber mood on their last meal together. As soon as she had finished eating, Ruby excused herself to go finish her packing, leaving the two Johns sitting at the table.

"We are very grateful to you for inviting us to stay here with you," Smyth said. "It has been a very good holiday for Ruby. You are a gracious host."

Robinson shrugged. "I was glad to have you."

"It's almost been like living in a luxury hotel."

Again Robinson shrugged and smiled.

Smyth took a deep breath. "That's not entirely a compliment," he continued. "What I'm trying to say is—this visit has felt somewhat impersonal, like staying in a hotel or a bed-and-breakfast. John, I don't know whether I would say we are friends. We've known each other a long time. And we've talked about a lot of issues, but you hardly ever talk about yourself. I know you must be going through a tough time—first with Deirdre's death and then with this awful murder investigation, but you've kept it all inside. And John, I don't care whether you talk to me, but you need to talk to someone. It's just not healthy to keep everything locked up inside you."

Robinson stared fixedly at Smyth, sighed, pursed his lips, and looked down. Smyth thought he was not going to say anything, but at last he spoke. "I am a very private person, as you no doubt know, and I don't speak about personal things very easily. I learned a long time ago that you can get hurt that way. My family is well-off, and we always had to be careful not to say anything that someone could use against us. Deirdre used to complain about it, that I never told her what I was thinking. It was—" He paused. "It was one of my great failings as a husband."

Smyth said nothing, fearing that anything he said might stem the flow of Robinson's words.

"It was also difficult to discuss matters with the investigation going on because anything I said might only make things worse. I guess, now that the killers have been arrested, I can talk about it a little more."

"What do you mean, 'make things worse'?"

Robinson looked down as if arranging his thoughts. "You didn't know Deirdre, did you?"

"I think I met her once or twice, but I didn't really know her, no."

"Deirdre came from a family with an overbearing father. She was very insecure and suffered from chronic depression. I knew that before we married, but she seemed to grow worse afterward. She talked to dozens of counselors and had even seen a psychiatrist or two, but she never seemed to be able to overcome her depression. That was one reason we never had children. I didn't think I would make a very sensitive father, and I didn't think Deirdre was stable enough to handle the responsibility. But she was never really able to work, either, which left her with too much time on her hands—and that just made matters worse. I was busy with my work, and I think she felt irrelevant. I wasn't very good at talking with her about it. She complained that I wasn't very communicative, and she was right, but it's not that easy for a man to change who he is."

Robinson paused again and then continued. "Before I met Deirdre, while I was still studying at Assiniboine University in Winnipeg, I had been seeing another woman. Her name was Sylvan Harwood."

"Sylvan . . ."

"Yes, she later became Sylvan Halvis. I'll get to that. Sylvan visited the Christian club on campus, but she was not a committed evangelical Christian. I knew I could not marry someone who was not committed to Christ, couldn't live with someone who was going in a completely different direction on the fundamental issues of life. But she seemed genuinely interested, and so I dated her for a while. Strangely enough, I found I could talk to her more easily than I could to Deirdre, and we talked about a lot of things. I think she never became a Christian because she never believed in sin. She saw herself as a basically good person who didn't need forgiveness . . ."

He paused and looked momentarily confused, as if he had lost track of what he wanted to say. Then he shook his head very slightly. "At any rate, eventually we stopped dating, Sylvan stopped coming to the campus Christian club, and a few months later I learned she had become engaged to Thomas Halvis. I don't think I had ever met him, but he was about my age and was finishing his law degree while Sylvan was finishing her B.A. I went off to Harvard to do my doctorate, and I never heard what had happened to them. I finished my degree, I married Deirdre, and we moved to Abbotsford. We bought a little house near the college and then later had this house built. It was only after we had moved in that I discovered Sylvan and Thomas were living next door."

"That was . . ."

Robinson nodded. "Yes, an amazing coincidence, but maybe not as much as it first appears. A lot of people from the prairies were moving to B.C. then, and a lot of them were coming to Abbotsford, and this is the neighborhood of choice for those who have the means to live anywhere they want. It actually makes sense that both Thomas Halvis and I would end up here."

"Sometimes coincidences are part of God's plan."

"I've wondered about that since, but at first all I felt was shock. I decided to not do anything about it, just stay clear of the Halvises, and I never told Deirdre about Sylvan and me. She was insecure and depressive enough without that. But one day she came across one of my old photo albums and figured it out. I was writing a book that winter and had just taken on an extra course at the college, so I spent a lot of evenings working in my office. And it pains me to admit it, but I neglected my wife. I didn't know how to help her, so I ended up giving no help at all . . ."

His voice trailed off again as Robinson lowered his face against one hand. Smyth waited, hardly daring to move. Then Robinson resumed without raising his head. "One night the pressure just built up inside her, and she stormed into my office. She accused me of deliberately moving here to be near Sylvan. I didn't know what to say. I think I felt guilty because I realized I might still have feelings for Sylvan. Deirdre grabbed a coat and ran out of the house, and I didn't stop her. I had been in my office, and I hadn't realized there was freezing rain coming down. I still don't know whether the car skidded on the ice or she deliberately drove off the side of the mountain. I'm not even sure it matters. Either way, I still feel responsible."

"But it wasn't your fault," John said. Robinson didn't answer, just sat quietly for a long moment.

"There was a police inquiry into Deirdre's death," he finally said. "They couldn't believe she would go out so late in that kind of weather, and they suspected me of . . . arranging her death . . . for the insurance money. They had no proof, of course—because I didn't do it—and the investigation was dropped. But I know they never quite believed I was innocent. So you see why I could not talk openly to the police when Sylvan was murdered and they had started to suspect me of killing her. The police already thought I was a murderer.

And anything I said would only cause them to suspect me even more. Calvin Henderson agrees. He counseled me not to lie to the police, but not to volunteer information either."

As a journalist and a Christian, John Smyth had always insisted it was better to tell the whole truth, but he recognized the reality of Robinson's dilemma.

"I had always been careful to avoid Sylvan since moving here, and I was even more careful after Deirdre died. I didn't feel like talking to anyone anyway, so I became even more of a recluse." His mouth quirked into a small, sardonic smile. "An academic in an ivory tower, if you will, observing but not participating in human life."

"But you did step out of the tower," Smyth said quietly. "You did talk to Sylvan."

Robinson nodded. "About a year ago, Sylvan enrolled in one of my courses at the college, and I could no longer avoid her. We talked as before—nothing romantic, mind you—but simple talk. And I became aware that something had changed in Sylvan. I'm not sure what it was exactly, but it seemed like . . . a fundamental change in attitude. While before she had refused to accept the idea of sin, she now seemed racked by guilt. No, that's not quite right. She now seemed convinced of the reality of evil. So I suggested some books she could read, and a month or so ago I even bought a couple of books for her. We talked in my office at the college and sometimes over the back fence when we were sure Thomas wasn't around. But I made sure I never invited her into the house, and I never went into hers."

"That was wise, I think," said John.

"I don't know if it was wise or not, but it was necessary. I think we both realized the temptation might have been too much, so, as much as possible, we tried to pretend we didn't know each other. I know she didn't tell Thomas we had known each other before. But he was my neighbor, and he seemed interested in becoming friends. He came into my house once. He had given me his business card, and I invited him into the house so I could get one of my cards from my office, and then I was glad I had never invited Sylvan in."

"But you continued to talk to her—over the fence, I mean."

Robinson nodded. "And as time went on, she seemed to grow more troubled. Just a couple of days before you got here, we had a long talk over the back fence. I told you she was worried about evil, so I talked to her about forgiveness from that best-known verse in the Bible: 'For God so loved the world that he gave his one and only Son, that whoever believes in him shall not perish but have eternal life.'"

"John three-sixteen," Smyth murmured.

"But she seemed to have trouble believing in forgiveness and raised all kinds of questions, such as, did accepting forgiveness mean you had to stop committing the sin? I got the idea she had something specific in mind, but didn't ask her what it was. I didn't want to get any more involved. Then I remembered Joyce Barker. Joyce was the one who brought Sylvan to the campus Christian club all those years ago, and I got the idea that maybe I could ask her to contact Sylvan, help her understand."

"Couldn't you just ask some of the women in your church to help her?" John asked.

Doctor John looked chagrined. "I probably could have done that. But to be honest, I've more or less isolated myself from my fellow Christians here. After Deirdre died, I just withdrew, and I haven't really gotten to know any women at church. At any rate, Joyce was the only person who came to my mind. But I had lost track of her, and the alumni association at the university in Winnipeg was reluctant to give me her address over the phone, so I decided on the spur of the moment to fly to Winnipeg and try to track her down, along with some of the other women who had known Sylvan."

"We wondered why you flew out so suddenly."

"I hoped maybe some of them could give her the help I felt was inappropriate for me to give. Besides, I had gotten the impression that maybe you and Ruby might be happier alone here, so I decided to go right away. I had wanted to drop in and see my parents sometime this summer anyway. I spent the weekend and Monday morning visiting them, and on Monday afternoon I was on my way down to the university when I turned on the radio and found out Sylvan had been murdered.

"Needless to say, I was stunned. But there was no longer any point in looking for Joyce or any of the others. And to tell you the truth, I was reluctant to be in the vicinity of another police investigation. So I spent a couple of days visiting and doing some research at the university before I flew back here."

"I see," Smyth said. He wondered what the police would have made of all that if they had known.

"So that's the story," said Robinson. "And thank you for listening. I did need to talk to someone. Besides, you have a right to know how things stand, since you are also involved."

"What do you mean?"

"You have been interrogated by the police, haven't you? And I got the impression that since they suspected me of killing Sylvan, they also suspected you of helping me kill her."

"They did?" Smyth asked, thinking of an earlier occasion when he had been a suspect in a murder case.

"I got that impression," Robinson continued. "Anyway, now you know. But please understand that I have told you all this as a friend, not an editor. I would appreciate your keeping all this to yourself—and certainly not printing any of it."

Smyth nodded a little stiffly. "Of course I won't tell anyone else, and I would never publish such a thing without your permission."

But there was another reason, he admitted to himself. John Robinson's story was a powerful one, one which Smyth might indeed be interested in publishing. He preferred to publish stories in which people wrestled with real issues. But maybe that was the problem. It *sounded* like a story, and that made him hesitate to trust it. He thought of Bob Young and his wariness about believing David Black's story. How could you know when anyone was telling the truth? Maybe that was an occupational hazard, the curse of being a journalist (or a policeman?)—the tendency to distrust anything you were told.

On the other hand, maybe it wasn't his problem at all. Maybe Ruby was right, that you could never really tell what Doctor John was thinking.

At one thirty that afternoon, John and Ruby piled their well-worn, mismatched luggage into their old gray station wagon, waved to Doctor John at the window, and backed out of the driveway. John Smyth rolled his shoulders as they drove away, trying to work out the stiffness. In spite of what he had told Ruby, he knew that working vacations weren't really vacations.

They wound their way down Sumas Mountain, turned onto the Trans-Canada Highway, and headed toward home. It was an hour down the Trans-Canada Highway to Hope, so named by the gold prospectors who first opened up British Columbia to white settlement. Then for another hour they turned northeast into the mountains, their old car chugging up the long, steep climb of the Coquihalla Highway. At Merritt, they turned east for another hour, climbing up and over another range of mountains before descending into a brown, arid landscape—their destination for the night.

The Okanagan Valley is a hot, almost desertlike region between two mountain ranges. Little rain falls, but the sandy soil is rich in nutrients, and irrigation from Okanagan Lake has turned acres and acres of it into a paradise of vineyards and apple and cherry orchards. In the middle of the valley, at a narrow point in the lake, sits Kelowna, a rapidly growing farm and industrial center that also caters to tourists and retirees, advertising itself as a playland of warm beaches and easy living.

It took the Smyths another half hour to wend their way through Kelowna's suburban streets to an average-looking house on a quiet street. Stretching, they got out of the car and approached the front door, which suddenly swung open to reveal a man of average height and weight and an above-average smile. A thatch of blond hair, going gray, topped his square face, and he looked comfortably cool in pressed slacks and a white short-sleeved shirt.

"John, Ruby," he enthused. "Welcome, welcome."

"Hello, Walter," John Smyth answered.

A neat, slightly overweight woman in a print dress and apron bustled through the doorway and welcomed the Smyths with a hug.

Walter and Arlene White were warmhearted people who had run into the Smyths at the Grace Evangelical Church convention and insisted they stay overnight at their place on the way home. Doing so meant a short drive the first day and two very long days of driving after that to reach Winnipeg by Saturday night. But the Whites were people it was hard to say no to—and very good people to relax with after a stressful three weeks in Abbotsford.

Walter had been pastor of Kelowna First Grace Evangelical

Church for fifteen years. He was known in the denomination as a mediocre preacher but a good pastor. He genuinely loved the people he served, and his people loved him as well, happy to overlook his lack of charisma and dynamism. Under his leadership, First Church had grown from two hundred to two hundred thirty-five members over the past fifteen years and had never had a serious disagreement in that time—an amazing accomplishment in John Smyth's eyes.

Dinner was served in a bright yellow dining room with white lace curtains just off the kitchen. Just before they said grace, they were joined by a sandy-haired teenager with a wide grin.

"This is Tyler, the last of our six sons." Walter beamed. "He's working up at the Ogo Inn this summer and plans to go to Grace Bible College in the fall."

"What do you do at the Inn?" Smyth asked, somehow feeling he was expected to make conversation with this remarkably unremarkable young man.

"Just about anything that needs doing," Tyler answered.

"Tyler is a valet," Arlene explained.

"I park cars, carry in luggage, give directions, and sometimes take extra towels or pillows to rooms—whatever the front desk tells me to do. I get lots of exercise and some fresh air and meet a lot of people. And I get to drive some great cars. A couple of weeks ago, I got to drive a BMW Roadster, a little silver convertible. The guy gave me a twenty-five-buck tip to take the car over to the car wash, wash it by hand, and vacuum the interior. He even insisted I wipe down the interior because he said he had cut his finger and wanted to make sure there were no stains on the seats. Like you would've seen 'em anyway on the black leather."

"It almost doesn't seem right," Walter said, "the boy getting a twenty-five-dollar tip for cleaning a car on a Saturday morning when he used to clean our car for free."

"Listen, Dad," said Tyler. "I *deserved* that twenty-five bucks. Car wasn't really too bad, but the guy was a jerk. Oh, and speaking of jerks, another time I helped clean a limousine that was owned by a movie star. You wouldn't believe that backseat—it was a mess. The guy was traveling incognito, and I never found out what his name was, but I kept a couple of napkins just in case I ever find out."

Listening, John Smyth grew thoughtful. What was it that made the difference between this enthusiastic young man and a lost soul like Dean Carpenter or his own struggling teenager Michael?

"It's the grace of God," Walter was saying. Smyth had lost the train of the conversation, but the comment seemed an appropriate response to his thoughts.

"What did you think of Abbotsford?" Walter asked as he helped himself to another slice of roast beef. "I always like visiting there myself."

"We had a good time," Ruby said. "Quite restful." She looked over at her husband. "Well, it was restful for me. John had to work."

"I'm writing articles on the two Grace churches there," John explained. "There's quite a contrast between Mountaintop and Shadow Valley and between Marv Andreason and Bob Young."

"Yes, isn't there?" Walter agreed. "I grew up with both of them in Calgary."

"Did you?"

"Yes, I knew them quite well actually. We all went to the same church. Bob's father was the richest man in the congregation."

"You said Bob's father. You mean Marv's father, don't you?"

John said, unable to resist the editor's compulsion to correct mistakes.

"No, I meant Bob. Bob's father was the richest man I knew. He owned Young Man Industries, one of the largest manufacturing conglomerates in the city. Bob himself was quite wild in his youth—drove a fast car, drank too much, and dabbled in drugs. He even got involved in street fights and that kind of thing. Finally he smashed the car up. Brenda was with him. She wasn't his wife then, just a wild girl from the poor side of town. No one was killed, but they both spent several months in the hospital. It gave them lots of time to think about life, and first Brenda and then Bob became Christians. It was Marv Andreason's father who convinced them. He was a youth leader in the church and had been trying to help them before the accident, but until the accident they hadn't been listening. Marv's father told them there must have been a reason God saved their lives. And he was apparently right, because they eventually went to Bible college and seminary, and Bob became a pastor. He spent a few years as an associate pastor at the church in Calgary before moving out to Shadow Valley."

"Why would he choose a place like Shadow Valley?"

"I've talked to Bob about that. The easy answer is the call of God. That's where he thought God was telling him to go. The more complex answer is that Bob had had money all his life and found it as much a problem as a solution. Money has never been all that important to him—especially since he became a Christian."

"What happened to his father's money?"

"Oh, he still has it. He's a wealthy man."

"Do Bob and his father get along?"

"Of course. Bob's father is very proud of him."

"What about Marv Andreason's father? Was he rich too?"

"Marv Andreason's father worked in one of the Young Man factories as a pipe fitter or something. Bob Young's father paid for a lot of Marv's education, partly in gratitude for the help Marv's father had given to Bob and partly because that's just what Bob's father did—his conglomerate offered scholarships to a lot of employees' families."

"So how did Marv end up becoming pastor of Mountaintop Church?"

"I don't know the complex answer to that. The simple answer is—"

"I know. The call of God."

Chapter 17

FRIDAY, JULY 23

Ruby woke early the next morning. The first rays of the rising sun were already streaming in through gaps in the curtains. She looked over at John. He lay on his back, his eyes wide open.

"John, what is it?"

"I've been thinking," he said. "We have to go back."

"Back?" she asked. "Back to Winnipeg or back to Abbotsford?"

"To Abbotsford."

Ruby was thoughtful for a while. "Yes," she said, "we should go back. Can we stay long enough to go to church there one last time?"

"Sure. That should be long enough. Then, if we leave Sunday afternoon after church and push it, we can probably make it back to Winnipeg by Tuesday evening."

As soon as the Whites were up, John made several phone calls to make arrangements in Winnipeg and in Abbotsford.

"Is everything okay?" Ruby asked when he was done.

"Yes. *Grace* magazine can get along without me for two more days, and Doctor John has agreed to renew his hospitality till Sunday."

"What about your parents?"

"They can stay with the kids a few more days, no problem."

"Good. That will give your dad more time to finish replacing the kitchen cabinets."

John's mouth dropped open. "How did you know about that? It was supposed to be a secret."

"I thought you said we don't have secrets, that we told each other everything?"

"This was a surprise, for your birthday."

"And a good surprise too." Seeing the look on John's face, she added, "What's wrong? Are you upset that I guessed your surprise?"

"No. It's Michael."

"Michael? What did he do now?"

"He didn't do anything. When I explained to Dad that we would be staying a few more days, I could hear him passing the word on to Mom and the kids. Then I could hear Michael saying, 'Right. Why not? His work is always more important than we are.' He sounded very angry." John sighed. "It's just so strange coming from a boy who hardly ever speaks to me. When I'm not there, he's angry about it, and when I'm there, he's angry too."

"Yes, I know," Ruby said, "but being away from the kids on this trip has helped me think more clearly about that. Remember what pastor Dave said back in Winnipeg—that the kids who are the troublemakers, the ones who sit at the back of the church youth group and act up, often grow up to be the most productive members of society—because they are the ones who have wrestled with God? They're the ones who have personally discovered the reality of right and wrong and have really searched for meaning instead of just accepting what has been handed to them. I think there's something to that."

"Yes," John said, "as long as they don't get lost in the search. Michael carries around such a heavy burden of anger, and I don't even know what he's angry about."

"Maybe that's just how teenagers are. I had a bit of temper when I was a kid."

He laughed. "You *had* a bit of temper?"

"Well, that's what you get for marrying a redhead. But don't you think all this just might be a normal part of growing up for Michael?"

"How would I know? I've never parented a teenager before. Now that we have all four kids in school, I feel pretty competent about parenting preschool kids, but I haven't a clue how to parent a teenager."

"Don't worry about it, John. Twenty years from now, you'll be an expert at parenting teenagers."

"But by then we won't have any."

"No, but you can give advice to our children about raising the grandchildren."

"What's the point? They probably won't listen anyway."

The phone on the desk rang, and the tall man reached for it.

"McNoll."

"Thomas Halvis is here to see you."

McNoll looked up, but Sandhu had already started for the reception area. He returned with Halvis, and McNoll rose to greet him.

"Good morning, Mr. Halvis," he said. "Have a seat."

The lawyer remained standing. "I want to know when you are going to release Sylvan's body."

"Very soon, Mr. Halvis. Probably in the next day or two. Please, sit down."

"Does this mean you are making progress in solving my wife's murder?"

"Yes. We expect to lay formal charges today or tomorrow."

"Against whom?"

"David Black and Kurt Hallbach. I believe they are clients of yours, inmates at Ferndale Institution. They were angry at you, felt you weren't doing enough to prepare for their parole hearings. And they were out of Ferndale on a weekend pass, so they decided to break into your place and rob it in order to get even. They knew you were away and didn't realize Sylvan would be home. She probably heard them and came down to investigate. We think they panicked and killed her."

Halvis had accepted McNoll's invitation to sit. He sank down suddenly, staring in stunned silence.

"You all right, Mr. Halvis?"

Halvis swallowed hard. "Yes. It's just such a shock. I never suspected that—I mean, when I started taking legal aid cases, I never suspected that they would come to my house and kill my wife."

Halvis stumbled to his feet. He reached out and shook McNoll's hand. "Thank you," he said, then turned and walked out the door.

The Smyths arrived back in Abbotsford shortly before noon. They grabbed a quick lunch at a fast-food restaurant; then John dropped Ruby off at the Robinson house and drove back down into old Abbotsford.

To John's eyes, Bob Young's house looked even shabbier than it had a few days earlier. He knocked on the door and waited alone on the front porch. It was Bob himself who answered.

"Hello, Bob. Can I talk to you for a few moments?"

"John! I thought you had gone back to Manitoba."

"Well, we started to, but something came up."

"The kids are still finishing lunch. Let's walk around to the back patio."

The "patio" consisted of a dozen cement slabs about two feet square with grass growing up between them. There was a sandbox in one corner of the backyard, a small garden, and a clothesline. The rest of the backyard consisted of a lawn that was even more worn and brown than the front lawn. The two men sat in white plastic lawn chairs.

"How are you holding up, Bob?" John asked.

Bob sighed. "Okay, considering. It's been a tough week. The government won't let me claim Dean's body, but I plan to hold a memorial service for him next week. I am trying to track down his family and friends, anyone who might have known him. Brianne is going to contact some of the kids from school, and of course the people of the church will come."

"What about Black and Hallbach?"

"The police haven't formally charged either of them yet, but they tell me it's certain they will as soon as they finish processing the evidence they collected from our house. They pulled a letter opener out of the drain in front of the Halvises' house, and it has David's fingerprints and Mrs. Halvis's blood on it. I'm afraid the evidence seems pretty substantial."

"Have they confessed?"

"Kurt is still refusing to see me, and David again tried to tell me that he had just tripped over the body and then carried the letter opener out and dropped it into the drain. I'm not having any of that, John. He needs to face up to what he has done. But that's not why you're here, I think. Come on. What's on your mind?"

John shifted in his seat. "When we left yesterday, we got

235

as far as Kelowna and stayed last night at Walter and Arlene White's place."

"Ah, good old Walter. I know him from way back."

"That's what he told me—that he knew you when you were growing up in Calgary."

Bob sighed. "I did a lot of things in those days I'm not proud of. I think that's why I can identify so well with people like David and Kurt and Dean."

"Walter also told me something I didn't know, that you come from a wealthy family. You never mentioned anything like that."

"It's not something I talk about a lot. It wouldn't necessarily be helpful in the work I do."

"But don't you ever wish you were wealthy now? Don't you ever envy people like John Robinson or Thomas Halvis?"

"Not really. When I see my kids and my friends, all the people I'm involved with and the wonderfully fulfilling ministry God gave me, I realize I'm far richer than both of those men put together."

"You don't ever wish you lived on Mountaintop Drive? You don't get angry with people like Thomas Halvis for the way they mistreat the poor?"

"Oh yes, I get angry with rich people who oppress the poor. But no, I have no desire to live on Mountaintop Drive, where you live in a golden cocoon and you never know your neighbors. I've lived in neighborhoods like that, and to tell the truth, I like this a lot better."

"But—"

"John, when I left home to enter the ministry, my father began transferring company shares to me. If I wanted a house on Mountaintop Drive, I could buy one outright. I have no mortgage on this house. I could buy a new car anytime I want.

But if I did those things, do you think the people in Shadow Valley would listen to me?"

Smyth let his breath out slowly. "No, I suppose not." He rose from his chair. "Thanks, Bob, for the conversation. I'm really sorry for the ways things turned out for David and Kurt and Dean."

"John," Bob called after him. "You won't print any of that information about my family's money, will you?"

Smyth paused at the corner of the house. "No, I won't print any of that. Good-bye."

"John, I thought you had left."

"I did, but I had to come back. There were some other questions I wanted to ask you, so I thought I'd take a chance on dropping in. Could you spare me just a few minutes?"

It had indeed taken some effort to convince Marv Andreason's receptionist to ask her boss if he would consider seeing John Smyth without an appointment. "I am glad to see you, John, and I can give you a little time, but I have a meeting in fifteen minutes."

"That's okay. This won't take long. I was just curious. Why did the Abbotsford lawyers group ask you to speak to them rather than Bob Young? He deals a lot more with crime and legal matters than you do."

"True, but most lawyers deal with contracts and finances rather than criminal law, things that I and my congregation work with every day. An organization as big as Mountaintop Church deals with legal issues all the time—contracts, mortgages, endowments. And it's sad to say, but lawyers aren't going to listen to someone who spends his time with lower-class criminals. They wouldn't believe Bob Young had anything to teach them. The truth is, I dress like the lawyers. I live in their neighborhood. I speak their language. So they're willing to listen to me."

"But are criminals really mostly from the lower classes? Don't rich people ever break the law?"

Andreason leaned back in his chair and smiled. "John, you know the answer to that as well as I do. Read the newspapers. It's lower-class people who rob liquor stores, shoplift, and steal cars. The people I work with would never do anything like that."

"But, what about—"

The pastor held up a hand, palm out. "Now, they might use a different interpretation of the tax laws than the government does. They might use their power and wealth to get more power and wealth, conveniently forget to abide by some government regulations, or use some creative accounting procedures. But they are certainly not criminals—oh no. They're not sinners, either, of course." He smiled again.

"You mean—"

"What I mean is that different circumstances call for different approaches. But underneath it all, the needs are the same."

Now John Smyth also smiled. "Thank you, Marv," he said. "I understand what you are saying."

McNoll, Sandhu, and Stantzky sat in the Abbotsford police station with Mangucci, going over evidence.

"So, there's a lot of blood evidence on Black's clothes, Young's car, Young's house. We also found a crowbar in the Youngs' basement that has traces of blood and Black's fingerprints, as well as Hallbach's fingerprints. The blood all matches Mrs. Halvis's DNA. Black's shoes match the smaller pair of footprints found at the scene. There was no blood on Hallbach, but you guessed right. We did find his fingerprint on the seat-adjustment lever on Young's car. His shoes, of course, didn't match the larger pair of bloody footprints we found at the scene."

"So we assume he borrowed John Robinson's shoes and rinsed off any blood with Robinson's hose?" McNoll asked.

"Hey," Mangucci said. "It's up to you to make those deductions. I just tell you what the evidence is. In my opinion, though, what we have certainly points to Black as the killer. He got blood all over him, and even rinsing with the hose wouldn't have gotten all the blood off Hallbach if he'd done it. If he was just there, maybe the hose would have washed off all trace of incidental spatter, depending on how close he was standing."

McNoll's phone rang. "McNoll." He listened a moment and asked, "What's he look like?" After another listening pause, McNoll thought a moment, then said, "Tell him to wait. I'll see him in a minute." Turning to Sandhu, he said, "John Smyth, Robinson's friend, is here to see me. Will you go and bring him in?"

A few moments later, Sandhu ushered Smyth into the crowded space where the others were sitting.

"Good afternoon, Mr. Smyth," McNoll said. "Sit down. What brings you here?"

"Well, umm . . ." Smyth started. He took a deep breath. "I've come to tell you who I think murdered Sylvan Halvis."

"We already know who murdered Sylvan Halvis," McNoll answered.

"David Black and Kurt Hallbach?"

McNoll nodded. "We'll be charging them shortly."

"I don't believe they killed Mrs. Halvis. I think David is telling the truth. They went there to rob the house, but Mrs. Halvis was already dead. David tripped over the body in the dark, got covered with blood, and ended up with the letter

239

opener in his hand. They ran out of there and dropped the letter opener in the drain."

"How do you know all of those details?"

"Bob Young told me."

"And just what is your relationship with Bob Young?"

"I'm editor of *Grace* magazine, which is published by the Grace Evangelical Churches of North America. Mountaintop Church and Shadow Valley Church are the two Grace Evangelical churches in Abbotsford. I came here to write an article about the Grace Evangelical Church convention, which was held here the weekend Mrs. Halvis was murdered, and to write articles about the two Grace Evangelical churches here. I became interested in David Black and Kurt Hallbach because they gave testimonies at the convention."

"They gave testimony? Was there a trial?" McNoll knew very little about church organizations and was getting strange pictures in his head.

"No, I mean they talked at the convention about how they became Christians through the prison visitation program of Bob Young's Shadow Valley Church."

"So they became Christians and then went out and murdered Mrs. Halvis? In that case, I hope nobody else ever becomes a Christian."

Smyth squirmed. "They were either lying about becoming Christians and were just telling the convention what they thought we wanted to hear, or they are Christians and succumbed to temptation anyway. Christians aren't perfect, and old habits die hard. In any case, Black and Hallbach may have gone to rob the Halvis house, but I don't believe they murdered Mrs. Halvis."

McNoll thought a moment. "What you're really saying is that you don't want anybody connected with your churches to be charged with murdering Mrs. Halvis."

"No. I am a journalist and a Christian—two reasons why I value truth. Christians above all people should face unwelcome truth, no matter how uncomfortable. Besides, we believe humans are basically sinful, so it's no stretch to believe that individual Christians can do wrong things."

"So, if Black and Hallbach didn't murder Mrs. Halvis, who do you think did? Not John Robinson? He belongs to your church too, doesn't he?"

"No, not John Robinson. Thomas Halvis."

McNoll rose. "Thanks for coming in, Mr. Smyth. Now stop wasting my time. Thomas Halvis has an alibi for the weekend Mrs. Halvis was killed."

"You mean because he was in Kelowna?"

"How do you know all these details?"

"You told me, and it was in the newspaper."

"Never mind. Just go away and stop wasting my time."

"Wait! I'm explaining this badly." Smyth was desperately trying to think of something that would be convincing to McNoll. "Mrs. Halvis was killed with John Robinson's letter opener, right? If Black and Hallbach committed the murder, how did they *get* the letter opener?"

McNoll stopped in midgesture. After a moment, he said, "It doesn't matter. Maybe they broke into Robinson's first. Maybe Mrs. Halvis had the letter opener. Or since they all belong to the same church, maybe Robinson invited Black and Hallbach into his house."

"No. Dr. Robinson didn't invite them into his house, and there was no break-in. He has a burglar alarm. For that matter, the Halvis house also has a burglar alarm, doesn't it? Dr. Robinson told me all the houses on that street have burglar alarms. If Black and Hallbach broke in, why didn't the alarm go off?"

Sandhu shot a glance at McNoll, but the four policemen

were silent. Finally McNoll said, "The alarm had been switched off."

"Anyway, Dr. Robinson also told me Mrs. Halvis had never been in his house, but Thomas Halvis had. In fact, he was in the office. He had asked Dr. Robinson to give him one of his business cards and he may have taken the letter opener then."

"It seems Dr. Robinson told you a lot. Why didn't he tell us this?"

"Because Dr. Robinson is a very private man, and he decided to trust me when he didn't trust you. I advised him that it is always the best idea to tell the whole truth, but he wasn't sure what you would do with the information. I think he was afraid you would just use the information to blame him."

"Why would he think that?"

"You already suspected him, and with good reason. I think Thomas Halvis tried to frame Dr. Robinson for his wife's murder. That's why he used Dr. Robinson's letter opener to murder her—David Black messed up that evidence by taking the letter opener away. And that's also why Thomas Halvis wore Dr. Robinson's shoes to commit the murder. He would have known the shoes were sitting there on the deck. Black and Hallbach did not."

"And did Thomas Halvis also write 'John 31' on the bottom of the coffee table? Mrs. Halvis wrote that, not Thomas."

"Absolutely. I think Mrs. Halvis did write that, and I think I know what it means. She wasn't trying to say Dr. Robinson murdered her. I think she was trying to give a message to Dr. Robinson, but she died before she finished writing it. You see, Dr. Robinson had been talking to Sylvan, trying to convince her to become a Christian, and one of the things he mentioned to her was a verse from the Bible, from the book of John. She wasn't trying to write 'John 31' but 'John 3:16,' which says: 'For God so loved the world that he gave his one and only Son, that whoever believes in him shall not perish but have eternal life.' It means that if we believe in Jesus, that death is not the end. I think Sylvan was trying to tell Dr. Robinson that she believed in Jesus and was forgiven."

"Forgiven for what?"

"I don't know specifically. Whatever bad things she had done."

"Fascinating, Mr. Smyth. But why would Thomas Halvis murder his wife, and why would he try to blame it on Robinson?"

"Well, Dr. Robinson had known Sylvan before she got married—had dated her, in fact. Dr. Robinson thinks he may have found out about that. Thomas Halvis might have been jealous, thought that Mrs. Halvis was having an affair with Dr. Robinson."

"And was she?"

"I don't think so. I think it was more that Sylvan was talking to Dr. Robinson about becoming a Christian. And maybe he was afraid that if she became a Christian, she might disapprove of some of the things he was doing in his legal practice or something, might try to get him to change."

There was silence. "Anything else, Mr. Smyth?"

"Oh, yes. Last night I talked with a young man in Kelowna named Tyler White. He is a valet at the Ogo Inn. He said that on the Saturday after Mrs. Halvis was murdered, a man paid him to clean blood from the black leather seats of a silver BMW Roadster convertible. The man gave him twenty-five dollars and told him that he had cut his finger."

"So?" McNoll spread his hands.

"Thomas Halvis drives a silver BMW Roadster with black leather seats."

"I've seen your car, Mr. Smyth. What do you know about BMW Roadsters?"

"Just because I can't afford one doesn't mean that I don't notice them. I'm an editor. We're good at noticing details."

There was another silence. The other three policemen had been watching and listening intently. McNoll spoke: "Thank you for coming in, Mr. Smyth. It has all been fascinating. You can go now."

"But what are you going to do with the information I've given you? Do you believe me?"

"We are going to follow the evidence." McNoll smiled. "Trust me."

Smyth smiled, got up, and walked out the door.

"Funny little man," McNoll observed.

"Do you believe him?" Sandhu asked.

"I believe the evidence," McNoll answered. "I think we should check it out."

"It's an explanation that fits all the known evidence," Mangucci said. Catching a look from McNoll, he added, "Of course, interpreting the evidence is your responsibility."

That evening, John and Ruby decided to go out for dinner, which meant that they were not there when McNoll and Sandhu arrived.

"Dr. Robinson, I wonder if you would be willing to answer a few questions?" McNoll asked at the door.

"I told you before that I will not answer any more questions without my lawyer present."

"Yes, Dr. Robinson. You can call him if you like, but I'm not really interested in you at the moment. I want to know what Sylvan Halvis told you about her husband, Thomas."

"What makes you think Mrs. Halvis told me anything about her husband?"

"John Smyth told us. Didn't he tell you he was coming to see us?"

"No."

"May we come in?" McNoll insisted.

Robinson hesitated, then ushered them into the living room. McNoll was mildly surprised the man didn't insist on calling his attorney first. But he seemed somehow different, calmer.

"I just want to check some facts, Dr. Robinson," said McNoll. "Did you give Mrs. Halvis one of your business cards?"

"I don't think so, no."

"Did you give one to Thomas Halvis?"

"Yes. Yes, I did."

"When was that?"

"A month or so ago. I was out in the backyard, and he came out and struck up a conversation."

"How often had you talked to him before?"

"Hardly ever. He had never seemed interested in getting to know me, and I—I tend to keep to myself."

"What happened that day?"

"He seemed very friendly—offered me a business card and intimated that he would like one of mine. He suggested it was good to get to know other professional people because I might be helpful to him as an expert witness in a court case sometime—one of the sections in one of my courses is on the sociology of youth gangs. So I invited him into the house and gave him a business card. He asked to see one of my books. I pulled a copy off my shelf, and he looked it over. He asked for a cold drink, so I got him one, and we talked about my work for about fifteen minutes."

"Where was Mr. Halvis while you were getting the drink?"

"He was sitting in my office looking at my book. Why are you asking about this?"

"Have you talked to Mr. Halvis since then?"

"I talked to him once or twice in passing, saying good morning on the front driveway when we were both going to work."

"When was it you misplaced your letter opener, Dr. Robinson?"

"I don't know. It was a month or so ago."

"About the same time Thomas Halvis came into your office to get your business card?"

"About that time, yes."

"Did Mrs. Halvis tell you she felt guilty about something?"

"Not exactly." Robinson's face tightened, and he pulled back a little.

"Your friend Mr. Smyth has told us that you knew Mrs. Halvis before. I'm not really concerned about that. He also suggested that she felt guilty about something, and *that* I am interested in."

"It was not like that. Sylvan came from a wealthy family. Her parents were older when she was born. Her father is a retired judge. We Christians believe that all people are sinful; all people do wrong things and need to be forgiven. But Sylvan always insisted that she came from a respectable family and was a good person and didn't need any of that. I think she thought my talk about sin was a little too dark or morbid, that people were just basically good. But when we began talking again recently after she took one of my courses at Abbotsford College, her attitude seemed to have changed completely. She seemed much more convinced of the reality of human evil."

"Did she say why?"

"No. She asked questions about the guilt of people who benefit from injustice even if they do not commit the injustice themselves—and of people who see evil being committed but don't do anything to try to stop it."

"Was she talking about something her husband did?"

"I didn't get that impression at the time, but it's possible. She phrased her questions in general terms, using examples like the Germans who knew the Nazis were killing Jews, that sort of thing. We did not talk about her husband. We had dated years ago, you see, and both of us were being very cautious not to do anything inappropriate that would threaten her marriage."

"So you didn't have an affair with her?"

Robinson paused and smiled. "No. I'm not denying the attraction was still there. We made very sure we were never anyplace where that would become likely. We never went into each other's houses, for instance."

"Did Thomas Halvis think you were having an affair?"

"I don't know. It's possible. I never knew him well enough to know what he was thinking."

McNoll and Sandhu sat in silence for a while. "Is there anything else that we should know?" McNoll asked at last.

"No. Nothing I can think of."

"Thank you, Dr. Robinson."

As they rose to leave, Robinson asked, "Do you suspect Thomas Halvis of killing Sylvan?"

McNoll turned back. "That's what we are trying to find out. Do you think he killed her?"

Robinson shook his head. "I don't know. I wouldn't like to accuse a man of such a thing."

On the way back to the station, Sandhu asked, "Do you believe him?"

McNoll shrugged. "Could be a story cooked up by Smyth and Robinson, but it doesn't feel like it."

When they got back to the station, a call was waiting for

them from Corporal Morrison in Kelowna. Sandhu switched the phone to "speaker" so they both could listen.

"I tracked down the kid, Tyler White," Morrison reported. "It appears it was Thomas Halvis's car he cleaned. No other guest had a BMW Roadster that weekend."

"What about the gas stations?" Sandhu asked.

"We're just starting to check those."

"Thanks," McNoll said. "Send us a full report on the Tyler kid and let us know what else you find out."

"Right." Morrison hung up.

"Well?" Sandhu asked.

"It's enough to get a search warrant for his car."

Chapter 18

SATURDAY, JULY 23

On Saturday morning, Ruby insisted on going for a walk around Mill Lake, alone. John, feeling tired, slept in. It would be a long hard drive back to Winnipeg.

The police did not sleep in that morning. They were at Thomas Halvis's house at dawn with a search warrant for his car. The Roadster was loaded onto a flatbed and hauled away, and a blue-and-white cruiser was stationed at the end of the Halvis driveway all morning.

At ten thirty, Sandhu received another call from Corporal Morrison in Kelowna. "What have you got?" Sandhu asked breathlessly.

"It took a lot of legwork, but we found the gas station," Morrison said. "Halvis bought gas Saturday afternoon at a station in Westbank, just across the lake from Kelowna. He usually bought gas with a credit card, but this time he paid cash. The kid pumping the gas remembers it because it was the first time he had touched a car like that, and then he slopped some gas on the car. He said, quote, I thought the man was going to kill me because the car had just been washed, end quote, but Halvis just handed him the cash and drove away."

"Thanks," Sandhu said before Morrison hung up.

"Funny thing," McNoll observed when Sandhu had told him. "On Mountaintop Drive, nobody notices whether Halvis's Roadster is there or not. All they remember is an old red mini-van. But in Kelowna, everyone remembers the BMW. It's the exceptions to the norm that stick out in people's memories."

At one thirty, Mangucci came in. "I think that Tyler White kid should give back his twenty-five-dollar tip."

"Why?" McNoll asked.

"We found traces of blood all over the front seat and the driver's floor mat. DNA tests will take some time, of course."

"Halvis will get a good lawyer, and a good lawyer will argue that Halvis got the blood on him when he checked his wife's body after he got home," McNoll observed.

"But we searched him after he found the body and before he got back into the car, and he didn't have any blood on him then," Mangucci said.

"Let that be a lesson to you, Sandhu. Careful police work pays off."

"Yes, but we have even better evidence than that," Sandhu answered.

"We do?"

"Yes, I just heard back from Corporal Morrison again. They got into Halvis's hotel room in Kelowna. It was vacant, and the hotel owner gave permission for a search. They have found minute traces of blood in the bathroom. It's enough for a DNA match."

McNoll smiled. Turning back to Mangucci, he asked, "Anything else?"

"Yes. We checked Halvis's fingerprints against the unknown

fingerprints in Robinson's house. We hadn't done it before because we had no reason to. We only had his fingerprints for elimination purposes in his own house. Anyway, we've matched Halvis to two prints in Robinson's office, one on the underlip of the desktop and one on the underside of a chair arm."

"That confirms Robinson's story and shows Halvis was lying when he said he had never talked to Robinson," Sandhu said.

McNoll nodded. "I think it's time we picked up Thomas Halvis."

"Do we have enough evidence to arrest him?" Sandhu asked.

"And convict him," McNoll answered. "I'm convinced he did it. Aren't you?"

"Yes. But what was his motive?"

"Not sure. Probably something to do with the drugs. We'll start tearing apart all of his records."

"If Halvis is as intelligent as he seems, won't he have hidden everything pretty well?"

"Sure, and if he planned to murder his wife, he would have made sure there was nothing in the house for us to find when we searched it. But nobody's perfect, and there's almost always some trace evidence. We'll search his law office too, and maybe we will get lucky. If not, we still have enough to convict him. We can always just say it was domestic."

"Domestic or drugs," Sandhu said. "That's what you said the motive would be. It turns out it could be both."

McNoll shrugged. "Benefit of experience."

One more time, the white police car parked on Mountaintop Drive. McNoll spoke briefly with the uniformed officers sitting in the car parked ahead of them. Then he and Sandhu walked up the driveway and rang the doorbell.

When Thomas Halvis answered, McNoll said simply, "Please come with us, Mr. Halvis. We are arresting you for the murder of your wife, Sylvan. You have the right—"

The tall, broad-faced man looked McNoll in the eye and cut him off. "Don't be ridiculous," he said. "I wouldn't murder my wife. I loved her. Besides, I was in Kelowna."

McNoll simply started again: "You have the right to—"

"I cannot believe your incompetence," Halvis sputtered. "You've taken all this time, and you still can't get it right. Don't you see—it was that self-righteous religious fanatic next door who killed her—can't you see that? John Robinson. It's obvious. He knew my wife years ago, and they were having an affair. He probably killed her in order to keep it secret, save his precious reputation. Stabbed her with his own letter opener and—"

Abruptly he stopped, recognizing what he had said.

McNoll allowed himself a smile. "That's right. We've never told you about that letter opener, have we? And thanks to David Black, it was no longer in the body when you came home Saturday afternoon. So with all the other evidence, we're left with the little question of how you know."

Halvis took a deep breath, tucking away his panic under his usual professional veneer. "You have not read me my rights," he informed them haughtily. "And I will not talk to you until my lawyer is present."

As Thomas Halvis was driven away from Mountaintop Drive, Robinson was standing in the living room window watching. John Smyth had come quietly down the stairs and was watching behind him.

"It's a strange thing, John," Robinson said. "I have probably looked out this window more in the past two weeks than I have in the past year."

"Maybe that's good. Maybe it means you're becoming more involved in what's going on around you."

"I'm a private man, John, and I'm an academic. Don't expect a miraculous personality change."

"I don't think you need one." Smyth smiled. "As far as I can see, you've done a pretty good job of loving your neighbor just as you are."

Robinson nodded. "Let's sit on the deck and talk awhile."

Looking out over the panoramic view of the lower Fraser Valley toward the magnificence of Mount Baker, Smyth outlined to Robinson the content of his conversations with the police.

After a time, Robinson rose and stood at the railing looking out at the Halvises' backyard. "There probably won't even be a funeral now," Robinson said. He stood there silently for a minute. Then his shoulders began to heave.

Smyth was not sure what to do. He stood and awkwardly reached up his arm, placing his hand on Robinson's shoulder blade. "I'm sorry, John," he said.

After a few moments, Robinson answered, "Someone should mourn her."

It was late Saturday night, and McNoll was still at his desk when Sandhu walked in.

"What's up?" he asked.

"I just heard back from Corporal Morrison in Kelowna again. They are sending down samples of the blood found in Halvis's hotel room."

"Good," McNoll said.

"And something else—last week, they picked up a homeless man in Kelowna named Harry Cider. He was well-known to the police there. A patrolman noticed he was wearing new clothes with brown stains on them. He thought the stains looked like blood and took him into custody. Cider claimed he found the clothes in a dumpster two blocks from the Ogo Inn. The stains did turn out to be blood, so they kept the clothes just in case something turned up. But they didn't connect this to our case at first because we had only asked them to check on Halvis's alibi. But now they've picked up Cider again and searched his belongings. Turns out he still has the garbage bag the clothes were in—and not all the fingerprints on the bag are Cider's . . ."

McNoll let a slow smile spread over his face. "I think Mr. Halvis is in deep trouble."

"Yes, he is."

"I've been going through Mrs. Halvis's personal papers again," McNoll continued. "Remember that research paper in her files that proved she took a course from Dr. Robinson?"

Sandhu nodded. "It's called 'Collateral Social Guilt in Complex Human Societies.'"

"Sounds fascinating."

"Not even close. It's full of footnotes and hundred-dollar words—which is why I never finished reading it before. Starts with whether those Germans who benefited from the extermination of the Jews by the Nazis were still guilty even if they were not personally involved. In that part, she just quotes what other people had to say about it. In the last part of the paper, though, she asks the same question about people now who benefit financially from the drug trade even if they aren't personally growing or selling the stuff themselves. Concludes that they're guilty too and even suggests that people who know about the activity have an obligation to report it to the police."

Sandhu was silent for a moment. "That's a rather dangerous position for a wife to take if her husband was doing real-estate deals for drug dealers."

"That's what I think too."

Chapter 19

SUNDAY, JULY 24

"Where do you want to go to church this morning?" Smyth asked.

Ruby smiled. "Shadow Valley, of course."

After breakfast, they loaded their mismatched suitcases into the old gray station wagon and shook hands with Doctor John.

"Thanks for everything," Smyth said.

"Thank you," Robinson answered.

Ruby reached up and gave Robinson a hug and a kiss on the cheek.

The old gray station wagon rolled down Sumas Mountain into old Abbotsford.

"Remember, we need to pick someone else up this morning," Ruby said.

"Yes, you told me that last night, but you wouldn't say who, and you didn't say where."

"Mill Lake Park."

They rolled into the parking lot, which had few cars in it that early in the morning. A woman stood near the edge of the parking lot—a scrawny woman with worn clothes, unkempt hair, and gaps between her teeth. She smiled hesitantly. Ruby got out of the car, approached the woman, and talked with her briefly, then walked with her back to the car and held the back door open for her.

"John, this is Mary," Ruby said.

John and Mary stared at each other for several seconds, recognition filling their eyes. "Hello, Mary," John said at last. "It's good to meet you."

Minutes later, the gray car rolled to a stop in the uneven parking lot as before. The three people got out of the car and walked slowly and silently toward the building, Ruby in the middle.

"Do you think they will let me in?" Mary whispered to Ruby.

Two women appeared in the doorway of the building. One wore her blonde hair in a shaggy cut, and the other, a few inches shorter, had long blonde hair with black roots. Both were thin and wore blue jeans and tank tops. As they approached the Smyths, the taller one opened her arms. "Mary," she enthused. "Welcome here!" The two women put arms around Mary and walked her into the church, leaving the Smyths standing on the doorstep outside.

"That's good," Ruby commented. "They must already know her." She slipped her arm into John's. "I'm sorry I didn't tell you about her," she said. "It was just something I felt I needed to do on my own, without any help from you or any other church leader. I met her at Mill Lake, and she looked like she desperately needed a friend. Talking to her was different from anything else I've ever done, much different from raising our kids. I think maybe I benefited more than she did.

I can't explain it, really, but in the end I had this strange feeling that if there was hope for Mary, maybe there would be hope for Michael too, that maybe I could learn something from helping her that might help us help him."

John Smyth nodded. He was silent, thinking of Bob Young's attempts to help Dean Carpenter—and his own reaction to Mary.

As the Smyths started to follow the three women inside, a fat man in blue jeans and a clean yellow tee-shirt intercepted them. "Welcome here," he said. "I'm Isaac Fellows."

"John and Ruby Smyth," John said.

"Are you new here?"

"Uh, no," John said. "We've been here before."

The fat man turned to welcome another couple into the building. John and Ruby passed on into the room, which was again filled with people milling about and talking. They found seats near the middle of the church but near the aisle so that they could see the overheads.

Music began to play, and people started drifting to their seats. The musicians were the same as before, except that a couple of the singers were new. The same redheaded drummer still looked bored and unhappy. The congregation stood and began singing the words projected onto the screen from an overhead projector, and Smyth smiled to see that one line read: "Our faith will never waiver." The congregation sang as enthusiastically and as inharmoniously as the last time. A swarthy man wandered up and down the aisles, either looking for a place to sit or trying to remember what he was there for.

After about fifteen minutes, a tall, thin, older man with wispy hair and spectacles stepped onto the stage, took a microphone from one of the singers, and said, "Good morning. I'm Ira Williams. Welcome to Shadow Valley Grace Evangelical Church. If you are walking in shadows this morning, I pray that you will experience God's grace before you leave here to-day." He went on to give several announcements about things like AA meetings, soup kitchen hours, and the need for various volunteers. Then he said a prayer and asked the ushers to collect the morning offering. "Remember that this is our exchange Sunday, so give as generously as you can." The band resumed playing and singing almost immediately, while deep buckets were passed down the rows to collect the offering.

After another fifteen minutes, the band members laid down their instruments and microphones, and Ira Williams returned to the stage. "As I mentioned before, this is a very special Sunday," he said, "our annual exchange Sunday. Pastor Bob is speaking in Mountaintop Grace Evangelical Church this morning, and we are pleased to welcome Marv Andreason, senior pastor of Mountaintop Church, to speak to us. Welcome, Marv. May God bless you and us!"

Andreason stood up from the front row and walked onto the stage. He wore a plain sports jacket and slacks, a white shirt, and a conservative blue tie. "Good morning," he said. Laying some notes on one of the music stands, he pushed it over in front of a microphone, dropping some pages in the process. He picked them up, said a short prayer, and opened his Bible. "I want to begin by reading from the Old Testament part of the Bible, the book of Proverbs, chapter thirty, verses seven through nine. Proverbs are wise teachings given by several wise men. This one is by a man named Agur: 'Two things I ask of you, O Lord; do not refuse me before I die: Keep falsehood and lies far from me; give me neither poverty nor riches, but give me only my daily bread. Otherwise, I may have too much and disown you and say, "Who is the Lord?" Or I may become poor and steal, and so dishonor the name of my God.'"

Andreason set down the Bible on a nearby speaker and

continued speaking. "In the matter of wealth, there are two great dangers or temptations. One is faced by those who are rich. When they become rich, they start to think they have everything they need and they can take care of themselves, so they don't need God, and they don't have a responsibility to help anyone else. The other temptation is faced primarily, although not entirely, by the poor. The poor are sometimes so desperate that they resort to crime, to dishonest and immoral ways to get money. Their sin is a failure to trust that God will take care of them, but it is also an unwillingness to suffer in order to obey God's moral law. Both temptations are temptations to commit sins and to not trust God. Note that both rich and poor are tempted, both rich and poor sin, and both rich and poor need the forgiveness offered to us by Jesus Christ. Moral questions are the fundamental concerns that all of us need to deal with. They are not the problem of somebody else in some other social class."

Andreason elaborated on what he had just said for another ten or fifteen minutes, using other Bible references and various stories and illustrations. "Now I want to read something that the apostle Paul wrote in the New Testament," he continued. "Philippians chapter four, verses twelve and thirteen." He flipped in his Bible for the place and read, "I know what it is to be in need, and I know what it is to have plenty. I have learned the secret of being content in any and every situation, whether well fed or hungry, whether living in plenty or in want. I can do everything through him who gives me strength."

Andreason put down the Bible again. "Paul was an unusual man," he said. "He experienced both poverty and wealth. He faced the temptations of both situations, and he overcame those temptations. When he was rich, he did not become proud and say he did not need God. And when he was poor, he kept trusting God and did not give in to the temptation to steal. It wasn't easy. He says it was something he had to learn. How did he do it? Through Jesus Christ. On your own, you cannot resist temptation, but Jesus can give you the strength you need to resist it."

After another ten minutes, Andreason finished the sermon, said a short prayer, and in closing invited anyone who wanted spiritual counseling to come to the front of the church and talk to one of the church leaders.

As before, the congregation began to mill about, talking and laughing in small groups, with many hugs given and received. "There she is," Ruby told John, pointing to a corner where Mary sat talking earnestly with the two blonde women. A few men and women began setting up the tables for lunch.

"Staying for lunch?" a voice asked.

The Smyths turned to see Marv and Nancy Andreason smiling down at them.

"Wouldn't miss it," John said.

A number of people wanted to talk to Andreason, and a couple of people surprised Smyth by wanting to talk about *Grace* magazine, so they were among the last to get their food. They sat together at a vacant table in the corner.

"Room for two more?" a familiar voice asked, and the Smyths looked up to see Bob and Brenda Young standing beside them. "We'll get our food and join you," Brenda said.

A few minutes later, when they were all seated, Bob asked Marv, "How did the sermon go here this morning?"

"Pretty well, I think," Marv answered. "The people here always give me a good hearing. How were the sermons at Mountaintop?"

"On the whole they went well, I think. As you say, the people listened well."

"Do you do this exchange very often?" John asked.

"Once a year," Bob answered. "We've been doing it for

about ten years. The last few years we have been preparing sermons on the same topic, so both congregations get the same message."

"It would be interesting to have heard that sermon in the other context," John observed.

"As I said, I think it went well," Bob said. "But afterward a tall man with white hair and a good tan came up to me and said, 'You don't have to worry about people being rich here. You can't get rich in Canada. The tax laws won't allow it.'"

Marv laughed. "That sounds like Calvin Henderson. He's an investor as well as a lawyer. And, well, let's just say Calvin is a work in progress. What did you tell him?"

"I told him that that was strange, since I live in Canada and I am a very rich man."

Everyone laughed at that.

"What is even stranger to me," said Marv, "is that no one at Shadow Valley complained that getting rich was impossible."

Bob shrugged. "The poor are sometimes less cynical than the rich."

"Yes," Marv said, "but isn't it odd that a well-to-do man like Calvin Henderson would have to make excuses for not being even better off? I have noticed that before, though. I think it's the insidious influence of the society Calvin travels in, where human worth is measured by how much money you have."

"Why did you start doing the exchange," John asked, "preaching in each other's churches?"

"Ours are the only two Grace Evangelical churches in Abbotsford, and we actually had a common beginning, so we thought it would be good to cooperate," Marv explained. "We're planning on starting a third church, by the way, geared to the Indo-Canadian community. The other reason we decided to do it was that we saw it as a teaching opportunity. People tend to get stuck in ghettos of their own social class.

We wanted to show them that Jesus is the answer for everyone, rich and poor, and that their common faith in Christ should overcome all social barriers."

"Ira Williams said something to the effect that people should give generously to the offering this morning because it was exchange Sunday," John said. "What did he mean by that?"

"Oh, that," Bob answered. "The second time we tried the exchange, Marv suggested we try switching offerings as well as preachers. So the offering collected at Mountaintop comes to Shadow Valley, and the Shadow Valley offering goes to Mountaintop. The offering at Mountaintop on exchange Sunday is usually the largest of the year, over a hundred thousand dollars. That goes a long way to helping us meet our annual budget. Of course, the people at Mountaintop also provide a lot of the stuff we need to stock our food bank and our thrift store."

"I knew our people would give generously," Marv put in. "But we decided it would be good to exchange offerings, not just have Mountaintop give money to Shadow Valley. We wanted to demonstrate that what we were doing was a two-way street, a mutual sharing of abilities and responsibilities. What surprised us is that exchange Sunday usually brings in the biggest offering of the year at Shadow Valley as well."

The room was starting to clear out as people drifted off home. Ruby turned and saw Mary still sitting with the blonde women at a table at the far end of the room. "I wonder if Mary still needs a ride," she wondered. "The woman over there is our guest," she explained to Bob. "I met her while I was walking around Mill Lake, and she needed someone to talk to. I thought she would be welcome here."

Bob looked over at the three women. "I believe I've met Mary. And yes, she'll be welcome here. Maxie and Sherri will take care of her. They have been off the street almost three years now. I believe they know Mary from when they were hooking."

"I know her too," John said. "She was the prostitute who tried to get into my car at the bank."

"I told you she needed more help than five dollars' worth of help," Bob answered. "But your gift may have kept her alive long enough to meet Ruby."

"The difference, I think," John said, "is that I saw a prostitute, and Ruby saw a woman."

"Takes a lot of practice to learn to see through Jesus' eyes," Bob said.

A half hour later, the Smyths' old gray station wagon pulled onto the Trans-Canada Highway and began the long, slow journey back to Winnipeg. At the wheel, John let out a long sigh.

"What are you thinking?" Ruby asked.

"I was thinking of how much work I have to do when we get back to Winnipeg, and our staying longer in Abbotsford is only going to make it worse."

"I know that," she said. "I'm sorry. I wish I could help."

"I was also thinking about the problems we have to face when we get home, the chief one being Michael."

"That's also true." Ruby sighed as well.

"And I was thinking . . . that it has been a good holiday. I feel good, like I have been refreshed and reenergized."

Ruby smiled. "I know what you mean. I'm glad we went."

She settled back in the seat, stretched out her legs, and clasped her hands behind her head. "But next year," she said, "I want to go to the Maritimes."

Acknowledgments

The city of Abbotsford, British Columbia, is real, and so is its description as Canada's Bible Belt. However, Mountaintop and Shadow Valley Grace Evangelical Churches do not exist, nor are they modeled on any existing churches. They are fictional creations, as is the Grace Evangelical denomination itself. There are a number of excellent Christian ministries to the poor in Abbotsford, including the Salvation Army and the M2W2 prison visitation ministry. However, none of these should be confused with the supposed ministries portrayed in this book. All characters in this book are also fictional and are not based on any real human beings.

I am grateful to Dick Poulton, a former corrections officer, for helping me to understand the atmosphere in correctional institutions.

A John Smyth Mystery

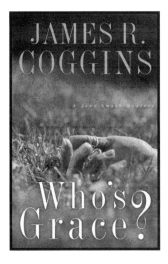

John Smyth witnesses what he believes is a murder as he is landing on a flight arriving in Winnipeg, Canada. No one takes him seriously until a woman's body is found with a pendant bearing the name "Grace."

Who's Grace
ISBN: 0-8024-1764-7
ISBN-13: 978-0-8024-1764-0

John Smyth is not anxious to get involved in another murder investigation. But when questions begin to multiply, he can't resist stepping in. What ever happened to his friend Jake? Will more bodies be uncovered? And why does that woman in the newspaper look so familiar?

Desolation Highway
ISBN: 0-8024-1766-3
ISBN-13: 978-0-8024-1766-4

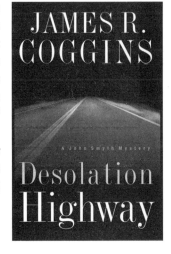

SINCE 1894, Moody Publishers has been dedicated to equip and motivate people to advance the cause of Christ by publishing evangelical Christian literature and other media for all ages, around the world. Because we are a ministry of the Moody Bible Institute of Chicago, a portion of the proceeds from the sale of this book go to train the next generation of Christian leaders.

If we may serve you in any way in your spiritual journey toward understanding Christ and the Christian life, please contact us at www.moodypublishers.com.

"All Scripture is God-breathed and is useful for teaching, rebuking, correcting and training in righteousness, so that the man of God may be thoroughly equipped for every good work."
—2 TIMOTHY 3:16, 17

MOODY
PUBLISHERS

THE NAME YOU CAN TRUST®

MOUNTAINTOP DRIVE TEAM

ACQUIRING EDITOR
Andy McGuire

COPY EDITOR
Anne Buchanan

BACK COVER COPY
Laura Pokrzywa

COVER DESIGN
Charles Brock,
The DesignWorks Group, Inc.
www.thedesignworksgroup.com

COVER PHOTO
Steve Gardner, pixelworksstudio.net

INTERIOR DESIGN
Ragont Design

PRINTING AND BINDING
Bethany Press International

The typeface for the text of this book is
Fairfield LH